ONE

LAST

PRAYER

BOOKS BY CARLA KOVACH

DETECTIVE GINA HARTE SERIES

The Next Girl

Her Final Hour

Her Pretty Bones

The Liar's House

Her Dark Heart

Her Last Mistake

Their Silent Graves

The Broken Ones

One Left Behind

Her Dying Wish

One Girl Missing

Her Deadly Promise

Their Cold Hearts

Her Hidden Shadow

Her Last Goodbye

What She Did

Find Me

The Houseshare

On a Quiet Street

Meet Me at Marmaris Castle

Whispers Beneath the Pines

Flame

ONE

LAST

PRAYER

CARLA KOVACH

bookouture

Published by Bookouture in 2024

An imprint of Storyfire Ltd.
Carmelite House
50 Victoria Embankment
London EC4Y 0DZ

Storyfire Ltd's authorised representative in the EEA is Hachette Ireland
8 Castlecourt Centre
Castleknock Road
Castleknock
Dublin 15 D15 YF6A
Ireland

www.bookouture.com

ISBN: 978-1-83525-599-5
eBook ISBN: 978-1-83525-598-8

To anyone who has ever felt abandoned. Life can be a tough journey.

PROLOGUE

She gripped the doll as she tried to force the stained dress over its head. Her nanny had to leave to catch her bus to work, but it was okay, she had a plate of custard creams and a glass of squash. She wouldn't be alone for too long, so she wasn't scared. Nanny had told her she was a big girl and she had to be brave, and that her sister would be back in a while. After getting the doll's dress in position, she pulled the arms through the holes and smoothed the hair. The doll had once been her mother's when she was little, and her name was Suki. She loved the doll. The other children were mean to her because of Suki. They had nicer toys and their clothes were new looking but Suki was special to her.

Nanny always talked about not having any money. She worked a lot and her house was always cold. Shivering, she grabbed a bobbly old blanket from the sofa that smelled of her nan's washing powder.

The hamster ran around in circles on its wheel. Swish, swish, swish it went as it ran faster and faster.

She flinched as a thudding sound came from the other side of the door. Nanny wasn't due back for ages, not until around teatime after she'd cleaned the offices. Placing Suki on the rug, she stood from her cross-legged position, her checked school dress falling over her bony knees and the blanket falling in a crumpled heap beside her. She was told to never answer the door. Nanny had a key so there was no need.

Biting her bottom lip, she wondered if she should have a look to see who was making the noise.

Whoever was behind the door used the knocker this time. She flinched and stepped into her plate of custard creams with bare feet, the crumbs bedding between her toes. She shook her foot and swallowed. What if it was important? Maybe something had happened to her sister or maybe Nanny was back or maybe she'd lost her key. She glanced around to see if Nanny had taken her bag and umbrella. They had both gone.

She crept over to the chair under the net-covered window and went to lift it. If it was Nanny, she could let her in. If it was anyone else, she could hide until her big sister came home. As she created a tiny gap by lifting the net, she peered out onto the rainy path, but she couldn't see anyone at all. The only things she could see was their dustbin. It had fallen over.

Pulling the whole net over her head, she glanced up and down the road. She wasn't allowed to do that normally as people talked about them and Nanny said that they'd get into trouble for her being home alone. She was meant to hide and let people think there was no one in.

A scraping sound came from the back garden. Maybe whoever was at the front door was now at the back trying to get in. Her heart banged, making thud sounds in her ears as she thought of the alleyway that went under the bedrooms. Their gate was broken and there wasn't a lock on it. Then she heard a dog barking, and she remembered that Nanny had let Freeloader out for a pee before she left. Everyone else mocked her for having a dog called Freeloader but her silly sister had named their dog. Freeloader was a stray and he'd run in. From that day, he'd been their dog. The scraping noise had to be his claws on the door. 'I'm coming,' she called as she dropped the nets and slid off the chair and headed to the kitchen.

As she kicked her sister's pumps out of the way, she reached for the door handle. Her hand lingered as she watched the huge silhouette move behind the mottled glass. It was too tall to be Freeloader or her nan and it looked like a man. She crept back, hoping that whoever was behind the door hadn't seen her. She gasped for breath as the door handle rattled. She was so relieved that Nanny had locked it but where was Freeloader? The last time a stranger came to their door was when her sister had accidentally scratched Mr Golding's car by leaning her bike against it. Then there was the man who came for the money every week, who said if payments weren't made we would all cook inside the house, whatever that meant. He had a friendly voice and seemed nice because he gave her a sweet.

Freeloader yelped and she flinched and let out a short shrill scream. What if the man was hurting their dog? She loved the little terrier so much. The man vanished and reappeared at the kitchen window. As she held her breath, she stepped forward just enough to see out. That's when her eyes locked on his. He gripped Freeloader under a meaty arm, the little brown and white wire-haired dog whining to be let down.

She knew who he was and she'd been told to never let him in. The man held the dog out and she knew that if she didn't unlock the back door right there and then, he'd hurt Freeloader. Being brave is all she could be. Her nan would understand and he wasn't scary at all. She struggled to break his stare, so much so that she hadn't realised her mouth was wide open. She closed it and held a hand over her pounding heart. He held up something in his hand. It was a purple notebook with a smiling horse on the front of it.

The dog yelped again. The streetlamp just beyond the end of their garden came on, lighting up the dusky kitchen. 'Open the door,' he said gently. 'I have a present for my little Bright Eyes.'

He wouldn't hurt her, would he? She smiled at him through the window as she unlocked the door and Freeloader ran through her legs. She was going to be in trouble, big trouble. 'Nanny said I'm not meant to let you in.'

He didn't say another word as he closed the door and locked it behind them.

ONE

Wednesday, 3 July

Sally wiped the kitchen worktop of all its crumbs and hurried back into the nave. She loved the days when the community came together to offer support to each other, and this morning had been another winner. Very soon, the parents and children would leave the church and Sally would be heading back to the vicarage with a smile on her face to walk her dog, Jerry. The sun cast rainbows of colour through the stained-glass windows. The beautiful spectrums reached over the altar and touched almost every pew. Sally loved this time of the year and instantly felt a spring in her step.

The babies and toddlers laughed and shrieked as they played together with the wooden train set on the floor. Sally had laid it and a lot of other fun toys on the huge striped rug at the back, while the parents chattered away with cups of tea and cakes. She glanced at the new woman, Nell Craven. Another parent called Kira had mentioned Nell to her and Sally was glad she'd managed to join them. Although Sally had said hello and asked her a few basic questions, Nell had seemed slightly timid and had barely spoken. Sally knew that some people took their time when it came to mixing and she was also aware that not all were believers or churchgoers and at first some avoided her, thinking she might try to get them to come along to a Sunday service. That wasn't her aim. A happy and connected community was all she wanted. If they came to church for other reasons, that was a bonus. Nell would warm to her soon, if she made an effort. As she walked over to speak to Nell, Shayla stopped her. In fact, Shayla had been struggling and had needed to talk every week since Easter. She didn't mind. It was part of her job to listen. She knew that new parenthood was the hardest job in the world and Shayla's baby never stopped crying.

'I'm so tired,' Shayla said as she bobbed her shrieking baby up and down in her arms, tears beginning to slip from her eyes as the baby's scrunched hand yanked her necklace. 'She never sleeps and I can't think, I can't...' Shayla shook her head, losing the thread of what she was about to say.

Sally smiled and offered to take the tiny baby and Shayla was more than happy to pass the little one over for a few minutes. 'Did you go and see your doctor, for you and the little one?'

'I have an appointment when we're finished here.'

'That's a good start. I tell you what, shall I walk around with this cutie, try and soothe her while you enjoy the rest of your cuppa? And remember, I'm always here if you need to talk.'

The woman wiped the wet from her eyes. 'Thank you so much for everything.' Shayla smiled. 'I've forgotten what it's like to have a hot drink.'

Sally rocked the baby in her arms but the baby shrieked

louder. She knew that she'd just been fed and winded and her nappy didn't feel bloated, and it didn't smell. A sour scent came from the crease of the baby's neck. Sally wiped the milk with the damp bib. As she glanced up, she saw Nell running from the corridor and she wondered where she'd been. The toilets were down that way, maybe she'd just been to the loo. Phone gripped in one hand and a *Community Matters* magazine in the other, she seemed to be visibly shaking. Nell placed the opened-out magazine, face down, onto a rack of Bibles. Nell then sat down and brushed a hand through her messy brown bun, releasing some of the hair from the grips that secured it.

The baby in Sally's arms had quietened down and was now only whimpering sporadically as she fought the sleep she needed so badly. Maybe now was a good time to speak to Nell, see if she needed any extra support. She carefully walked over, one Doc Martens boot in front of the other. Her thick black fringe flopped forward, almost covering her eyes but she daren't move as much as a little finger while carrying Shayla's precious little baby, even though her own hair was tickling her nose. 'Nell,' she said, startling the woman.

With visibly shaky hands, Nell placed her phone face down on the wooden back row of pews. She glanced back to check on her toddler, Alfie, who lay on his back with the corner of a large wooden block in his mouth. The placid little boy seemed amused by all the slightly older children who were pushing the carriages back and forth while making choo-choo sounds. Nell went to reach for her phone but changed her mind, leaving it exactly where it was before finally acknowledging Sally's presence.

'Are you okay?'

'Err... Yes,' she replied in a whisper as she glanced at the main doors.

'You're new. How are you finding it?'

Nell turned her wrist over and rubbed the tattoo of Alfie's name that sat just under the leather friendship bracelet she wore. 'Err, nice.'

'I like to think we're a friendly group. Early parenthood can be lonely and hard. People come here and make friends, find people to share hardships with and you can always talk to me. I'm a great listener. And I won't try to make you join the church.' She shut up, knowing that she was wittering on but making everyone feel included, regardless of their personal beliefs, was her priority. Shayla's baby made a slight suckling noise and then her rosebud lips opened as she fell into the deep sleep that her body had been craving. Sally glanced at Shayla who was now smiling and in deep conversation with the only father who came to the group. The warmth of the bundle against Sally's chest made her feel warm and fuzzy. A tiny wash of sadness passed through her. She doubted she'd ever have a baby. She'd never met the right person and up until the last five years, being a foster carer had filled the gap a little. The Cleevesford community and her role in it was now her life. She'd have to enjoy moments like this where she got to cuddle other people's babies.

Nell turned her head and stared at the door. Sally wondered if something was worrying her, something more than being a parent to a toddler. 'Nell?'

'Sorry.' Nell faced her again and swallowed.

This time, Sally took her features in. The large black mole on Nell's forehead was quite distinctive. Nell pulled her fringe over it as if self-conscious. It was a hot day. Most people were wearing T-shirts, shorts or summer dresses. Nell wore a jumper and leggings. Sally had dug out a thin black lace skirt to go with her aubergine-coloured summer blouse, along with her dog collar. As for the boots, she wore them all year round so maybe Nell's clothes were just part of her identity in the same way that Sally's were. Not even being a vicar could remove the goth from her. The dark circles under Nell's eyes made Sally wonder if she'd had any sleep at all since her little boy was born. It was the shaking that was disturbing her more though. She wondered if Nell was detoxing from a drug or drink problem. Her frame was so slight, Nell looked like she'd snap like a dried-up twig if she did the laces of her trainers up. If Nell was having drug issues, or any other issues, Sally knew she'd have to tread carefully so as not to scare her away. She looked back at Alfie who was now up on his feet and playing with the other children. He beamed away, had the cutest chubby arms and legs and his clothes and body were clean. He looked so well in comparison to his mother. 'You seem a little worried.'

'I... I...' Nell paused for a second, closing her eyes, then she opened them to try and speak again. 'I can't sleep. I don't sleep. I get so worried something will happen...' She spoke in a whisper, the fallen strands of hair almost covering her mouth. 'And then...'

So that was it. Sally had come across parents like Nell before. In fact, most parents went through what Nell was going through, except not this extreme and it normally improved after the first few months. 'I see. You can't sleep because you worry something will happen to Alfie?'

She nodded.

'I can see Alfie now and he's a gorgeous and healthy-looking little boy and you deserve a good night's sleep. Do you live alone or with a partner?' She never assumed what someone's family set up might be.

'It's just me and him.' She flinched as her phone beeped.

'Do you have any family close by?'

She glanced back at the door, again. 'No. My half-sister lives in Birmingham, which I know isn't too far but I don't drive.'

'How about parents?'

'My mum is dead and my dad...' She paused. 'I can't talk

about him. I don't want to talk about him.' A tear streamed down her face. 'I can't trust anyone.'

One of the children dropped a wooden train station onto the flagstone tiles and Nell let out a cry and stood. Her body trembling as she stared wide-eyed at the children.

'It's okay. It's just the children playing. Can I get you another drink?' Sally knew she had to keep Nell talking a bit longer if she was to get to the bottom of why she seemed so on edge. It was more than insomnia; Sally was experienced enough to know that much. Nell was scared of something or someone. Sally glanced at Nell's phone as it buzzed.

'No. I need to go.' Nell snatched her phone and hurried towards her son. 'Alfie, come on.' She held out her arms and her son toddled over towards her. She scooped him up and he began to cry as Nell carried him to the main doors, grabbing her pushchair.

'Nell, wait,' Sally called, but Nell had already left the building. She was about to try and run after Nell but then she remembered Shayla's sleeping baby in her arms. Sally reached the doors to catch Nell and call for her to wait, but Nell was nowhere to be seen. She swallowed, knowing that she'd have to go and visit her as soon as the group had finished and after she'd walked Jerry. There was no way she could ignore the signs of someone in distress. All the attendee details were logged on forms in her office and she'd filled one out for Nell on her arrival.

'Sally, thank you so much. You seem to have the knack,' Shayla said as she held her arms out to take her baby girl back.

'I hope you both get on okay at the doctor's. As I said, if you need to talk or need any support, you know where I am.'

'Thank you. You're a gem, Reverend. Don't know what I'd do without this group.'

The now dried-up tears had been replaced by a smile on Shayla's face; that made everything worthwhile for Sally.

Almost. She needed to help Nell. She reached for the magazine that was strewn across the Bible rack. As she went to close it, she gasped as she saw three words scrawled across an article about a litter pick and she knew those were Nell's words.

'Help me, God!'

TWO

SALLY

Sally ran through the streets of Cleevesford, holding her phone out in front of her as she followed the map. Several people who recognised her had stopped her along the way to chat but all she'd been able to think about was Nell and the note, which is why she hadn't given them as much time as she normally would have. The walking instructions coming from her phone were dire and she'd been going around in circles for at least ten minutes. One of her wheelchair-bound parishioners waved and called out from his front garden. 'Hi, Tony. We must catch up soon,' she called as she continued. Beads of sweat gathered at the bottom of her back and her blouse was now stuck to her skin. The heat was sickening as the sun pounded against her head. She slipped down a thin path that divided two houses and gardens and came out onto a quiet road that sat opposite to a wildflower meadow.

'Morning, Sally,' a woman called out of her bedroom window as she cleaned them. Sally waved and smiled as she passed. She was sure the woman was called Elaine.

Her phone buzzed, telling her that she'd arrived at Nell Craven's home. She walked towards the tiny fenced off front

garden, the gorgeous meadow view now cut off by a row of
garages. She knew she'd reached Nell's place immediately. The
pushchair she'd ran out with had been ditched on the slabs
underneath the front window. She nudged the wooden gate
open and hurried towards the open concrete porch. That's
when she saw two doors. They were flats and Nell's was downstairs. Sally rang the bell and stood back but no one answered.
She knocked and heard clattering coming from the letter box.
Alfie peered through the door and smiled at her.

'Hello, Alfie. It's Reverend Sally. Can you get Mummy for
me?' He was so young; she wasn't even sure Alfie knew what
she'd asked him to do. In fact, she was certain he had no idea
what she needed him to do.

'Mammamama,' he garbled, his cobalt-coloured eyes striking
against his olive skin tone.

'Yes, Mamma.'

The letter box dropped but the little boy didn't come back.
Sally hurried over to the front window. The neighbour waved
back while straightening her curtains. Her name was definitely
Elaine. Sally remembered now. She had a husband called Reg.
Sally recognised her from the church carol service last Christmas. She peered through Nell's kitchen window. She couldn't
see Nell or Alfie but she did see Nell's handbag on the cluttered
worktop.

A minute passed and no one had opened the door. Sally's
stomach began to churn. She knew something had happened,
but what? Had Nell left Alfie alone? *Help me, God!* She was
sure Nell had written those words in the magazine. That's what
Nell had been doing when she'd wandered off. While they were
speaking, Nell had been looking at the door and shaking. Sally
puffed out a breath. She should have handed the baby back to
Shayla and ran after her.

Running from the front garden alongside the flat, she
stopped at the gate to the back garden. It wasn't locked. She

nudged it open and as she stepped through, her legs almost buckled. She stared open-mouthed in horror as the young mother lay in the middle of the garden, sprawled out. The sight of blood was turning her stomach. Sally couldn't believe what she was seeing. She'd never been convinced that the devil existed in a literal sense but the scene in front of her was as close as she was ever going to get to that thought. Only someone evil could have done that to another human being.

'Mama.' Alfie half-opened the back door.

Sally ran towards him, blocking his view of Nell's body on the lawn. She scooped the toddler up, taking him back into the flat. The sound of blood pumping through her body filled her head as she called the police. 'There's been a murder, you have to come now.'

THREE

Gina pushed her trolley up and down the supermarket aisles. So far, she'd only filled it with fruit and veg, knowing that she needed to eat a little healthier. A blood test at the doctor's had revealed that her cholesterol was slightly elevated and she knew she was to blame. The endless fast food they ate at the station and Detective Constable Harry O'Connor's wife's delicious cakes were totally to blame. From now on, she was going to get ten portions of fruit and veg a day, not the five the doctor had hoped she might try to eat. Didn't current advice suggest eating thirty different veggies per week? It was all so confusing. How the hell does someone eat thirty types of veg per week? She was going to batch cook, start power walking, and make time for herself; do whatever she could to get that cholesterol number back to normal. Maybe she'd take up yoga or meditation or whatever new age chill-out trend was in at the moment. It was either that or a heart attack and she didn't fancy the latter.

As she turned into the next aisle, someone crashed into her side, almost knocking her over. As she regained her footing and turned to give them a piece of her mind, they'd already hurried off down another aisle. Shaking her head, she grabbed a bag of walnuts and her mind began to wander back to her health. She was catastrophising. It was just raised cholesterol. But then again, she didn't want to have a heart attack. She passed the coffee and grabbed a jar of decaffeinated. Now she knew she was being serious. She hadn't had a decaf in years.

Her phone buzzed in her pocket. 'Hello,' she said. The signal wavered and dropped before she had a chance to get a reply from Detective Chief Inspector, Chris Briggs. She hurried to the till and tried to call him back as she loaded her shopping onto the conveyor belt. She now had a signal. She pressed his number.

Briggs answered immediately. 'Gina, I know you're not due in today but Jacob is stuck at court giving evidence. He should be back within the hour. O'Connor is here but I don't want to send him alone. It's not a pretty sight, from what I've heard. Uniform and forensics are at the scene and have been feeding back in real time. Bernard Small is managing the crime scene.'

'Wait, what's happened?'

'The vicar, Sally Stevens—'

'Sally? Is she okay?' Gina knew and liked Sally. Her heart started to pump as she battled to stop a rogue avocado from falling off the conveyor belt. The cashier began to buzz her shopping through.

'Yes, I mean, maybe. She called nine-nine-nine.' He paused. 'One of her parent and toddler group mums has been murdered. Sally and the toddler are now at that neighbour's house. A neighbour of the victim saw Sally turning up so we are not considering her to be a suspect. Sally also spoke to several of her parishioners as she walked to the victim's flat and was recorded on a Ring doorbell chatting to one of them. For obvious reasons, the team have already checked her version of events and they easily managed to verify her statement. We are already liaising with a social worker with regards to the child, and the police safeguarding team are involved too. The victim's name is Nell Craven. Are you able to attend? I really need a senior detective at the scene.'

Gina felt for Sally, the vicar who'd helped them on a previous case. The cashier tutted and shook her head as Gina continued speaking on her phone. She knew she was coming across as rude when the cashier rolled her eyes while asking Gina for thirty pounds and fifty pence. She pulled her card out and tapped it, nudging the phone between her ear and cheek as she packed and mouthed the word sorry to the cashier. 'Yes, I can go. How is the toddler?'

'He's been medically examined and seems okay. No injuries and he doesn't seem to be aware of what's happened. I know his clothes, along with Sally's, have been bagged for potential evidence transfer. We should have more details on what will happen with the child when we know the outcome of the urgent strategy meeting, but the boy is with Sally and an officer as we speak.'

'I've just finished shopping. Let me get outside.'

Moments later she hoicked the bags back into the trolley and hurried out into the blazing sun. 'Right, I'm at my car. Do I need to know anything?'

'Yes, it's not pretty, I'm afraid.'

'Are they ever?'

Briggs paused. 'Sally said that the victim has a sister in Birmingham. Her mother is dead and, at the moment, we don't have a location for her father. Obviously, locating the victim's sister is a priority.'

Gina slowly let out a breath. Cases that involved children were the worst. 'How old is the boy?'

'Sally said he's eighteen months old.'

She almost choked on the next question as she thought of her own granddaughter, Gracie, when she was that age. It would break her heart if Gracie ever saw a scene like that. She swallowed. She and her daughter Hannah barely spoke. A previous case putting Gracie in danger had put distance between them. 'Was her son there when it happened?'

'The victim is in the garden and the little boy was inside their downstairs flat. Sally managed to scoop him up just before he saw anything. Sally also went into the flat with the little boy. Bernard and our team will be taking her DNA and fingerprints as we speak, to eliminate her from the scene.'

Gina closed her boot and pushed the trolley into the trolley shelter. 'Right, I'm on my way.' She glanced down at her lemon-coloured T-shirt, pumps and ankle-length gypsy skirt. It wasn't ideal clothing to wear at a crime scene but she had to get there, now.

'There is something else you need to know.'

'What?'

She heard Briggs exhale. 'The victim's eyes have been removed.'

FOUR

The sun had been replaced by a few grey clouds as Gina pulled up opposite a row of garages. A forensics van and several police cars had filled the road. A group of people huddled on the path in front of the wildflower meadow. One woman stared as she pulled the petals from a pink foxglove. Her creased brow and pressed lips gave off an anxious vibe. She walked over, holding a little boy's hand. 'Hey,' she called out as Gina closed her car door.

'Can I help you?' Gina asked.

'I don't know. I hope so. Are you a social worker? The police won't tell me anything.' She threw the long flower stem onto the road. The boy sat on the kerb and began to play with it as he gabbled a few words.

'I'm DI Harte from Cleevesford Police.' She pulled her identification from her bag and slipped the lanyard over her neck.

'Oh, sorry. Can you tell me anything, only my friend, Nell, lives in that flat and I'm really worried.'

Gina pulled a pen and notebook from her bag. Bernard walked over to his van and carried out a huge box, ready to preserve and examine the crime scene. He held a hand up and nodded. Gina returned the gesture, knowing that her time was probably better spent talking to the victim's friend right now until Bernard could tell her more. 'Can I get your name?'

'Kira. Kira Fellows.'

'You say you're a friend of Nell Craven?'

'Yes. We live close by and we both have children who are the same age. Is she okay?'

Gina knew that no formal identification had taken place as yet and that family hadn't been informed of Nell's murder. 'I don't know much yet as I'm just about to attend the scene. I'm sorry to say that a young woman has been found dead but I can't confirm who or any details.'

'But that's where Nell lives and she's not answering her phone. I know it's her. She answers when I call her. I sent her a message and she hasn't replied...' Kira's eyes began to water.

'Can you tell me how long you've known, Nell?' Gina tilted her head and bit her bottom lip. She could tell that Kira was struggling and she wished she knew more.

'Only a month, in person. We met before that in a Facebook parenting group. Nell moved in just before me. I live just over there, the flat with the hanging basket at the porch.' Kira pointed. 'I'd just pulled up with my car full of boxes and she came over and helped me carry them into my flat. Alfie, that's her little boy, started playing with my son, Leo. They were so happy playing, she invited me over and made me a drink. Then I started going to the parent and toddler group and I invited her. She was meant to be there today.'

'Did she go with you?'

'Today was her first day but I didn't go.'

'You were at home?'

Kira nodded. 'Leo had a sickness bug; I think it's stopped now. He had me up all night. I didn't want to take him as I thought he might pass it on.'

Gina glanced down at the little boy who was making the stem walk along the pavement while he giggled.

'He's feeling a bit better now, thank goodness.'

'Have you been in all day?'

Kira nodded. 'I finally managed to get to sleep about ten this morning and Leo was so tired after being ill so we slept through lunchtime and I woke up to see police cars everywhere.' She flattened her blonde frizzy hair down. 'Sorry, I haven't even had a wash yet. I was just so worried; I came straight out to see what was going on.'

Gina thought at first the woman had been wearing track bottoms but now she'd spotted the ribbon drawstring at her waist, she knew they were pyjama bottoms. Without knowing the approximate time of death or any more details, she decided that she'd need to speak to Kira when she had more information. 'Is it okay if I come over to yours to take a statement in a short while?'

'Yes, of course.' She bent over and picked Leo up. He hit her on the shoulder with the stem and giggled. 'I just hope it's not Nell. I mean... she's, err.' She pulled her phone from her pocket. 'I still haven't had a reply.' Tears began to drizzle down her cheeks.

'Do you worry that something might have happened to Nell?'

Kira inhaled sharply. 'Over the past week she's seemed different. Nervous, weird. When I asked her what was wrong, it's like she'd forgotten I was there. I can only describe her as staring right through me. She hasn't been sleeping, I can tell that much. She did say one thing and it scared me. I asked her about it but she refused to say anything more.'

'What did she say?'

'I think she'd moved to get away from someone and she wouldn't talk to me about it. She said, "They always find you in the end."'

FIVE

Gina watched as Kira walked back to her flat on the other side of the road, holding Leo closely. The other neighbours huddled together, gossiping as their children played on the meadow and dogs panted at their feet. It wouldn't be long before the press arrived, hoping for a photo to go with the press release Briggs was no doubt preparing after she reported back. She hurried past the garages and saw PC Smith standing by the outer cordon that had been taped from lamppost to lamppost. She glanced back. All she could see was a wall of garages. Nell's view wouldn't have extended to the beautiful meadow just beyond them from her ground floor maisonette.

'Alright, guv,' PC Smith said as he passed her the log sheet on a clipboard. She took the Biro from him and signed in. She took a crime scene suit pack from the bag just behind him and wondered how she was going to tackle wearing the all-in-one over a long skirt.

DC Harry O'Connor wiped a line of perspiration from his brow as he turned away from one of the neighbours and hurried back over. His bald head had caught the sun and the skin had started to peel from the top of one of his ears. A wet patch had formed under the armpits of his white short-sleeved shirt. 'Guv, I've spoken to a couple of the neighbours but the man who lives above the victim hasn't come home yet. Most people are still at work.'

'Have you spoken to Bernard yet?'

'No, guv. He's been too busy setting up. They've erected a tent in the back garden after catching a teenager trying to peer over and take a selfie with the body. Can you believe it? Anyway, the body is still there. Bernard was saying that he hoped they could remove it without too much of a delay or this heat and the flies would cause a lot of trouble.'

'Have we managed to get any details of any relatives?'

'We have a phone and PC Shaf Ahmed is going through it now. There isn't anything obvious in it, like contacts marked up as Mum, Dad, Sister. The phone is a bit strange, though.'

'In what way?'

'It's a basic phone with barely anything in it and only a few messages from someone called Kira and she's made a few phone calls but the contact details haven't been stored. We're hoping that there is a laptop or a tablet in the flat, but we can't go in yet.'

'Where's Sally, and the victim's little boy?'

'They're at a neighbour's house. I was just leaving the house as you arrived. Sally is in shock and is currently sitting in their kitchen with a glass of water. As we've bagged her clothes, the neighbour has kindly given her something to wear. Same with the boy. She had some clothing that she keeps at hers for her grandson. I've spoken to Sally. She said that the victim, Nell Craven, had attended her parent and toddler group this morning. Also, she said that Nell had seemed worried about something and had run off. Sally found a magazine that Nell had left open on a page. It had the words "Help me, God" written in it so she walked her dog and headed straight to Nell's after the session had finished around lunchtime. When she arrived about one this afternoon, she found Nell's body in the garden and called emergency services.'

'Thanks for the update. I wonder if Bernard is in a position to talk to us yet. I guess we should tog up.'

O'Connor nodded. He walked back over to the cordon with her and grabbed a crime scene suit pack. Gina fed both of her sandalled feet into the foot holes and pulled it up. The bulk of her skirt had got bunched into the one leg. As she glanced up to see Bernard peering out of the front door, she slipped the shoe covers, face mask, hair cover and gloves on.

'Come through,' Bernard said. 'Stay on the stepping plates.'

Gina glanced down, her feet clunking on metal as she walked the plates up to the front door.

Bernard towered over them both as he led the way. 'I was going to lead you in through the back but we have got stepping plates down in the flat and I thought you might both want to see the flat too.'

'Have you found any tech?'

Bernard shook his head causing his beard to escape slightly. He pulled his face mask a little wider over his face to gather it up again. 'Not a thing. There is still a lot to search through as you'll see.'

Gina glanced into the kitchen. 'Gosh.' Each work surface was covered with something. Pots and pans that would have been better placed in cupboards had been left everywhere. Store cupboard food had been stacked up on the flat hob top.

'There's nothing in the cupboards. They're empty.' Bernard stepped ahead. 'The bedroom and bathroom are to your right.'

Gina peered into the bathroom. Again, there was an open medicine cabinet, emptied of everything. Shampoo, creams, make-up had been strewn all over the floor. She stepped back onto a metal plate and glanced into the bedroom that Nell would have shared with her son. His toddler bed had been pushed against the back wall and a single bed was next to it. Clothes covered every bit of the bed.

'The wardrobe is empty. You'll see that there's an indentation in the clothes on the bed. It looks like someone has been sleeping on them. Follow me to the lounge and garden.'

Gina felt her underarms getting sticky in all the gear. She hated the summer months more than the colder months. Since the menopause was still creeping up on her and despite HRT, she still found too much heat unbearable. A wave of dizziness caught her by surprise. She reached for the doorframe.

'Are you okay, guv?' O'Connor asked.

She raised her eyebrows and breathed out slowly. 'Yes, I'm just sweltering. It's a bit on the stuffy side today.'

O'Connor nodded in agreement. 'Let's check out the lounge and head outside.'

She let O'Connor lead the way as she composed herself and followed. The tiny lounge sofa had been piled up with toddler toys. A dinosaur and teddy poked from the top of a plastic box. 'She hasn't got many things for someone with a toddler.' There weren't many toys, only a box full. She'd been to other people's houses with children of a similar age and they seemed to have toy mountains in their lounges.

They always find you in the end. Kira's words rang through her mind. Had Nell escaped an abusive relationship? Is that why she had a basic phone with no internet access? Had she bought that and a SIM card to tide her over? Gina pictured the young mother leaving her life and belongings behind to escape something awful. She swallowed the sick feeling that had risen in her throat. The only thing left to see was the victim. Sally said that the body was that of Nell Craven but then again, Sally had only met Nell for the first time that day.

'Bernard?' He turned around as Gina spoke and went to step out of the door into the garden. 'Have you found any identification at all?'

'There is a passport in a drawer and the picture and distinguishing features match those of our victim.'

Gina stopped and glanced around the room. 'We have to find out who she was calling on her phone and I need to speak to Sally.' Her heart began to boom. The thought of Nell's little boy being taken into care filled her heart with sadness. No doubt, the social worker and the safeguarding team would have an answer on what would happen to the little boy soon. Nell's sister had to be contacted, and fast.

She stepped out onto the slabs and gazed through the gap in the white tent that had been erected. A tangled mess of shrubs lined the back of the garden and an upturned sand pit leaned against the fence. Gina struggled to control her nausea as she saw the victim lying on her back. The hair that had fallen from a bun framed her face in tangled tendrils and her leggings were covered in dust and dried grass as if she'd been in a struggle. The young woman's missing eyes were a shock and the flies buzzing around the blood made her turn away.

'From what the vicar said to us, we know that the victim left the play group about midday and the vicar turned up around one in the afternoon. Her murder happened between twelve fifteen and one. That's a forty-five-minute window. The state of the body is in line with that,' Bernard said. 'It is also a bloody scene so whoever did this must have either got blood on them or had a change of clothing with them.'

'You mentioned distinguishing features.'

'Yes, she has a tattoo on her left wrist with the name Alfie entwined in a small row of leaves and flowers, and she has a large black mole just under her hairline but it is covered by her fringe.'

'Thanks for that.' Gina turned away and saw that O'Connor was choosing to look at his feet. 'Guv.'

'Yes.'

O'Connor furrowed his brow. 'Did you see what I saw in the kitchen, pushed back against the skirting board?'

Gina remembered seeing all the food over the worktops but she hadn't looked at the floor. 'What was it?'

'Dog bowls. That means she has or had a dog. The food one wasn't clean either. It looked like it had some dried-up dog food stuck around the inside. And there was a water dish too.'

She grabbed her phone and called Briggs. What had happened to the dog?

SIX

SALLY

After loosening a couple of buttons on the polo top that Elaine had given her, she took a deep breath as little Alfie lay sleeping in her arms. She held the toddler close to her heart. His mother had been murdered. Sally had seen Nell's face, stripped of both eyes and all that blood, it would haunt her forever. While waiting for the emergency services to arrive, she had whispered a prayer. Hatred was an emotion that Sally refused to feel on a normal day but right now, she loathed whoever had done that to Nell. It was beyond hate. She always thought that everyone deserved a second chance and that the path to redemption should be there for any person who wanted to change, but whoever murdered Nell was an animal. Only the worst kind of evil could hurt another human being like that. She swallowed the lump in her throat and stroked the little boy's soft damp hair. The police officer who had walked her over remained at the back of the room, occasionally casting a sympathetic glance her way.

'Can I get you another cuppa,' Elaine asked as she swiped Sally's half-finished cup of tea from the coffee table.

She looked up at the woman who'd shown her and Alfie

such kindness by taking them into her house, giving them clothes and looking after them. Her throat felt like sandpaper. Alfie's comfort had trumped her need for fluids. She nodded. 'Thank you. You've been very kind.'

'You can lay him down on the other side of the sofa if you want? Your arm must be going numb.' Elaine pressed her lips together.

'It's okay. I really don't mind.' The poor boy would need all the comfort she had to offer. She wondered where Alfie's dad might be. Nell had mentioned a sister. She hoped the police would soon find someone to come and take Alfie from this awful situation and look after him. Until then, she would do everything she could to keep him with her. She'd already mentioned that she was available to look after him to the officers. The knock at the door made her flinch.

Elaine hurried out of the lounge in her flip-flops and went to the front door with her husband, Reg.

'Hello, may we come in and speak to you all?'

Sally recognised that voice. It was Gina or DI Harte as she was known in her professional capacity. Sally had always liked Gina and she was glad that she in particular was involved in solving the case. The DI stepped into the living room, her lemon-coloured T-shirt slightly damp under her breasts and her brown hair frizzed up from the humidity. Her long cotton skirt was creased and almost reached her sandals. It looked like she'd been called to the scene on her day off. She acknowledged the officer in the room and turned to Sally.

'Gina. I wish I could say it was nice to see you today but the circumstances—' Sally exhaled and looked up.

'I'm so sorry,' Gina said. 'What you saw, it must have been such a shock. This is DC O'Connor.' She gestured to the man standing next to her. 'How is the little one?'

'Thankfully, I don't think he saw his mum in the garden.

He's been asleep for about half an hour now.' Tiny bursts of air came from the sleeping boy's mouth and tickled Sally's arm.

'We're just trying to locate his relatives and social services are on their way to assist.'

Sally bit her bottom lip. She might be impulsive in saying what was on her mind but she was going to do it anyway. She tilted her head to take in the little boy's closed eyes, his eyelashes catching the top of his cheeks. 'If no one is available to take him straight away, I've already told the other police officers that I can look after him in the interim. I've had all the necessary checks because of my job and I have room and toys, nappies, a cot. We keep those kinds of supplies at the church. I also used to be a foster parent so I've had all the training. I have everything he could need.'

'That's a really kind offer, Sally. I'm sure we'll hear something soon. Is there any way you can pop him down so we can talk in the kitchen?' The DI glanced at Elaine. 'Would that be okay?' Elaine nodded in agreement.

Sally placed him on the sofa as if he was made of bone china. He barely stirred. 'Could you both please watch him, so he doesn't fall?'

'Of course, love.' Elaine sat in the armchair next to the boy. Sally followed the DI and the other detective into the kitchen. The police officer nodded.

After sitting around the tiny circular table, the DC took a notepad out and Gina sat opposite. Reg went to the fridge and took a jug of cold orange juice out and placed it in the middle of them all with three glasses. 'I'll leave you to it.' He pressed a switch on the wall and the ceiling fan came on. Sally poured juice for each of them and she took a huge swig, enjoying the coolness slipping down her throat. Even though evening was looming now, it was still quite humid.

'Sally, can you talk me through earlier, when you were

running the parent and child group?' Gina loosened her T-shirt away from her body and sipped her drink.

'Yes. It started off like any normal day. I opened up at ten. A couple of the parents were already waiting. Nell turned up about ten minutes after that. She seemed really nervous and kept checking the main door. At first, I thought she might be waiting for someone. I know that another parent, Kira, had mentioned that her friend, Nell, would be coming along one week. Kira had messaged me to say she wouldn't be attending as her son had been sick so I told Nell to put her at ease. I then got her to register, which is how I knew where she lived.'

'Did she give you an email address or a phone number?'

'No, she only gave me her address and said that she was friends with Kira.'

'I just spoke to Kira outside. Can you tell me more about their friendship?'

'Last week, Kira said that she and Nell hadn't known each other for long but they'd just clicked and become friends. Kira mentioned that Nell was nice and that their children got on with each other.' Sally paused. 'Nell was scared of someone and when I saw that message in the magazine, "Help me, God", it confirmed that thought. Nell ran off fast and at the time, I was holding a group member's baby. I couldn't chase after her, otherwise I would have. As soon as everyone left, I went to see to my dog and hurried to Nell's place.' The lump in her throat felt as though it might choke her. She swallowed a bit more juice. 'That's when I found her and called you.'

'Did Nell mention having a dog?'

Sally shook her head.

'Did you see anyone suspicious hanging around by the church or by Nell Craven's flat when you arrived?'

'No, but I wasn't looking for anyone. It just seemed like a normal afternoon up until I saw Nell. It's fairly quiet around here. It's not busy but, then again, the children haven't broken up from school yet either.' Her hands were shaking. She placed them in her lap.

'How close were Kira and Nell?'

'From what Kira had said to me, I'd say they were getting close quickly. They were both lone parents and new to the area. Kira seemed really excited to have met Nell. They'd planned to help each other with childcare. Kira mentioned applying for jobs but she'd been struggling to find childcare. Nell had offered to look after her son while she got on her feet. I think Kira was worried for Nell.'

'In what way?'

'Kira confided in me and I never break a confidence. Please could you ask Kira? I know she'd want to help.'

Gina nodded. 'Of course. I'm heading over there in a minute. I know you have my number so if you remember anything else or need to talk, just call me, okay?'

'I will do, and thank you. I think there is someone else you need to speak to.' Sally paused. 'Reg was looking out of his bedroom window a couple of nights ago and he saw a figure in Nell's garden.' A shiver ran through Sally's body. She held a hand to her heart and imagined some creepy person watching Nell through her window. She glanced at Reg who had heard his name mentioned and stood at the door.

'Did you want me for anything?' he asked.

SEVEN

Reg took Sally's seat at the table. Gina listened as the toddler in the other room woke up and cried for his mother. Sally's soothing tones calmed him down slightly.

'Mr Hampton, would you mind talking me through what you saw two nights ago and can you confirm that date?' His drawn jowls made him look ever so slightly like a bloodhound, Gina thought. She guessed he was in his early to mid-sixties.

He nodded as he rubbed his stubble. 'Yes, it was the first of July, Monday just gone. Actually, it was early Tuesday morning, so the second of July.' He furrowed his grey brows and stared at the juice jug. 'Let me get this right. I woke up to pee. Elaine and I sleep with our curtains open. Anyway, my idiot neighbour leaves a lot of scraps out for the foxes and I heard them fighting in her garden. We get into so many arguments. She leaves all this food out and we have to deal with the rats. It cost me over a hundred pounds to get a pest controller out.'

'You said you saw someone in Nell's garden?' Gina wanted to bring him back on track. She was very aware that time was slipping away and she wanted to check in with PC Smith and PC Ahmed before speaking to Kira Fellows again. She checked her watch. Clumps of grey-looking clouds filled the sky. Gina turned away. Thunder had been forecast and it always made her feel a deep itch inside, one that made her want to shed her own skin. Ever since that stormy night when she helped her abusive ex-husband plunge down their stairs to his death, thunder brought back the memory of his dying eyes as he took his last breath.

'Erm, yes.' Gina flinched and Reg continued. 'I was tutting to myself and making a note in my diary by the light of my phone torch, when I spotted the figure enter the garden. They never keep their shared gate locked and anyone can access it from the walkthrough, with it being on the side of the garden too. Not safe if you ask me.' He paused. 'Sorry, I need to remember that the poor woman lost her life. My wife is always telling me to think before I speak. I'm too blunt for my own good. Anyway, it gave me the creeps but I kept thinking that it was probably the man who lives in the flat above. He likes to go out for a drink and he's even fallen asleep in the back garden before after a night out. The idiot probably can't get himself up the steps. I remember assuming it was him and going back to bed.'

'Did it look like him?'

'I can't answer that. It was dark and they don't have a security light. All I saw was an outline, a black blob in the darkness. The dog had started to bark, though.'

Gina made a mental note to come back to the dog in a short while. 'Can you describe the shape of the person?'

'Ah, actually. I remember seeing a light flash at one point. It was like whoever it was had received a message and their phone had lit up. The person was about average height but it's hard to tell from up here. They might have been bulky but they could have also had a coat on. Who knows?'

'What time was that?'

'I don't know. I know it was the earlier part of the night. I'd say around one in the morning.'

Gina went to ask him why he hadn't called the police but he'd covered that. He thought the man living above had been drunk. 'Is there anything else you can tell me? Have you noticed anyone hanging around or anyone displaying suspicious behaviour?'

'Wait.' He hurried upstairs and came back down with an exercise pad. 'Like I said, I keep a diary, logging all antisocial behaviour.' He flicked through a few pages and stopped on one. 'Earlier on the Monday, maybe around lunchtime, I saw Nell running out of her flat crying. I was just heading to my garage. I asked her what was wrong. She stared at me, stared at her flat and then went back in when her son cried for her.'

Gina almost gasped under her breath. That was unusual behaviour. 'Was the dog with her?'

'Yes, the tiny mutt was yapping around her feet.'

'When did you last see or hear the dog?'

'I popped out at maybe ten this morning and I heard it yapping like mad which was unusual. It isn't a noisy dog, normally.'

'Did you see anyone hanging around?'

'Despite what people think, I'm not on the lookout all the time. I'd just got up and was going to my garage. I wasn't looking and a dog barking isn't really anything to worry about.'

'What breed of dog did Nell have?'

He scratched his nose and leaned back. 'I don't really know much about dogs. It's short-haired, tan in colour and tiny, like one of these toy dogs that dopey celebrities carry in bags.'

Elaine entered carrying a tray of empty cups. 'Sorry, I didn't mean to listen in. The dog is a chihuahua called Toffee. Is he okay?'

Gina watched as O'Connor tried to write chihuahua. She

couldn't even help him with that spelling. 'We haven't managed to locate the dog yet.'

'Oh, my goodness,' Elaine said. 'Do you think it was a dog theft gone wrong? I mean, those little dogs are really sought after, aren't they? They're worth a lot of money.'

'We don't know as yet.' Gina doubted that the murderer removed Nell's eyes as part of a dog theft, but she definitely wasn't about to share that detail with Reg and Elaine and she hoped that Sally hadn't either. 'Is there anything else either of you can tell us?'

Reg shook his head and Elaine spoke. 'I don't think so. Can't think of anything.'

Sally peered around the door, her clunky boots giving her presence away. 'Is it okay if I head back to the vicarage? I can take little Alfie with me for now?'

'I'll arrange for an officer to take you and they will stay with you for the time being. Thank you for taking care of him.' Gina knew that Sally was one of the most trusted members of the community. Alfie was in safe hands. She tried to swallow her own emotion down. Alfie was so vulnerable right now. Gina owed it to that little boy to find out who murdered his mother.

'Come on, little man, we're going to mine for a bit and you can meet my dog, Jerry. He will absolutely adore you.'

'Doggy,' Alfie said as he made a barking noise and giggled.

Gina's phone rang. She nodded to O'Connor, letting him know that he could tie things up with Reg and Elaine for now. She opened the front door and stepped into their porch. 'Sir.' She waited for Briggs to speak.

'The dog has been located not too far from where you are. I've just called Bernard to get a crime scene assistant over there. The dog is at the woods behind the wildflower field. Looking at the map, it's just out of distance for any of you to hear it barking. It has been tied to a tree in the shade and someone left a plastic dish of water next to it.'

'Is the dog, okay?'

'Thankfully, yes. As soon as we've taken some swabs from the dog, we'll have to call the RSPCA.'

'Damn, I wonder if Nell's friend Kira would take the dog for now, while we sort something out.'

Sally came into the hallway with Alfie. 'I don't mind looking after the dog too.'

Gina mouthed the word, thank you. Sally really was being wonderful, given the situation they were in. 'Bear with me.' She took the phone away from her ear and spoke to Sally. 'I'll pop by later to see how you're getting on.'

O'Connor joined them while slipping his notebook into his pocket. Gina turned to face him. 'Could you please arrange for a specially trained officer to go back with Sally and interview her, and also can you make sure you get the magazine and book it into evidence?'

'Yes, guv.'

Sally took a deep breath and followed O'Connor. 'I'll see you later.' They walked the little boy in the opposite direction to his home that was surrounded by police tape. Gina watched how Sally had swallowed her own upset and turned what she and the boy were doing into a game as she picked him up and carried him down the path towards the waiting police car.

Gina returned to her call with Briggs. 'Sally, the vicar, said she'll look after the dog too. When we've finished with the dog, who is called Toffee by the way, he can be dropped off at the vicarage.'

'Great. There is something else. We found one of those Turkish lucky eyes attached to its collar. It doesn't look like it belongs there as the safety pin it was attached to has been forced through the leather collar.'

EIGHT

DIARY EXTRACT

I need to be available for him and it's ridiculous that I crave his love and approval, but I do. I can't help it. I wish with all I had that I could just walk away from this but I've spent too long feeling invisible. He did a bad thing, that's not up for debate, but don't people deserve forgiveness? The last visit went well and he now phones me instead of writing. Writing feels so old-fashioned now in the age of email and WhatsApp but I understand that he has his limitations.

He's been so full of regret when it comes to the past but it has me thinking. I'm not sure whether all this attention he's giving me is because no one else speaks to him. Right now, I'm shaking my head. I believe he's genuine. He's changed and I believe he deserves a second chance.

He too has had a hard life. I'm not making excuses for his crimes, honestly. I would never do that, but he told me about how his brother was abused at the hands of their mother, how she beat and neglected them. It almost made me cry when he said how he'd gone four days without any food. She left them locked in their terraced house and told him not to say a word or the authorities would send them both to a home. Damn, thinking about all that has started me off again. I don't know how people can be so cruel.

Am I being gullible here, Diary? Damn, why can't you be a person. I feel as though I'm talking to no one in a dark room. Is he genuine or is it all an act? I guess at least I have some time to ponder that question. It's not like I'll be seeing him in person anytime soon.

He always gifted me notebooks and like some crazed writing addict, I kept buying more and filling them with utter shite about every aspect of my life. That gift of journaling was given to me a long time ago but it's what has always connected me to him and, I guess, I hoped he'd be interested in the small details of my life at some point. After all, he told me to keep the journals because he didn't want to miss a thing. Then, the fear of forgetting these things turned me into a writing obsessive. And I did it for him.

Please don't let me down, that's what I want to tell him. I want to say this out loud but I'm scared I'll drive him away. I know he told me how much he loves me and I know he'll call me tonight, which is why I'm glued to my phone.

As for what he did, this is what I will say to him. I forgive you. I FORGIVE YOU!

NINE

Gina kept mulling over the Turkish lucky eye attached to the dog's collar. That and the victim's missing eyes was enough to link the two but what was the killer trying to tell them? O'Connor huffed, muttering something about the humidity under his breath. She knew they were both a bit sticky and all she wanted to do was have a shower but that shower had to wait. The ever-darkening sky made it feel later than it was. Another low rumble of thunder filled the air but, given the weather forecast, it wasn't set to come to much. As they reached Kira's front door, Gina rang the bell.

'Ouch,' O'Connor said as his head nudged the hanging basket. He began rubbing the red patch that was forming just above his right eyebrow. 'That'll teach me to look where I'm going.' A speck of rain caught Gina's cheek.

Kira opened the door and held a finger to her lips. 'My son's just fallen asleep,' she said in a hushed tone. 'We can talk in the kitchen.'

Gina and O'Connor followed the woman along the hallway of a flat that mirrored the layout of Nell's. She glanced through the open living room door and saw the little boy lying on the sofa covered in towels with a bowl on the floor next to him.

'Sorry you've had to come into the sick house. I thought he was better but he kept saying he had tummy ache again. I'd wash your hands well before you eat. All the kids seem to be coming down with one bug or another. I feel like I'm living in stomach flu hell lately. Can I offer you a drink?'

O'Connor went to say yes but Gina interrupted. 'No, we're good, thank you.' The last thing she needed was to lose him on the case because of a virus. Instead of a drink, he settled for getting his notebook out. Gina quickly checked her phone and saw a message saying that Jacob was back at the station. 'We've spoken to some of the neighbours and witnesses and I have a few questions that I think you'll be able to help us with.' She thought of what Sally had said, about Nell confiding in Kira.

'Anything, fire away.'

'Did Nell confide in you about anything?'

Kira sighed and sipped from a can of iced tea. 'Nell was quite a closed book but her behaviour worried me. At first, she seemed quite positive but a couple of weeks ago she started pulling her flat apart. I tried to speak to her about it. I asked if there was anything wrong but she kept saying no. I don't think she's been eating properly or sleeping. Whenever I saw her, she'd be yawning all the time. I think she thought someone was spying on her. She thought that her flat was bugged.'

'Did she find anything?'

'No, that's the thing. She pulled the place apart and found nothing at all.'

'Have you noticed anyone suspicious hanging around?'

Kira shook her head. 'Not at all. Darrah, the man who lives above her, seems to come and go at all hours, but I know he likes the pubs and clubs.'

Gina watched as O'Connor made a note to interview him.

'Have you heard her dog barking today?'

'Toffee? No, but I have had *Hey Duggee* and *Bluey* on rerun all day and Leo tends to have a tantrum if the TV isn't turned up loud when he's watching it. If Toffee was barking, I wouldn't have even realised. I think with the road between us, I'd be too far away to hear the barking anyway.'

'Do you know if Toffee has any type of pendant attached to his collar normally?'

Kira frowned. 'He has a name tag on a disk but that's it.'

'Apart from Nell's sister do you know if she has any more relatives?' Gina glanced around at the kitchen. It seemed uncluttered, which was a stark contrast to Nell's. The kitchen looked a bit old-fashioned with its set of three watercolours of herbs adorning the main wall, and the dado rail with floral wallpaper above it and eighties peach paint.

Kira bit her bottom lip and leaned back. 'She did actually speak to me about Maeve and they're actually half-sisters. They shared the same mother. I know Maeve is older and her father died of a drug overdose before Maeve was even born. I remember thinking how sad that was. When Maeve was little, her mother moved in with Nell's father, then Nell came along soon after so it was the four of them then. That's all I really know. I don't know Nell's father's name and I don't know where he is, or if he's even alive. Nell didn't say much more about Maeve either. They kept in touch but I sense they didn't get on. I don't know why. Whenever she mentioned Maeve's name, she'd shake her head and tut. I asked her what had happened between her and Maeve but she always shook my questions off and said it was all in the past and nothing to worry about. Just sister things, she said. I totally get that, I mean, I have a sister too and we fall out over such silly things.' Kira smiled and shrugged.

'Do you know where Maeve lives?'

'Birmingham, right in the centre. I think she has an apartment. I know she has her own fashion brand and from what Nell said, she's rich. I don't know the name of it, sorry. Oh, I do know that Nell's mother changed Maeve's surname to Craven, the same as Nell's father. Nell said that her mum had wanted them to all have the same name. So, her full name is Maeve Craven. That should make her easier to google.'

Gina waited for O'Connor to catch up with his notes. He wasn't as fast as her usual partner, Jacob. O'Connor looked up and smiled, letting her know he was ready to continue. Another rumble of thunder came from above and the kitchen had darkened even more. Gina tried to push it to the back of her mind. Kira stood up and turned up the main light with the dimmer switch. 'Did Nell ever mention Alfie's father?' Gina asked.

Kira shook her head. 'I asked her if Alfie's dad ever saw his son, but she said no. It seemed like something she didn't want to talk about so I dropped it.'

That rang true with Nell's behaviour. From what Sally said, it seemed Nell was worried that someone was following her or looking for her. 'Did Nell mention anything else?'

'I told her that I was keen to find a job and we spoke about childcare. In fact, I've had a lot of interviews and Nell looked after my little one while I attended them. She was so kind to me.' Kira paused. 'Anyway, Nell said that she was a chiropodist and wanted to work for herself and go back to treating clients in their own homes. She offered to help me out with childcare for a while, until a local nursery place became available. She said she was okay for money so I know she wasn't too worried about having to start work straight away. I did wonder if she was getting maintenance from Alfie's dad. Like I said, she wouldn't talk about that aspect of her life so I didn't push her. All I know is she wasn't hard up. She wasn't rich enough to be able to rent anything bigger than the flat, but she wasn't that poor she had to worry about paying the bills.' Kira paused. 'Apart from what I've already told you, our time together was spent either sitting outside my door on a couple of kitchen chairs or in her garden while we watched Leo and Alfie play. We didn't go out together as we hadn't been here long enough to find a babysitter. All I know is, I really liked her and I was so happy to find such a great friend. When I moved here, I thought it would take me ages to meet people and form connections but meeting Nell' – she paused and swallowed – 'and the stay and play group. I was happy. Now, I'm really sad and...' Kira clenched the coaster on the table until her knuckles turned white. She held her breath for a few seconds.

'I'm really sorry for your loss.' Gina realised how hard talking about Nell must be for Kira. It seemed they'd become close.

'I'm so angry and I want to cry and tear my bloody hair out. I can't get it out of my head that someone took her from us and from Alfie. I don't know what will happen to him. It's so sad.' Kira stood and walked over to the sink. She began to run the tap before splashing her face with a handful of water. 'Sorry. It's really hitting me now. I'm never going to see her again. She was scared of someone. She was running from something. You have to find out why and who.'

Gina heard Leo calling for his mother from the living room. 'Biscuit.'

'I need to look after my son, sorry. At least he's asking for food now, that's a sign of him getting better.' She folded her arms. 'I have one last thing. I don't know who her ex was but I know she got rid of her smartphone and bought a really basic thing. It has to be because of him. I bet he found her.'

Gina stood. 'Thank you for your time. Can you tell me anything else about her neighbour, Darrah?'

'He seems like a lovely guy despite that he drinks a lot. I know that because I've seen him staggering towards his flat. Anyway, he's single and I guess he goes out enjoying himself. He doesn't seem to be too rowdy. He's one of those guys who offers to help anyone with anything and always shouts hello across the street. On the day I moved in here, he hurried over and helped me all evening after I left Nell's flat. He saw me leaving after I'd had a drink at hers. He must have seen us carrying boxes into mine earlier that day. He put my flat-pack together and helped me arrange everything in each room and he set up my TV. It's not like I can't do these things, it was just much quicker with him helping and I had Leo to entertain. Nell later told me he did the same for her too. I joked that he fancied her but she brushed it off, even though he asked her if she wanted to go out to dinner with him. As far as I know there was no relationship there, or even a date. I don't think Nell was interested.' Kira paused in thought. 'I remember Nell having a problem with one of her taps. The letting agent said that they couldn't get a plumber over immediately. Anyway, long story short, Darrah fixed the tap for her and then I think he fitted her new toilet seat. He did look after her dog sometimes when she had to go out, just until Toffee settled into the new flat.'

'Did he look after the dog in his flat?' Gina tried to picture the same neighbour standing in their garden in the early hours of Tuesday morning. She noticed that Darrah didn't have a door that led into the back garden. He'd have to come out of his front door and walk around the back of the building to use it, even though it was shared.

'No, he sat in her flat as Nell didn't want Toffee to damage any of Darrah's furniture. I remember her saying that she was taking Alfie out and that it was going to be a long day. She'd left him a couple of cans of lager and a pizza to cook for himself.' Kira frowned. 'She got back several hours later and found lots of empty cans on the side and Toffee and Darrah weren't in her flat. She told me how much it had panicked her. He'd left the door on the catch and gone back up to his flat with the dog, and was in bed. She knocked and knocked before she eventually woke him up. After that, he kept offering to help her but she couldn't forgive him for leaving her door unlocked all afternoon.

She didn't fall out with him, she decided that his help was more trouble than it was worth.'

'When was this?'

'A couple of weeks ago. I don't know which day.'

'Which friend was she seeing?'

'She didn't say, but she'd curled her hair and put perfume on. I wish I knew. I only hoped she hadn't gone to see a violent ex, letting him know where she was now living. That could have happened.'

They needed to find out who Nell had met up with that day. Maybe Darrah had the answers.

Gina's phone beeped. She glanced at the message from a withheld number.

> *It was lovely to see you again earlier. It's good to see you're taking such an interest in your health with all that salad. You're looking well or should I say, too well. Anyway, I know I'll see you again very soon. I'll make sure of it.*

She frowned. She hadn't met anyone she knew at the supermarket. Despite how stuffy she felt, a slight shiver worked its way through her. A rumble of thunder made her stiffen and she gasped slightly for breath.

TEN

SALLY

Now home and back in her own clothes, Sally sipped her tea and placed it back on the hearth, way out of Alfie's reach. The interview had been brief, and one of the police officers had left, promising that a family liaison officer would arrive at some point. The box of toys from the church collection seemed to be occupying Alfie nicely. Her Cairn Terrier whimpered from behind the kitchen door. Jerry had been a little bit bouncy, excited by the toddler's presence, so she'd closed him in there with the police officer.

Alfie sat with his legs parted in front of him. He played with the plastic dinosaur and the red train, making noises as the two collided. He placed some of the sheep from the Noah's Ark animal set into the carriage. A gentle breeze blew through the bay window that she'd opened on the latch. The thundery weather seemed to have passed, thank goodness. She knew how nervous Jerry was when it thundered and she didn't know how Alfie would react to it either if it got bad.

She glanced at her phone and saw several Facebook messages pop up from the church members group. Everyone was upset and scared about what had happened to Nell. Word had certainly got around quickly. Someone tapped at the door and PC Benton stepped into the room, her hair in a bun and uniform pristine. Thankfully, the officer had shut Jerry in the kitchen. 'There has been an initial strategy meeting. It's all been arranged for Alfie to stay in your care for the time being. There's an emergency contact number for the social worker on the side, should you need to speak to someone about it.'

Sally exhaled. She loathed the thought of Alfie being pulled from pillar to post. He now needed his aunty. 'Have you contacted Nell's sister yet?'

'No, not as yet. I'll keep you updated. Can I get you a cup of tea or anything else?'

'Look, I'm fine. I can manage. You have the magazine and your team has been through the church. I know how busy you are. Alfie and I will be fine now.' She wanted the police officer to go. PC Benton had a job to do but Sally wanted her home back and seeing a uniformed officer constantly being present wasn't good for Alfie. He'd need some food and a sleep.

'Okay, I'll head back to the station. If you need anything, please don't hesitate to call us. You have the information I gave you about victim support?'

'Yes, but I'm okay. I get over things by helping people. That's what I do. I know I saw something today, something I'm never going to be able to erase from my memory—' She gasped and took a few deep breaths. 'I'm okay though. All I want to do is look after Alfie.'

PC Benton walked a little closer. 'It's okay to not be okay, you know. I get that you're everyone else's strength through hard times. You're the person people share their problems with, but you're entitled to be sad, upset, angry and definitely not okay.'

Sally had no idea where her tears came from. She stood and faced PC Benton. 'Thank you for your kind words. When little Alfie has been sorted, I'll call them.'

'Okay. I'll leave you and Alfie to it, then. Is there anything I can help with before I go?'

Sally shook her head. 'I've set up the cot in the box room. I have nappies, lots of food and milk. I'm good, really. I forgot to ask. Is there any news about Nell's dog? I said Toffee could stay here. Jerry is good with other dogs and I think it would be good for Alfie to have his pet here with us.'

'Ah yes. Forensics have nearly finished with him. Someone will deliver him to you later. I don't know what time that will be though. I know it's getting late.'

'Don't worry about it. I somehow think I'm not going to get much sleep tonight.'

'I'll let myself out.' PC Benton smiled sympathetically and left. A few minutes later, Sally heard the front door close. She left Alfie playing on the rug while she peered out of the window. Soon the PC disappeared down the path and past the church. She was soon out of view. Sally closed the window to the darkness outside that almost felt suffocating. The wall lamps made the place feel cosy and she hoped Alfie would wind down soon. The toddler was definitely getting tired.

Sally headed to the kitchen, carefully prising the door open as she listened to Alfie playing at all times. He'd started making choo-choo sounds, which was cute. Jerry whined and tilted his head. Sally reached for his treats. 'Sit.' The dog sat. 'Give Mummy a paw.' Jerry obliged. He was being good and cooperative. It was time to introduce him to Alfie. She gave him a treat which he instantly gobbled. 'Heel,' she commanded, and the excited dog did exactly as it was told.

The choo-choo sounds Alfie was making had stopped. Heart banging, Sally entered the room, scared that Alfie was into something he shouldn't be. The toddler was up on his clumsy feet trying to peer out of the window as he held on to the window ledge with his chubby little fingers. 'Man,' he said.

'Sit, Jerry.' Sally hurried over, scooping Alfie up in her arms.

She stared at the back of the church. She couldn't see anyone. She glanced alongside the old building, there was no man. Maybe Alfie meant something else. Maybe he was trying to say Mum. She shivered. Someone had murdered Nell in the most horrific way. She caught a slight movement from the corner of her eye but when she turned to see what it was, all she could see was a slight gust whipping up a bush. Or had there been a man? She one-handedly drew each curtain in turn. At least no one could see in now. With Alfie in her arms, she darted back into the kitchen and pulled the blind down, blocking out the grave-yard. That's when Jerry began to growl at the front door. One step after another, she crept towards that heavy door. Alfie began to whimper and say Mummy. She held him tight and brought him even closer to her. As she neared the door, she leaned forward and peered through the spyhole. She flinched as her outdoor lights came on. It was nothing, just a response to the timer she'd set. That's when she saw the dark shadow stretching along the path. Alfie cried and tugged her hair. She moved her eye away to reassure him. 'Did you say man or Mum, Alfie?'

She leaned forward again to look through the spyhole. There was no shadow. Maybe her overreactive mind had conjured it up. She bobbed up and down with the now grumpy toddler in her arms and went back into the living room. On the hearth was her huge black wooden cross. 'Is someone out there?' she asked, almost hoping for a sign.

'Man, man, man,' Alfie shouted.

ELEVEN

Gina yawned as she crossed the road with O'Connor. That message had sent her anxiety simmering. She felt her heart rate ramping up as she tried to picture walking around the supermarket. Why had the messenger referred to her health and how could she be looking too well? As for them making sure they saw her again, very soon – that was a touch creepy.

PC Smith guarded the inner cordon and the small crowd that had formed earlier had grown. A sea of people stood at the end of the garage row and they reached all the way to the wildflower meadow. Groups huddled. Lots of people frowned, some wiped a few tears away and a local news van had parked up at the end of the road. A woman turned her back to them as she spoke into a microphone to the camera. The social media bandits had let everyone know about the murder. 'Has the neighbour above returned yet?'

PC Smith nodded. 'Yes, we've let him through and asked him if he'd be so kind as to stay in his flat until you arrived. He also agreed to give us elimination prints as they share the entrance area. Bernard has finished out here and the victim's body has been removed from the scene. I told him to expect you soon.'

'Thank you.' Gina signed in again and knocked at Darrah's door.

O'Connor stood next to her. 'That crowd grew fast.'

'I think it was that teen lad this afternoon, taking a photo over the fence. I bet the news is all over the place. I know we won't have released our victim's identity as yet. I just hope Nell's sister doesn't get wind of her murder before we've even managed to locate her. Sometimes, I really hate people.'

Darrah fought with his stiff front door for a few seconds before he managed to fully open it. 'You must be the detectives on the case. I was told to expect you,' he said in a slight Northern Irish accent. He held a can of lager in one hand. The white vest he had tucked into his jeans looked like it had seen better days. 'Come through.'

Gina entered first, following him up the brown carpeted stairs as O'Connor closed the door and followed.

'You'll have to excuse the place. I only rent it. The décor is hideous.'

'Thank you for speaking to us.'

'I'm sorry about this too,' he said as he pointed to the three empty cans on the coffee table. 'I just can't take it in. Nell was such a lovely woman.' He slumped onto his brown leather sofa. 'How's her little boy and Toffee the dog?'

Gina knew the dog would be released soon, if it hadn't already been. 'They're being taken care of.'

'Take a seat.'

Gina and O'Connor sat on the kitchen chairs that were next to the small dining table in the multi-use room. 'Thank you. Can I confirm your full name, please?'

'Darrah Liam Kelly.'

'Where were you today between twelve fifteen and one this afternoon?'

'Wait, am I a suspect?'

'We're just asking routine questions. We'll be asking all your neighbours the same.'

He went to take a swig from his can but placed it on the table instead. 'I need to stop drinking so much. Sorry. Of course, you need to ask questions and I want you to ask questions so you can find the bastard who did this to her.' He leaned back. 'I was at work.'

'Where do you work?'

'I'm a gardener at Cleevesford Manor. I was there from eight this morning and I finished about five, then I went to the Angel Arms for a couple of drinks before heading home. Actually, rumour was going around about a murder that had happened on my road and I couldn't believe it when I got home. I thought it would be at the block of flats a little farther down the road. There's always trouble happening there. I didn't think for one minute it would be Nell.'

Gina paused so that O'Connor could catch up. 'Can anyone confirm you were at work between twelve fifteen and one?'

'I don't know. I don't exactly work in an office around other people. Some of the guests may have seen me if they were walking around the grounds, or the manager might have been checking up on me.' He scrunched his brow. 'At that time, I stopped to eat my sandwich. I'm a creature of habit when it comes to lunch.'

'Where do you go to eat?'

'I always sit in the rose garden to have lunch, weather permitting. They have cameras there. One of them might have caught me walking around. I didn't hurt Nell. There's no way I'd hurt her.'

Gina thought back to what Kira said about Darrah asking Nell to go out on a date with him. 'What type of relationship did you and Nell have?'

'We didn't. I'm just her neighbour, and her friend. I did a bit of plumbing for her, that's all.'

The wooden chair creaked as Gina leaned back. The stark light in his lounge was starting to give her a headache and her mouth felt like she'd been chewing on sawdust. 'But you asked her out on a date.'

'Oh, come on. I was just being friendly; thought she might want to get to know the locals in the pub. She was new, that's all.' He paused. 'Okay, I liked her. She was nice and her son is a lovely little boy. He reminds me of my own son who lives with his mum in Northern Ireland.' Gina saw a wash of sadness cross his features. 'Less about me, I hoped she might want to go on a date with me, but she didn't. I'm a big boy, I get over rejection easily.' He scratched his dark stubble and ran a hand through his shiny brown hair.

'You looked after her dog a couple of weeks ago.'

'Are you asking me or telling me?'

Gina sighed. Interviewing Darrah was becoming hard work and she had to get back to the station for a briefing. 'Did you look after Nell Craven's dog a couple of weeks ago?'

'So, I did. Yes.'

'Can you remember the date?'

'I can. I booked a day off.' He pulled his phone out from down the side of the settee cushion. 'I'll check my diary for you. It was Tuesday the eighteenth of June. I looked after the dog from early morning, I can't remember what time I went to Nell's. She knocked at my door and told me she was ready to go. I kept the dog with me until evening. Again, I can't remember what time Nell picked him up.'

'What happened that day?'

'Absolutely nothing. Toffee slept most of the day.'

Gina needed to drill down a little. 'Where did you look after him?'

'I was in Nell's flat, then I got tired around lunchtime. I took

him upstairs to mine and had a sleep. It was my day off so I'd
had a few drinks. Silly of me, I know, especially as I said I'd look
after Toffee. But Toffee was fine. Like I said, he went to sleep
most of the day.'

'Did you leave Nell Craven's door on the latch?'

He bit his cheek, then continued. 'Yes. I walked Toffee
earlier that day, just on the patch of grass next to the garages
and I didn't have her key so I left the door on the latch. Problem
is, I forgot to take it off the latch and Nell wasn't too happy
when she got back and I understand why, so I do. I just wanted
to help and I messed up.'

Gina tried to recall what Reg had said. O'Connor saw her
furrowed brows and flicked a few pages back in his pad. She
leaned over and read his notes. 'Can you also tell me where you
were at approximately one in the morning this Tuesday?'

'One in the morning?'

Gina nodded.

'That's easy. I was asleep because yesterday, like today, I
had to be up at six. If you'd asked me about Sunday morning, I
would have been staggering back from a pub but not Tuesday
morning. I was definitely in bed.'

'Were you alone?'

'Do you think I'd bring anyone back here, to this dump? I'm
looking for something nicer by the way. It's just these letting
agents seem to want six months up front and a huge deposit.
I've got a decent job but that isn't good enough for those types.'

Gina glanced around at the yellowing woodchip paper and
the old damp stains in the corner of the room. Nell's and Kira's
flats were much nicer. 'Have you ever seen anyone suspicious
hanging around?'

'Now you mention it, yes. I woke up with cramp about a
week ago and saw a gangly boy, possibly in his late teens,
walking up the path to our shared porch. It was around
midnight. At first, I thought he was delivering a takeaway as

he'd pulled up on a bike, but he didn't have one of those boxes attached to the back where they usually keep the food, and he wasn't carrying a pizza box or a bag. It did strike me as a bit odd.'

'Did you see his face or can you describe him?'

'No to the face. He was wearing a black or grey hoodie and I think he had baggy track bottoms on. I can't remember anything else about him. He knocked on Nell's door. She answered and then he left, all in the space of a few seconds.'

'Which night was that?'

'Wednesday or Thursday, around midnight. I don't know which night exactly.'

'Is there anything else you can tell us that might help?'

He scrunched his brow and picked his vape up from the table. He went to suck on it but gripped it instead. 'I did go out on Saturday night and when I came back from the Angel Arms about two on the Sunday morning, I was staggering around the estate, trying to get home and when I got to the end of our front garden, I dropped my keys. I fumbled around on the floor. Was on my hands and knees trying to find them, then all I saw were these huge trainers with the biggest feet ever in them. I must admit, I was seeing double by this time but a huge man was standing there holding my keys. He really freaked me out. He had these shovel hands, and this unruly beard. Not wanting any trouble, I snatched my keys and said thank you as I staggered to my door and let myself in. When I managed to finally get up the stairs, I looked out of my kitchen window and he'd gone.'

Gina tried to process everything. They had a youth on a bike and a bearded man with huge hands and feet to look for. 'Thank you for your time.' She placed her card on his coffee table. 'If you think of anything else or see anyone suspicious hanging around, please call me.'

'I will do. As I said, I just want to help. I hope you catch whoever did this. She was a young mother, she had everything to look forward to in life and it's been taken from her, just like that.' He shook his head and grabbed his can off the table, where he continued to drink. 'Can you let yourselves out?'

As Gina stepped out of Darrah's flat, she glanced at the back of the crowd, wondering if the killer was amongst them, watching everything unfold while working hard to blend in. No one was standing out. Phones lit up in the darkness and another group huddled under a lamppost. A youth on a pushbike caught her eye, his hood pulled over his head. He began nudging through the crowd on his bike as if trying to escape. Gina turned to PC Ahmed who was standing near the outer cordon. 'Shaf, we need to stop that kid on the bike,' she said in a hushed tone.

With O'Connor on her tail, all three of them jostled through the back of the crowd without arousing too much suspicion amongst the press and onlookers, then they all ran as fast as they could. Gina's heart thudded against her ribcage as she sprinted alongside the wildflower meadow towards the end of the street that led to a maze of other streets. As Gina took a left and then a right before darting down a path between gardens, she heard a rustling sound. A bike flew over a wooden fence and the youth followed it. Darting ahead, Gina threw herself against it with a jump. As she gripped the top of the fence she hauled herself over, dropping breathlessly into a bed of shrubs. She then saw the youth's figure in the darkness. He was headed towards an old building and turned alongside it. Gasping, Gina struggled to move, every muscle in her body protesting. They had lost the youth. As she followed the building round, she noticed that there was a metal fence around it. She heard heavy breathing coming from behind a skip. Grabbing her phone, she called O'Connor. 'Get backup here now. Lavender Lane, the large house with the metal fence around it. I have him. Hurry.'

Heart still banging, Gina held a hand over her chest, willing it to calm down. She heard voices approaching. 'You can't run, you're surrounded.' She only hoped the youth believed her.

Until O'Connor and Shaf arrived, there was no one else. A twinge of pain almost made Gina sick as it travelled its way up the left-hand side of her chest. She inhaled and exhaled slowly and the pain went. It was nothing, nothing at all.

He came out, wheeling his bike by his side. Strings of stingers had caught in the bike's spokes. 'I haven't done anything. I was just watching, that's all and you chased me.'

Gina walked over, sure now he wasn't going to run. That's when she saw a handful of tiny baggies lying in a pile where the youth had been hiding. It was time to make an arrest and question him.

'I swear I didn't kill her. You've got to believe me.'

PC Ahmed came up behind him with his handcuffs out and O'Connor walked up to Gina panting. 'I see you caught him, guv?'

'Book him in and we need to log those baggies in evidence,' Gina said, her gaze fixed on the teenager. 'I'm arresting you under suspicion of supplying a controlled drug under the Misuse of Drugs Act 1971. You do not need to say anything. But it may harm your defence if you do not mention when questioned something which you later rely on in court. Anything you do say may be given in evidence. What's in the bags?' she addressed the youth.

'I have the right to remain silent.' He shrugged.

TWELVE

MAEVE

Maeve kneeled on her bed and began tugging at the man's belt. She had no idea what his name was or if she'd ever see him again. All she knew was that she'd had a big day, things had got tense and she craved some release. It was tough being at the top. If she had to bury her tension while waiting for the biggest decisions to be made, she'd do it by bringing this fit man back to her apartment after getting half smashed with her team at a cocktail bar in Brindleyplace. She'd felt the tension between them all day at the meeting and he was her key to forgetting, if only for a few hours. Talking about their new IT system had never been so exciting and this handsome expert had certainly made her hot under the collar.

Her phone rang again. She sighed and turned away from him. She didn't recognise the number at all. Again, it stopped and the caller had left yet another voicemail.

'Can you turn it off?' he asked, a crooked smile forming on his face.

He leaned into her and his lips brushed her neck, sending tingles through her body. He began to feel for the clasp of her bra and she saw her annoying phone flash again, just before it began to ring. *Ignore, ignore, ignore,* her inner voice kept saying. The phone kept ringing and it was putting her off. She almost wanted to grab it and throw it against the wall. No one had any business calling her at this time but that didn't always stop them. She thought of her team and all they'd been saying about how their new line was going to be held up at the factory because of a management issue and she'd tasked them with finding a solution.

'Maeve, are you okay?' The man backed off, sensing that her thoughts were elsewhere.

'Yes, it's nothing.' She pressed her mouth on his, trying to coax his tongue into hers but he nudged her back.

'Only you were in your own world then. Look, I think we should leave it tonight. I'll call you tomorrow, okay?'

Was he rejecting her? She had felt his hardness pressing into her thigh only a few seconds ago. Had her moment of thoughts turned him off that quickly. She grabbed her discarded white shirt from where he dropped it when he pulled it off her back and she covered her chest up with it. 'Just go.'

Without being asked again, he collected his trousers from her bedroom floor and stepped into them, dressing as he left her bedroom. Then he slammed her front door as he left.

'Shit.' She grabbed her stiletto and threw it at the door before snatching her phone up. She pressed the answerphone button and waited for the message to start.

The muscles on her face tensed up as she listened to the message from someone called Detective Constable Wyre from Cleevesford Police, asking for her to contact them immediately. She called the number, suddenly feeling more sober than she had all evening. The mojitos were fast wearing off now as she waited for them to answer. 'Hello, you've been trying to call me.'

'Hello, I'm DC Wyre. Could you please tell me who you are?'

'I'm Maeve, Maeve Craven. What's happened?'

'I'm so sorry. This isn't something we normally do over the phone but we didn't know who this number belonged to.'

'What? Tell me? Is it Nell?'

'I can send an officer over to be with you.'

'No, no, no. Just spill. What's going on?'

The DC paused. 'The body of a young woman was found in the garden of a flat in Cleevesford and we believe it's your half-sister, Nell Craven. I am so sorry for your loss.'

Maeve gasped several times until she caught her breath. Nell was dead. The DC rattled on about Alfie, that he was safe for now but she couldn't take in what had been said.

As soon as the DC ended the call, Maeve let out a small cry. She knew exactly who could have killed Nell, the same person who had murdered their mother.

THIRTEEN

Gina gulped down the cold bottle of water that Briggs had given to her. The incident room was buzzing. Briggs had run through the press release. Nell's name hadn't been mentioned to them but word had spread from social media. She hoped that the youth would be interviewed soon. They were just waiting for his solicitor to arrive. At the centre on the board was Nell's name. A map had been pinned up next to it and a red push pin marked out the location where Nell's body had been found. Another pin had been placed in where the church was located. O'Connor bit into the burger he'd popped out to buy, knowing it would be a long evening and the smell of fried onions hung heavy in the room. Briggs handed DC Paula Wyre the pen so that she could update the board. She turned to acknowledge Detective Sergeant Jacob Driscoll, who had just entered with a can of pop. He sat next to Gina.

'How did court go?' she asked.

'They had me up at the end of the day. I literally did nothing all day but I've done my bit now so I'm back. I've tried to catch up as much as I can.'

DC Paula Wyre retied her straight black hair into a ponytail and added the suspects onto the board. 'We have yet to find her son's father. One of the numbers Nell had been calling regularly was her half-sister.'

Gina turned to face Wyre. 'Great. I'm glad we managed to find her.'

'Maeve Craven is coming into the station tomorrow morning. A PC has gone over to see her in the meantime.' Wyre turned back towards the board.

Detective Chief Inspector Chris Briggs cleared his throat. Although they'd been in a secret on/off relationship for years, Gina had recently found his over the top concern for her a bit stifling. As much as her head was telling her to keep him at arm's length, she missed being close to him. 'Gina, could you update us? You're going to be Senior Investigating Officer on the case and, Jacob, I want you to work closely with her.'

Still in her summer attire, Gina stood. At least it had cooled down a bit and the low rumbles of thunder had subsided. She gave the briefest of thoughts to all that salad she'd left in her boot earlier. It would be like mush now. But that didn't matter. She discreetly held a hand to her chest, where she'd felt that pain. Her heart was humming rapidly. Dismissing it, she dropped her hand. She was in no way about to have a heart attack. Her cholesterol had been high but it was nothing. She had been running too fast, that was all. She had a job to do. A woman had been murdered and she wasn't going to stop until she found out who had killed her.

'We have a couple of leads. The man who lives in the flat above is called Darrah Kelly. We need to check his alibi. He works at Cleevesford Manor and claims that he was having lunch in the rose garden there at the time of the murder. O'Connor?'

'Yep.' He wiped his greasy fingers on a napkin as he swallowed the last of his burger.

'I'd like you to head over there and see if there are any witnesses or CCTV to corroborate this.'

O'Connor noted that down. 'I'll get on it first thing.'

'Wyre, any more information on Nell Craven's phone?'

'She received a call from another number but that number is no longer in use. It's a burner phone and the call log only shows a connection lasting ten seconds. There are no text messages from this number. Kira Fellows called a lot. The calls started just after Nell moved in. There is another phone number stored under Nell's contacts. It looked like she had several lengthy discussions with this contact. I haven't been able to get hold of this person yet, but we have traced the number to someone called Abigail Bretton. Nell called her twice a week, without fail, every Monday and Friday night. The calls lasted around twenty minutes.' Wyre continued. 'I did a little digging. Abigail is a nurse who works at a hospital in Warwick, and she lives in Redditch. I then checked her social media. She doesn't use it much but she did post a picture of her tired face after being on a night shift last week.'

'We need to keep trying to contact her. If you have no luck, Jacob and I will go and see her in the morning after we've spoken to Maeve Craven. It sounds like the two women are close if they spoke on the phone that regularly.'

Gina drank some more water, her body seemingly absorbing every drop. 'O'Connor and I went to Kira's flat. She claims to have been in all day with her sick son. She was meant to go to the stay and play group at the church with Nell. Kira said that Nell had seemed worried and had been behaving oddly. She also claimed that Nell thought someone was bugging her flat or watching her. O'Connor, once we're finished here, could you please enter all the information onto the system so we're all working off the same page?'

'No worries, guv.'

'Thank you. I know it's been a long day and I appreciate

that you must all be tired. Right, onto the second suspect. Identity unknown. One of the neighbour's, Reginald Hampton, saw someone suspicious in Nell's garden at around one in the morning on Tuesday. We don't have much of a description, just that of a bulky dark figure. On Monday, Mr Hampton was going out to his garage when he saw Nell running out of her flat crying. He said she looked at him and then ran back into her flat.' Gina paused so that Wyre could add the reports onto the timeline. 'Going back to Darrah. He described how he came back from the Angel Arms about two in the morning on Sunday, drunk. He saw a man by the back gate and described him as having big feet, shovel-like hands and a beard. We could be looking at the same person who Mr Hampton witnessed in Nell and Darrah's shared garden in the early hours of Tuesday. Have we managed to go through the door-to-door interviews?'

Wyre nodded. 'Yes, I've looked through those. No one suspicious has been mentioned except the boy on the bike. A couple of people living close by saw him talking to Nell on various occasions.'

'Do we know his name? He was refusing to talk when we brought him in.'

'Drake Spool.'

'Ah, I have heard that name brandished around the station,' Gina replied. 'I often hear the PCs talking about him. He was arrested last year for graffitiing the library right in front of the new street camera. Not the brightest of petty criminals.'

'That's the one, guv,' Wyre replied.

'Do we know what was in the baggies found at the scene?'

'Not yet. It's a white powder.'

'So, Drake has taken up dealing now.'

'It looks that way. We should find out exactly what's in the bags soon.'

'Keep me updated.'

Trainee DC Jhanvi Kapoor entered, her hand gripping the

end of a lead with a tiny tan-coloured chihuahua tugging at the other end. 'Forensics have released Toffee.'

'Take a seat for a moment. When we finish up here, I'll take him to Sally's. She's offered to look after him for now. Right, let's move on so we can get everything entered onto the board and system. The victim's eyes had been removed. They looked to have been cut out with a knife, but I'm hoping that after the post-mortem we will have a better idea of what went on. Do we know if our victim's eyes were found anywhere near the scene?'

Wyre shook her head. 'Bernard called in just after the victim's body was taken. They didn't find them.'

Gina scrunched her nose. The killer still had Nell's eyes and that sent a chill through her. She continued. 'Thanks for the update on that. Toffee, Nell's dog, was found tied to a tree in the woodland. He had a little Turkish eye attached to his collar. Eyes mean something to the killer. We need to bear that in mind.' She let that sink in for a few seconds. Toffee began to yap. 'I'm going to wrap this up for now. Tomorrow Jacob and I will speak to Maeve Craven, before heading off to Abigail Bretton's. Wyre, if you could forward me her address in the meantime, that would be great. Also, could you try to interview Drake Spool in the morning. The substance should have been tested by then, besides I think he's going to go no comment all the way but we can try. If you don't have any luck, I'll try again tomorrow afternoon. We can keep him for twenty-four hours.'

'Yes, guv. There were just six baggies of a very small amount of substance. I'm guessing his solicitor is going to push for personal use.'

Someone was calling on the main phone. Gina answered. 'DI Harte. Can I help you?' The room went silent.

'I, err, I think I know who killed my half-sister, Nell. You have to find him. It's Nell's father, Ross Craven. He was released from prison five weeks ago. He murdered my mother.'

FOURTEEN

SALLY

Thursday, 4 July

Sally parted her living room curtains and peered towards the church again, just like she'd been doing every few minutes since Alfie had gone to sleep in the cot upstairs. She'd tried to speak to him a little more about the man, but Alfie had then started saying Mummy. After reading him a story about a toad that turned into a boy, he'd fallen asleep in her arms. Glancing at her watch, she saw that it was now nearly twelve thirty and there was still no sign of Toffee. Her dog lay spark out on the rug that Alfie had been playing on earlier. She glanced up at the cross on her fireplace and whispered, 'Please take good care of Nell.'

A rattle of the back door made her flinch. She stood like a statue, unable to move as she listened out to see if she could hear it again. Deep breath in, deep breath out. She could stand there all night, fixed to the spot, or she could take a look. Her imagination was running amok. Like PC Benton had said, she needed to address her shock and her own feelings about seeing

Nell's body. But that was a rattle, she'd heard it. Jerry jumped up and ran out of the living room, growling. She called after him but he refused to come back. Had she locked the back door?

Running as fast as she could to the kitchen, she went to turn the key in the door but it was already locked. She'd locked it after letting Jerry out for a pee. She pulled down the kitchen blind and the door blind, needing to shut the whole world out. Making sure her phone was in her pocket, she stepped back and turned the kitchen light off. Jerry snuffled at the door and Sally knew he needed to go out again. She hadn't walked him all night. As soon as her eyes adjusted to the lack of light, she lifted the blind away from the windowsill and peered out across the graveyard. She couldn't see anyone.

Her door did rattle sometimes if there was a breeze. The vicarage was such an old building, it came with its squeaks and creaks. They'd never worried her before tonight. Maybe there was no man loitering earlier and, just maybe, no one had rattled the door. She stared at her knife block, grabbed it and placed it in the cupboard under the sink. Sally was a listener, not a fighter and if she had to get herself out of a mess, she'd do it with words. She thought back to Nell's body again and flinched as she imagined the knife being plunged into her eyes. No, Sally could never stab a person, not even in self-defence.

Jerry began to scratch the door as he got more desperate. She took two deep breaths and tried to rationalise with her over-active imagination. The door always rattles. There is no one there. No one knew that Alfie was staying with her. Alfie said Mum, not man.

Heart banging, she held her breath, unlocked and opened the door.

There was no one there, just as she suspected. She exhaled and glanced to the left and then to the right as Jerry ran to his favourite patch of grass and peed next to a gravestone. She stepped out. 'Hello.' She felt slightly silly calling out when there was no one around.

A loud crashing sound came from the bushes to her left.

'Jerry, get in now.' The dog started running towards the commotion instead of back into the kitchen. Sally stepped back inside, locking herself in and almost crying out with fear. Jerry came back and barked at the door. Then there was a loud crash against the wood.

FIFTEEN

SALLY

Another thud came from the other side of the wood. Sally let out a cry as she pulled her phone from her pocket. She hit call on Gina's number. That's when she heard the DI answering from behind the door. 'Sally, I'm out the back. Dammit,' Gina shouted as the call ended.

Maybe Gina was in trouble. Sally swallowed back her fear. If Gina needed help, she would not fail her. With shaky hands, she opened the back door. Jerry jumped at her before hurrying into the kitchen and gobbling up his food. That's when she saw Gina running after a tiny dog across the graves. 'Gina,' she shouted as the DI ducked behind a gravestone and came back up a moment later.

'Sorry, when I got Toffee out of the car, I let go of him for a second and he was gone. For a dog with such short legs, he can move.' Gina almost fell as she grabbed the end of the dog's lead. By now Jerry was barking like the place was under attack, then the little dog began barking back. Jerry then escaped through her legs and ran towards the dog before sniffing at its rear end.

Sally ran out with the lead and clipped it to Jerry's collar.

This wasn't the introduction between the two dogs she'd hoped for, but it had happened now.

Ten minutes later they were sitting at Sally's kitchen island enjoying a peppermint tea as the dogs sniffed around each other. They seemed to be getting along, which was a relief.

'How's Alfie?'

Sally sighed. 'He was a tired little boy. He kept saying Mummy. All I've told him is that he'll be staying with me for a short while. Have you heard from his aunt?'

Gina nodded. 'We have. I'm seeing her tomorrow so we'll have more news.'

'Well, Alfie can stay here as long as you need me to look after him but I'm guessing that his aunt might want to take him home with her.' Sally noticed that her hands had a nervous tremor. She placed them in her lap.

Gina smiled as if she was trying to put her at ease. 'It's so kind of you to look after Alfie, and Toffee too.'

'It's the least I can do.' A lump formed in her throat. She couldn't bring the little boy's mother back. Her mind was whirring with all the events of the day. Nell's eyeless face. The blood. Alfie in her arms and Alfie pointing out the window saying "man". She wondered if she should say anything to Gina. She should, even if he had said Mum and she'd got it wrong. 'Alfie was looking out of my bay window earlier. I thought he was shouting the word man but the more I think of it, the more convinced I am that he was saying Mum. I'm literally on edge and hearing things. Today, when I saw Nell... I can't believe someone could do that to her.' Tears began to spill again.

Gina slid off the wooden stool and placed an arm around Sally's shoulder. 'What you saw was horrible and I'm so sorry you had to see it. You are totally entitled to be upset. You think it gets easier when I do my job but it's worse, with each case I hate humanity a bit more.'

Sally sniffed and wiped her eyes. 'Sorry, I think I had that building up.'

'You cry away.'

She blew her nose on a piece of kitchen roll. 'That's enough of that. I told myself I wouldn't crack again and that Alfie and the community need me to be strong at a time like this. I will lead them through it as best I can, be there for everyone. There will be a lot of fear, a lot of worry, and until you catch whoever did this, people will need to be extra careful.' She shook her head and arms to shake her emotions away. 'As for me, I think Alfie was talking about his mum but as soon as he said it, and I thought I heard the word man, I've been scaring myself silly with every creak of the house. I keep seeing shadows that aren't there and I keep thinking the murderer is hiding in my bushes. It's ridiculous.'

'It's not ridiculous, Sally. Not at all.'

'Anyway, I need to stop this crying. Do you want a biscuit?'

Gina thought about her cholesterol but her groaning stomach won. 'I would love a biscuit. I haven't eaten all day.'

'Oh, in that case, I'll bust out the cake. I save the cake for really bad days.'

'Are you still scaring the kids with your white sheet on a broom handle?'

'Of course. They come to the graveyard to see ghosts; I make sure they see ghosts.' For the first time that day, Sally allowed herself to laugh but then the image of Nell came to the front of her mind again. 'Do you know why the killer took her eyes?'

'We don't as yet.' The detective went silent for a moment as if mulling something over.

'Is everything okay, Gina?'

'I shouldn't really be revealing any details of the case but a Turkish lucky eye was found attached to Toffee's collar. Again, we have an eye link. Please don't reveal that to anyone else. I could get into huge trouble but I trust you and I know you're a wealth of knowledge.'

'And I'm honoured that you trust me. I would not break your confidence under any circumstance.'

'What do you know about eyes?'

Happy to feel useful, Sally tried to think of what the Turkish eye meant and she tried to think if anything in the Bible talked about eyes being removed. 'There's the obvious, an eye for an eye. The murderer took both of her eyes. Was it revenge, who knows? There's Matthew 5:29-30. If your right eye causes you to stumble, gouge it out and throw it away. It's better to lose one part of your body than for your whole body to be thrown into hell. This is more literal. The intention isn't really for people to gouge out their own eyes. Besides, looking at Nell, she didn't do that to herself. Did she stumble and did someone decide to take it upon themselves to remove her eyes because of that, who knows? If so, how did she stumble and really if we were being literal with that passage, she would have gouged it out herself? No, I don't think it's that and I don't think I have anything else at the moment. My brain isn't really working that well and I'm waffling.'

'Not at all. You're being really helpful. Right now, talking this through is a real help. How about the lucky eye?'

'I know it's meant to be protective against evil and bad luck. It's meant to bring good fortune if kept in the home, which is why a lot of people display a lucky eye.'

The detective looked even more confused. 'Why put it on the dog? Was the murderer intending to protect the dog from evil? Are they suggesting that Nell was evil by doing that?' Gina paused. 'Not that I believe in evil. I believe some people do horrible things but not in a spiritual sense.'

Sally tried to simplify her thinking. 'Maybe the murderer didn't want to see Nell looking at them. Were the eyes removed before or after she was murdered?'

'I don't know that yet. I'll know more after the post-mortem. Sally?'

'Yes.'

'I know this sounds like a big ask, but is there anyone else who can carry out your church duties for a few days? I'd rather no one knew that Alfie was staying here for now.'

'Do you think we're in some kind of danger?'

Gina shook her head, reassuring Sally slightly. 'No one knows he's staying with you but until we know more, I'd like to keep it that way.'

Sally shivered. 'I'll see what I can do. I'm certain I can get someone to cover my duties.' Something else occurred to her. She noticed that Nell had wandered around the back of the building during the stay and play but where had she gone? She'd been away for longer than it would have taken to write 'Help me, God' in a magazine. What had Nell been doing around the back of the church, by her office and all the store cupboards? As soon as she was up in the morning, she was going to take Alfie to the church and have a good look around. There was nothing on until the afternoon so no one would see them there.

'What are you thinking?' Gina asked.

'Nothing. Just going over the day in my head.' She wouldn't bother Gina with what she was thinking just yet, especially as it might come to nothing, but it was possible that Nell had left her another clue and if she had, Sally was going to find it.

SIXTEEN

Gina rubbed her tired eyes. It was just after seven in the morning and Jacob had picked her up only forty-five minutes earlier. Her upper stomach was bloated from the huge wedge of chocolate cake she'd shared with Sally about one in the morning but, despite that, she'd still woken up hungry. After rescuing most of her shopping from the boot, she'd gone straight to bed, but sleep had evaded her. That message had been playing on her mind. She had no idea who had sent it and she'd felt the threatening undertone. It wasn't sitting well with her. She checked her phone but there were no more messages.

As always, Jacob looked awake and fresh. Quite his opposite, Gina ached from trying to throw herself over the fence and running like she was going for gold as she chased Drake Spool and then Toffee the dog. She bit into the apple she'd grabbed from her fruit bowl as she rushed out the door. She'd intended to have porridge or something equally healthy that morning to make up for the cake, but she'd needed sleep more.

'I hate driving into Birmingham at this time,' Jacob said as he pulled up at yet another set of lights on the Hagley Road.

Gina glanced at the Maps app. 'We're close. Just over a mile to go and still fifteen minutes.'

'That's the slowest mile ever.'

The red flag on the screen showing Maeve's apartment building was getting ever closer on the satnav.

As Jacob pulled up towards the block of apartments, he rolled his window down and hit the number twenty-four buzzer.

'Hello,' said the woman.

'Miss Craven, it's DS Driscoll and I'm with DI Harte.'

The buzzer released the parking barrier. Jacob drove in. Gina wrapped her apple core in a piece of tissue before putting it in her bag. Once parked up in the private courtyard, Gina stepped out, stretching her arms and legs, trying to wake her stiff muscles up. The sound of a boat chugging behind the large brick wall gave way to quacking ducks after it had passed. Gina loved the canal side and Brindleyplace.

Once they were buzzed into the block, she almost smiled with relief as she saw a lift. While waiting, Gina inhaled the subtle jasmine scent that filled the lobby. It was the plushest block of apartments she'd ever been in with its floor-to-ceiling glass doors and real plants that looked well pruned. It reminded her of a swanky hotel. She imagined Alfie coming to live here and toddling through it all. The lift doors opened and they were soon heading up to the penthouse. The doors opened out onto a spacious landing, again a selection of plants neatly edged the walls, and floor-to-ceiling glass gave them a full view of the canal and towpath.

'This place is amazing,' Jacob half whispered as he rang Maeve's bell.

The woman answered and rubbed her red-rimmed eyes. Her sleek shoulder-length red hair caught a ray of sun that reached through the skylight above. Her yoga pants and vest top showed a perfectly toned frame underneath. 'Come through.'

She led them into a large living room. Large bifold doors led
to a fully decked balcony. With the doors open, a warm gentle
breeze danced through the room. Several scrunched-up tissues
had been piled on the coffee table and an empty wine glass had
toppled on the floor. A photo had been left next to the tissues
and Gina recognised the two girls instantly. The one on the left
had Maeve's high cheekbones and her large brown eyes. Her
hair was brown in the photo, the same colour as the other girl.
The girl on the right had her hair pulled back into a tight ponytail, revealing the mole on her forehead. Her eyes were blue.

'We'd like to offer our condolences. I can't imagine what
you're going through right now.'

Maeve shrugged and sighed. 'Have a seat. Can I get you a
drink?'

'I'm fine, thank you.' Jacob shook his head too. 'Did an
officer visit last night to speak to you?'

The woman nodded. 'A PC from Birmingham sat with me
for a while and said you'd be coming this morning. I think she'd
have stayed all night but I told her to go home as I just needed to
be on my own. Have you found her father yet?'

Gina sat. 'No. One of our officers made a few calls. He was
actually meant to be staying at a hostel and having a probation
meeting weekly, but he hasn't been back for nearly two weeks
which means he's breached his conditions.'

'So, he went AWOL and killed Nell. I can't believe he's out
of prison.' Maeve sat in a chair opposite them, partly obscuring
the view. 'I was ten when that man killed my mum. I don't
remember too much, I just know he scared me. He'd get so
angry and shout at her all the time and I would run away and
hide in my bedroom. Hours later, Mum would come and get me
after he'd stormed out, and we'd cry together.' She paused. 'It
wasn't always like that. There were times he'd try hard, like
when he took us on cottage breaks. I remember holidays by the
sea and him bringing me and Mum gifts. I know what that was

now, she was in this cycle of being love-bombed then abused. It just went on and on. A few months later I remember Mum taking my hand and holding it to her tummy, she explained that I was going to have a brother or sister. I was so angry. All I wanted was for us to go back to our little flat away from him. After her announcement, I knew we were never leaving his house, then Nell came along. You'd have thought he'd have been happy but all he did was shout and yell at Mum and one day, when Nell was three and I was ten, he killed her.' Maeve swallowed and looked away.

Gina paused. 'Do you know why he would kill his daughter?'

'The man is just a psycho. If you'd met him, you'd know. He doesn't love anyone but himself. Maybe she didn't write to him in prison or visit him. That would make him angry. I found some photos for you.' Maeve grabbed the photo on the table and a couple of others that were turned over. She passed them to Gina.

She glanced at the photo of the two of them at a party. 'Did Nell have any tattoos?'

'She had Alfie's name written on her wrist. She didn't have it in that photo as Alfie wasn't born then. That was taken at Nan's eightieth, three years ago. She's dead now but she brought us up after he killed Mum. She tried her best to make everything feel normal but it never did. We never had much but she did her best. We ended up living on the estate with her. It was all graffiti and gangs. I couldn't wait to leave and go to uni and as bad as this might sound, I wanted to leave Nell. She reminded me of her dad and it was too painful.' Maeve hiccupped a sob. 'I blamed Nell for Mum's murder. If she hadn't come along, we'd have left him and Mum would still be alive. I'm ashamed to say that I did my best to distance myself from her, which is why we didn't speak that often. Whenever I saw Nell, it made me think about what happened to my mum.

That's it. That's me and Nell for you. I left her with Nan when she was only eleven and I didn't come back for the holidays. I feel horrible now. I shouldn't have blamed her but I was so angry and I held on to that anger, and it's still in me now.'

'I'm sorry. I can't begin to imagine what you went through, losing your mother like that.' Gina paused for a moment. 'We're trying to locate Alfie's father.'

Maeve let out a huff. 'You've got no chance. He was probably a waiter on a holiday she went on. When she tried to call the hotel he'd been doing some work at to tell him she was pregnant, he wasn't even working there anymore. The hotel wouldn't give his personal details out. She decided she was going to go it alone when it came to her pregnancy. She didn't love him; it was just a drunken night. We didn't talk often on the phone, but Nell did like to tell me everything when we did.'

'Do you know where she met the waiter?'

'No. She used to go away a lot. I think it was Ibiza or maybe it was when she did the weekender to Lisbon. She travelled a lot so I really can't remember. I don't think you'll ever find him though.'

Gina undid the top button of her short-sleeved blouse to let some air flow over her body.

'What's going to happen to Alfie?'

'If we can't locate his father, you're his next of kin.'

Maeve crossed her legs. 'You know, I've never even held a baby or looked after a friend's kid. I don't know the first thing about them, and I swore I'd never have one. I swore I'd never end up like Mum and I know she stayed with him because of me, because she had nothing. Having children makes a person desperate. If it wasn't for me or Nell, Mum would still be alive, I'm sure of it.' She began to hyperventilate and ran outside onto the balcony where she gasped. Gina followed her. 'I can't do it. I can't bring Alfie up. I just can't. Look at me. I'm not a mother. I work all hours, I drink a bit too much, I party hard. I do what I need to forget the past and...' Tears flooded her face. 'Why wasn't I there for her? I spent all these years blaming her for what he did to my lovely mum. It wasn't her fault. She was a victim too and she needed me, and I let her down. It's my fault she's been killed because I wasn't there for her.' Maeve broke down.

'Maeve, do you mind me calling you Maeve?'

She shook her head and sobbed into her arm.

'This isn't your fault. You weren't close and that's fine. The only person to blame here is the person who killed your sister.'

Several minutes later, Gina had led Maeve back to her chair. 'Where's Alfie now?'

'He's still in Cleevesford. The local vicar, Sally Stevens, is taking good care of him. Nell had attended her stay and play group earlier that day. Alfie is safe. He's being very well looked after. She also has a background in foster care.' Gina paused. 'Would you like to see him?'

'I can't think right now. Can I just take some time to let this sink in?'

'Of course.'

Maeve leaned back and fanned her damp eyes with her hands. 'I know what it's like to feel alone, to lose the only person you love by an act of extreme violence. I should be there for Alfie but I don't know if I'm what he needs.' She paused. 'I'm not what he needs.'

Gina saw through Maeve's tough exterior and she saw the scared child she once was. 'When you're ready to talk about it, please call me. I can put you in touch with the social worker. You know where he is and you know he's safe.'

'Thank you.' She huffed out a breath and sat up straight.

'There's something I need to show you both and I wished I'd called the police but I didn't. A part of me was in denial so I just buried it.'

'Has something happened?'

Maeve nodded. 'Over the past couple of weeks, I've had this feeling. It's strange as I can't see anyone who is out of place when I look around but I jog along the towpath most mornings. I'm normally out there early, so there aren't many people around, but on a couple of occasions I've glanced back and... I don't know, I felt like I was being watched. I don't know whether I thought I heard a footstep under the bridge, but then saw no one there. One day I was so convinced someone was behind me, I ran even faster to escape them and I bumped into a poor woman with a pushchair and almost toppled into the canal. I was that panicked. Maybe it's because I heard the news that he was out of prison. I thought I was imagining it, allowing my mind to toy with me, then something happened. I don't know if you saw our letter boxes, they're built into the wall outside the gate. No one can enter unless they're buzzed in, not even by foot. Well, I found a note in my letter box a few days ago. It had been hand delivered.' Maeve got up and left the room for a minute before coming back in. She handed the piece of paper to Gina.

Opening it, Gina read the words, written in scrawled capital letters.

YOUR BITCH MUM DESERVED WHAT SHE GOT.

SEVENTEEN

SALLY

A squirrel darted across the grass with an acorn in its mouth. Alfie pointed and giggled with the sticky hand that wasn't holding Sally's. It had been a pleasure to watch him eating honey on toast, giving her a few moments to take her mind off what had happened to his mother. Her long black dress flowed as the breeze caught the bottom and blew it up like a balloon. She pulled out the huge brass key and opened the back door to the church, the entrance that led her straight to the offices, toilets and storage cupboards. If Nell had left something behind, Sally was going to find it. She stepped onto the wiry green carpet and inhaled the damp smell that the church always emitted. If funds had allowed, she'd have ripped it up and replaced it with new tiles years ago. Alfie toddled along, laughing as he pressed his honey-dabbed fingers on the cream walls. She forgot to wipe them clean but that didn't matter right now. What mattered was searching around to see if Nell had left anything else for her to find, a clue as to why she'd been so scared.

'Door.' Alfie went to push the door open to the ladies' loos. He didn't have the strength, so he banged on it with both hands.

'Shall we go in?' Sally smiled at him and he nodded in an exaggerated way. It was as good a place as any to start. At least the place wasn't due to be cleaned until the next day so everything would be as it was left yesterday. She glanced around. Both cubicles were empty apart from a stray empty toilet roll that had fallen on the floor. 'Alfie, come with me. Let's try another room, lovely.' He staggered back to her and held her hand.

'Door,' he yelled again as he excitedly pointed to the men's loos. Again, they went in and there was nothing.

After leaving, she tried several cupboards which she knew were all locked, and only she had the key. Nell would have had no access to those. There were another three locked rooms, all containing furniture used for events such as spare chairs and trestle tables. Then, she hurried towards her office.

'Door,' Alfie said again, pleased with himself.

She smiled at him. 'You are so clever. Shall we go through the door?'

He nodded and pushed as Sally pressed the door handle. It was the one room, with exception to the toilets, that she hadn't locked. Her cassocks and cinctures were all hung up, not as neatly as other members of the clergy would hang them but she kept them in order. Alfie ran over and stepped into her old black Crocs before giggling at how big they looked on his feet. Everything was one big adventure to him and that saddened her. He was playing and had no idea that his mother had been murdered. Sally had prayed all night for both Nell's soul and for Alfie. Eventually she had fallen asleep, sickened to the stomach for eating the rest of the cake when Gina had left, but like a lot of people, eating was how she dealt with upset. The toddler fell onto his bottom and began hiding behind her long cassock.

While he was occupied, she darted over to her large wooden desk and rifled through the drawers. Nothing seemed to be disturbed. Her Sunday sermon still sat on the top, begging for her to finish it. That was what she'd planned to do after the stay and play group. She glanced at what she'd written and took a moment to think of the message that she'd been working on. She was going to talk about random acts of kindness and how if we were all kind to everyone, including people we don't know, then the world would be a better place. She was going on to say that no one could possibly know what other people were going through and that silent battles were just that, battles that people didn't speak about. Turning the sheet over, she wondered what battles Nell was going through. Nell had probably been silent until she decided to write help me in a parish magazine. She felt herself choking up. Nell had reached out to her and Sally had failed to help her. She'd been too late. If only she hadn't walked her dog first or maybe she should have handed the baby back to Shayla and run after Nell, leaving one of the parents in charge for a short while. Her mind kept screaming out the words, if only, and it was hurting so much. Her sermon would now be placed on hold and the Reverend Ernest Langham would temporarily take over her duties when he arrived.

She took a few seconds to compose herself and continued searching for clues, any clues. Her shelves were overflowing with books, magazines and every note she'd ever made in no particular order. Even her old university work still had a place amongst all her important things. She got rid of nothing. If Nell had touched anything on her shelves, the whole lot probably would've toppled. When all this was over, she was going to have a sort out. Cobwebs hung from the ceiling, reaching all four corners of the room. Sally blushed, knowing that her office was in a complete state, but she didn't have time to clean it and the lady who cleaned a couple of times a week never came into her office. Besides, she couldn't deal with the cobwebs now, she had to look after Alfie and the reverend would understand. 'I can't see anything here, lovely,' she said to Alfie.

'Mummy,' he said as he hid under her dangling cassock, still on his bottom as he babbled away, playing peek-a-boo with the material.

Sally swallowed, sadness welling up again. She had no idea what she hoped to find. A great big piece of paper with the name of the person who killed Nell written on it? 'Alfie, shall we go back to the vicarage and see Toffee and Jerry. I bet they're missing us and I know Toffee will want a cuddle from you.'

'Mummy.' This time the toddler didn't peer from behind the material.

Sally was going to have to go over and pick him up. Maybe his little legs had tired of toddling around. She reached down and shouted peek-a-boo as she pulled the material back. That's when she saw Alfie holding a bracelet made of plaited leather. Sally had seen Nell wearing an identical bracelet but maybe she had been wearing two when she arrived before losing one in Sally's office.

'Mummy.' Alfie thrust it towards her.

Nell must have been in her office, but why? There were pens and magazines out the front. She glanced around again and nothing else was out of place. Not a thing. She lifted the cassock up and Nell hadn't left anything else on the floor. Sally guessed she must have been rummaging before accidentally losing it. What for? What did Nell want or do? She furrowed her brows, confused as to her motive for coming into Sally's office.

The back door slammed. Sally snatched the toddler in her arms and held him tightly. 'Hello,' she called as she crept back out into the corridor. One of the cupboard doors looked to be open slightly. She grabbed the handle and it opened with ease. Had she locked it last time she looked in it? She tried all the others and they were definitely locked. All except the one she was now staring at. She glanced inside and it was full of Bibles, candles and kneeling cushions. Nothing more, nothing less. She pushed the door closed and grimaced as she gazed up and down the corridor, listening at the same time for any sign of a person being in the building.

After checking the whole church, she couldn't see anyone. Confused, she hurried to the back door, key in hand ready to lock up and she shivered as she stepped out into the sunshine. As she locked the door a crow squawked, making her flinch with fright. Her heart began to bang. She hadn't felt that scared, ever. Glancing in every direction, she could see that there was no one around and a slight breeze was whipping up the leaves. Bushes rustled in the breeze and the squirrel was back.

Alfie gripped the bracelet and laughed as she ran with him in her arms back towards the vicarage. 'Sally.'

She gasped as she placed Alfie down on his feet. 'Reverend Langham.'

'Oh, Sally, do call me Ernie,' the short man with the bulbous red nose said with a smile.

'Thank you for coming.' She glanced back at the church. 'Did you come into the church just now?'

He raised his eyebrows. 'No, I came straight here. Straight out of my retirement and onto your patch.'

'Did you see anyone around?'

He furrowed his white brows. 'Er, no, but that gust did nearly blow me up the path. Are you okay?'

Sally exhaled. 'Yes, it's just all this business, you know. It's been unsettling.' She bent down to pick Alfie up and she hugged him close. Whatever it took, she'd do everything she could to protect this little boy. She popped the leather bracelet in her pocket.

EIGHTEEN

As Jacob drove them to Redditch, Gina called the station and updated them with what Maeve had said and about the note.

'All units are on the lookout for Ross Craven. We do have a photo which I'll message to you now,' Briggs said before Gina ended the call.

'Everything okay at the station?' Jacob asked as he turned into Brockhill and pulled up on the road outside Abigail Bretton's house.

'Yes. An officer has been stationed at the entrance of Maeve Craven's block of flats for the time being. Given that she received such a threatening note and her sister has been murdered, it seemed like the best course of action. Hopefully we'll locate Ross Craven soon. O'Connor also called Maeve and she confirmed that she's definitely not going to work for the time being. We've checked our database with regards to Maeve Craven and she has no previous at all. Her details have been passed to Children's Services too. The post-mortem is scheduled for late this afternoon and I want to be there so we have to stick to the plan today. Are you good to attend with me?'

Jacob smiled. 'Of course. But you know who really needs to attend a post-mortem as a part of her training?'

Gina nodded. 'I'll send Kapoor a quick message. You're right. She's excelling so I think she's ready. I just hope she's not a vomiter.' She hit send and Trainee DC Kapoor messaged back instantly.

'We all remember our first PM.'

'That we do.' She unclipped her seat belt and got out of the car. The late morning sun had come out beautifully. A few blue tits fluttered around a pile of nuts in the neighbour's garden. Abigail Bretton's house was a neatly presented detached, red-brick building. Small but pretty with its tiny bench under the front window and a parking space to the right of the house. All the curtains were drawn and Gina knew she was about to wake a nurse who was sleeping off a night shift to deliver some awful news. 'I checked with the others, they still haven't managed to get hold of Abigail Bretton and she hasn't called the station back.'

Gina led the way up the garden path and knocked the brass lion head knocker. No one stirred. 'Car's on the drive.' Gina glanced at the red Micra before knocking again. A couple of minutes later, a woman who looked to be in her late twenties answered the door, wearing a thin dressing gown. 'I don't want to buy anything and I don't talk politics on the doorstep.' She rubbed her bleary eyes.

Gina and Jacob held their identification up. 'I'm DI Harte and this is DS Driscoll. May we come in?'

'Err, okay.' She opened the door wide and yawned, allowing them to step into the light airy hallway, then she led them into the kitchen. Up against the back wall stood a white plastic high chair. Gina wondered if Abigail had a child. 'What's going on? Is it about the kids on electric scooters who ride up and down the close or the burglary at number four? I spoke to another officer and I told them that I didn't see anything on those nights as I was at work. My partner at the time didn't either. This was a couple of months ago now.' She looked confused.

'It's not about those incidents. We've been trying to call you. One of my colleagues left you a message.'

Abigail pulled her phone from her dressing gown pocket. 'Damn, it's on airplane mode. I started my shift earlier yesterday as one of the other nurses had gone home ill. I then worked my shift too. I got home in the early hours, exhausted, and went straight to bed. What's happened? Why were you calling me?'

'Would you like to sit down?' Gina gestured to the kitchen chairs and Jacob stepped aside.

'No, I'd like to know why you're here. People ask if you want to sit when they have bad news, I know I do. Please just tell me.'

'Do you know Nell Craven?'

Abigail sat. 'Yes.'

'Who are you to Nell?'

'Nell and I were in a relationship. She moved in with me several months ago but we split up recently. Is she okay?'

Gina sat next to Abigail and Jacob squeezed through at the other end. 'I'm really sorry to have to tell you this. Nell was found dead at an address in Cleevesford yesterday. We are treating it as suspicious.'

'Nell, dead?' Silence descended upon the room as the news sunk in with Abigail.

'I am so sorry. Is there anyone I can call to be with you?'

'I need my mum.' Abigail pressed a number on her phone and waited a few seconds until the other person answered. 'Mum, I need you to come to mine, now. I can't talk.' She began to hyperventilate. 'Just come.' She ended the call and leaned over the kitchen table as she got her breath back. 'You can't be right. Maybe it's not Nell.'

Gina thought of the mole and the tattoo, and the photos that

Maeve had given them. Identification was nothing more than a formality.

'Where's Alfie?'

'He's safe. Children's services have arranged for him to stay somewhere for now and we've located his next of kin.'

'Maeve? I can't see her looking after Alfie. I don't know her that well but what I do know is that she's never spent any time with him. What do I know, though? Maybe she'll step up. I hope she does. He's a lovely little boy.' She took a few more breaths.

Gina stood and walked over to the kitchen and grabbed a box of tissues that were on the side. She brought them over and placed them in front of the distraught woman. 'I know this is hard, but we really need to ask you a few questions. Whoever did this to Nell is still out there and we need to catch them.'

Abigail sniffed and blew her nose. 'I can't believe it. I spoke to her on Monday. She was fine.'

'You say you and Nell were in a relationship and she's been living with you for several months, and that you recently split up.'

'We were in a relationship but I really hoped we'd get back together again. I've never loved anyone like I loved Nell.'

'I know this is really hard, but can you tell me what happened between you?' Gina wondered if their break-up had been acrimonious.

'Nell has had it hard and I guess I expected too much of her. She was struggling to commit and I wanted more. I wanted her to marry me and I thought I was doing really well getting to know Alfie. A part of me dreamed that one day soon we'd be a family but Nell moved in and she never properly settled. That's never going to happen now, is it?' Abigail blew her nose again and rubbed her watery eyes. Her blonde hair fell over her shoulders as she slumped forward.

'Did she tell you much about her past?'

'Only that she barely spoke to her sister and that she grew up with her nan. She said her mother had died when she was a child. She didn't say how but I assumed that maybe she had been ill.'

'Did she mention her father?'

Abigail took a couple of deep breaths then nodded. 'He is not a good person.' Her brows furrowed.

'Did you know he was in prison?' Gina didn't want to influence what Abigail had to say.

'Yes, and Nell told me he'd been released. That's why Nell and I had argued so much. It was over him. At first, he'd sent her these letters saying how sorry he was for letting her down. She told me he'd murdered someone in a drunken argument years ago, and that it was an accident. She'd bounce from wanting to communicate with him to being scared and apprehensive of him. All I wanted was for her to open up to me but she shut me out and didn't want to talk about him. I tried to help her with Alfie and she pushed me away, saying she could manage. I don't know what I did wrong. All I know is she started spending a lot of time in her own head, writing in her diaries while Alfie played. It didn't seem healthy. I wondered if she needed some help. I told her that she should visit her doctor and she went mad at me.' Abigail scrunched her brows. 'I don't know what changed for her to go from happy and looking forward to a future with me to being so cagey and shutting me out. She left me just over a month ago. I got back from work, she'd taken all her stuff and left me a note saying that she needed some space, and that she'd call me.'

'And she called you twice a week, every week.'

Nodding, Abigail sniffed. 'Without fail. Same days and same times. I just wanted her to come home but I knew I couldn't keep saying that as she'd withdraw even more. Alfie seemed happy and healthy and she seemed to be looking after herself so I kept it light. We talked about what we were watching on telly. She mentioned a friend called Kira and I will confess to being jealous so we argued. She was also messaging Kira on Facebook before she got rid of her account. They were in some parent forum but I don't know which one. Anyway, I thought maybe she'd left me for Kira but then I kept thinking, why is she talking to me twice a week if she's with someone else? I asked her about Kira and she said that Kira told her about an empty flat, that was all. That's the one she moved into. My head is all over the place. I'm sorry that nothing makes sense. It doesn't make sense to me either. Maybe I was wrong to suggest she see her doctor. She started thinking I was conspiring against her, suggesting she was mentally ill. But the diaries and the constant writing and withdrawing, it was getting out of hand. Then she kept saying that she thought someone was watching her, but it came across as paranoia.'

'Miss Bretton.'

'I should have been more sensitive. She was murdered and I accused her of being paranoid. No wonder she left me. She was scared and I didn't listen.' She slammed her hand on the table, making the salt pot jump.

Gina felt for the woman. She could see how much Abigail cared for Nell and the realisation that Nell had been scared enough to leave her home, was just hitting her. 'Do you have Nell's diaries?'

Abigail shook her head. 'Nell burnt them on the barbeque just before she left. She said she'd had enough and that they were a reminder of her dad.'

That was a blow. Gina had hoped that there would be a lot of information in Nell's diaries had she still had them. Gina cleared her throat. Nell's sister had no idea who Alfie's father was. Right now, Ross Craven was the most likely murder suspect. Nell hadn't told Abigail the truth about her father killing her mother. Maybe Nell told Abigail more than she told Maeve about Alfie's father. As a previous partner, she had to consider him. 'Do you know who Alfie's father was?'

'Alfie was a result of a drunken night on holiday, I don't know where but I know she'd contacted the hotel where he said he'd worked recently as she wanted Alfie to know his father. She left her details in the hope that the staff would pass them on to him but no one got back to her as far as I'm aware. Maybe someone called her after she left me. Who knows?' Abigail paused. 'I told her it didn't matter and that she was doing a great job on her own but Nell being Nell, she wanted to do the right thing by Alfie.'

'I know this is hard for you, but can you tell me where you were between midday and one yesterday afternoon?'

Holding her chin up, Abigail stared at Gina for a moment. 'Do you think I could hurt Nell?'

'It's procedure. We have to ask everyone.'

'I was in bed, asleep and I was on my own. At around four in the afternoon, I headed to work and that's where I stayed until the early hours of this morning.'

Gina waited for Jacob to note the times down.

'My car was here until four yesterday. I only have one car.'

'Thank you.' Gina knew she needed to bear in mind that Abigail Bretton had opportunity and she would ask O'Connor or Wyre to dig a little further into her. They could check the Automated Number Plate Recognition cameras to see if Abigail's car had been spotted in Cleevesford at the time. As it stood, Nell and Abigail had argued. Nell had left her and she was jealous of Kira. Nell's phone was bugging Gina. 'Did Nell have another phone?'

'Yes.' Abigail shrugged her shoulders and slumped over the kitchen table. 'She had a smartphone just before she left, then she came off all social media and bought a basic one, stating that she didn't want it to be traceable, which again was odd as she was trying to locate Alfie's father. After destroying her SIM, she got rid of the phone. I think she may have sold it. I really think she didn't want her dad to find her.' Abigail paused. 'She didn't talk about him much but I wondered why she was so worried about him coming out of prison. I mean, she said he killed someone in a drunken fight, and I know that's bad but she said it was an accident. I think she was holding something back.'

Gina knew that a google search of the name Nell Craven would bring up the details of Ross Craven's crime. 'Ross Craven was actually convicted of murdering Nell's mother.' She hated delivering that fact to Abigail but she knew that the woman would find out soon. It was better coming from her than from the media.

'Shit.' She leaned back. 'I don't think I knew Nell at all. That's huge. No wonder she panicked about his release. I mean, why would she even communicate with a man like that?' She swallowed. 'I wish she'd talked to me. I could have been there for her. All she kept doing was writing in those diaries that she kept locked away in a case. I kept asking her why she wrote so much and she said it helped, that she missed her mother some-times and she wrote letters to her mother in them, telling her about Alfie and about Maeve. Then she destroyed them saying that she hated them and she hated him, that's her father. Do you know he was on the run for years before he got caught?'

Gina hadn't delved into Ross Craven's case yet but she'd be surprised if one of the team wasn't bursting to share that infor-mation when they returned for a briefing.

Abigail continued. 'I don't know how long for but Nell told me he used to hang around when she played out by her nan's house. He used to give her fancy notebooks, saying how much he missed her and he'd tell her to write everything down so that they could read them together one day. That's why she started writing everything down and I guess it became a habit.' Abigail shook her head and breathed out slowly. 'He made her promise not to tell her nan that he'd made contact with her. That it was their secret. I think it was creepy if you ask me and I think Nell thought the same when she told me that.' She began biting the inside of her cheek. 'I still can't get over that she didn't tell me he'd killed her mother.'

Gina pulled out her phone and opened up a photo that they had on the system. She placed it on the table in front of Abigail. 'Have you seen this man around?'

'Is that him?'

Gina nodded. They needed to find Ross Craven. She wanted to bring him out of wherever he was hiding. She thought back to the day that Darrah had looked after Toffee.

Abigail stared at the photo, then looked away. 'No, I don't recognise him.'

Gina had hoped for a sighting. A recent one would have been better but the most recent sighting of the large-footed, bearded man was from Nell's neighbour, Darrah. 'Did Nell leave any belongings behind?'

Abigail shook her head. 'Not a thing. Only one of Toffee's bowls and Alfie's high chair. She must have got the van around to collect her stuff as soon as I left for work.'

'Did you meet up with Nell on Tuesday the eighteenth of June?'

Abigail swallowed. 'Yes. I picked her up and we took Alfie to Stratford-upon-Avon for a picnic. It was my idea. I thought a day out would help us. We argued because I didn't do as much as she wanted me to do with her and Alfie, but I was always tired. I work a lot of nights and she didn't quite understand how those hours zapped my energy. And I had to do all the shifts I could as it was only my wage coming in. I hoped that by arranging the picnic, Nell could see that I was trying. Nell also told me she had some savings but we didn't want to deplete them.'

'Savings?' Gina remembered what Kira had said about Nell not having to find a job soon.

'Yes. Nell's mother had either life insurance or some savings and she and Maeve had been given their respective halves when each of them turned eighteen. Nell left her nan's house to study chiropody. She always wanted to work in a caring or nursing role but she also wanted to be able to work for herself. She studied until she was twenty-one. Got a job in a clinic and quite soon after got pregnant with Alfie. Before she moved in with me, she lived in a studio flat. It was something she could afford without worrying too much about money.' Abigail creased her brow. 'I know I shouldn't have done what I did but Nell had left her phone logged in to her bank account one day so I looked.'

'And?'

'She was receiving regular payments every month from someone.'

'Do you have her bank statements?'

'No, they were all online. I wanted to say something to her there and then, but she'd have known that I'd seen her account and I'd never breached her trust before. Not once did I look in those diaries. I must admit, I was really upset as I'd been struggling to keep the house going, what with everything Alfie needed too. She never told me she had so much money accumulating in her account. I was led to believe she had a couple of grand and I saw that as our emergency backup.'

'Did you see any of the details on the payments?'

'She received two thousand pounds a month from the mystery account and she had sixteen thousand pounds in her savings. I swear my jaw hit the ground.' Abigail turned away. 'On the day we went to Stratford-upon-Avon, I confronted her about the money.'

'What did she say?'

'What she said and the truth were probably two different things because even I find this hard to believe. She said she had no idea who'd been sending her the money, which is why she hadn't told me. As for the reference, it simply said, "For Alfie," next to the payment. I think she lied to me about not knowing who Alfie's father was.'

NINETEEN

MAEVE

Maeve slipped on her hugest sunglasses and left out of the main gate. The police officer smiled. 'I'm going to the shop.' For a moment she thought he might ask to go with her but he went back to scrolling on his phone as she walked away. She had made it clear enough that she wasn't sure about the police officer being posted outside her home. Yes, she was a bit scared of whoever sent the note but really, the police officer was overkill. Ross Craven had probably found out where Maeve lived and followed her to see if she'd lead him to Nell and now he was on the run again. After killing their mother, he'd successfully been on the run for ten years. The man was an expert at avoiding the authorities.

However big and luxurious her apartment was, she felt as though it was closing in on her. Processing all the news of the last twenty-four hours was suffocating. She needed to get out, to walk and think. As she reached the towpath, she headed towards her favourite canal side café. A strong coffee might even clear her head.

'Maeve.'

She turned to see a man in joggers, panting.

'Do I know you?' There was a vague familiarity.

He half jogged closer to her. 'I hope so.' He walked closer and smiled.

The crooked smile gave him away. She barely recognised him with his damp tangled hair and casual clothing. He'd left her place last night, slamming the door behind him as her phone kept beeping. 'Err...' Did she even ask him his name when he came back to her apartment last night? There had been a lot of wine, then he'd come over to her later that evening as they drank even more at a bar in the Mailbox and they talked and laughed.

'Matty.' He laughed. 'Matty and Maeve. We sound like a pair in a sitcom.'

Tears welled in her eyes. She couldn't even begin to laugh or even pretend that everything was okay.

'Damn, I don't normally have that effect on people. Oh, sorry about slamming your door when I left. I can be a bit ham-fisted. Are you okay?'

'No,' she said as her eyes watered. 'Those calls on my phone, they were from the police.'

'I am so sorry. Has something happened?' He tilted his head.

'My sister was murdered yesterday and the police are now standing outside my apartment block because I had this horrible note and I don't know what to do.'

He stood open-mouthed before continuing. 'That's horrible news.' He stepped closer. 'Do you want a hug?'

She nodded and placed her head against his damp T-shirt where he stroked her hair until she managed to compose herself. 'Sorry, I'm not normally like this.'

'Nothing about today is normal. I'm surprised you're even out and about. Can I get you a drink? There's a great little café just ahead.'

She nodded. 'Are you sure you have time? Do you have a lot of work on?'

'Knowing that we'd be drinking last night, I decided I was
having today off. The joys of being the boss. I'm not one of these
people that can burn the candle at both ends. I woke up with a
raging head and normally I cure it with a run, although I don't
normally run along the towpath. I like running towards the
Bullring.' He sounded like he was nervously chattering.

She wiped her eyes. 'I thought I hadn't seen you around.
This is where I normally run, most days before work.'

'You run too?'

She nodded. Before she knew it, they were at the café, the
one with the small round tables covered in red-checked table-
cloths. He pulled a chair out for her. 'What would you like to
drink?'

What she needed was a double espresso but the last thing
she wanted was to be jittery. She thought of Alfie, alone in the
world now that Nell was dead. Today, she had to think long and
hard about him. There was no way she could give him what he
needed.

'Maeve, drink?'

'Oh, thank you. I'll have a latte, please, a large one made
with oat milk.' She placed her sunglasses on her head now that
her tears had dried a little.

He smiled sympathetically and went into the café.

She leaned back and stared up at the blue sky, ignoring the
barking dog on the barge that slowly chugged by.

'Do you mind if I take this chair?'

She flinched and looked at the woman with the toddler in
her arms, then she noticed that the table next to them had no
chairs around it after a group of five on another table had taken
them all. 'Of course not.' The woman struggled to drag the
chair. Maeve stood and carried it over to the table for her. She
wondered what the hell she looked like with her smudged
make-up and puffy eyes. 'Do you need a highchair?'

'Yes, please. Thank you so much for your help.'

She popped into the café. Matty smiled at her as the barista finished making their coffees. She grabbed a highchair and popped it next to the woman, who thanked her again.

Matty came out and as he spoke all Maeve could do was watch the woman with the toddler. She pictured herself with Alfie but she wouldn't be as competent as the woman in front of her. She'd already juggled getting her own drink and drinking it while passing apple slices to her toddler. Despite the stress, she kept smiling and speaking warmly.

'Anyway,' Matty continued. She could tell he was just making small talk, not knowing what to say to the woman whose sister has been murdered. He lifted his arm up and sniffed. 'I'm just popping to the loo to get cleaned up a bit. Do you want a cake or anything?'

Maeve shook her head. 'No, thank you.' As he went back into the café the toddler held her hands up, making a grabbing motion and laughing. The woman lifted her out of the highchair and wiped the child's sticky fingers as she cooed and sang. She placed the toddler down, keeping a close eye on her as she clumsily walked around, thankfully keeping away from the edge of the canal. The tiny girl in the pink sundress toddled towards Maeve, giggling and pointing. She naturally returned the child's smile. 'Hello.' She didn't seem to care that Maeve looked upset.

'Leave the lady alone, sunshine.' The woman hurried over and picked her up. 'Gotcha. She just loves people,' she said.

Maeve saw her own bedraggled reflection in the woman's huge sunglasses. The woman's straw hat had scooped up all her hair and her thick sun cream lay like a sticky film on her shoulders. 'She's no problem at all. You're very cute, aren't you?' A heaviness spread throughout her chest. She began to choke up and gasp as she thought of Alfie. Which was screaming louder; avoid the responsibility or live with the heavy weight of guilt?

'Are you okay?' the woman asked, her diamanté heart necklace catching the sun's rays.

Maeve held a hand up. 'I'm fine,' she gasped. The panic attacks she thought she'd got rid of were threatening to come back. All those years she'd forced the memories of her mum to the back of her mind. Maeve had been the one to find her mother's body. She still remembered coming home from school and seeing blood on the lino, spread out like a small crimson halo around her mother's head. Nell's dad did that to her and he was out there somewhere.

The woman placed her free hand on Maeve's back and rubbed it gently. 'They come when you least expect them, don't they? Always there, bubbling under the surface, ready to attack. Just feel the air, listen to the boats and try to control your breathing.'

The tiny girl held her hand out to Maeve and she took a few deep breaths, not wanting to alarm the little one. She was winning her battle with the anxiety attack, and the girl's smile was helping her in more ways than one. Decisions had to be made and only she could make them.

'Is everything okay?' Matty asked as he came out of the café, looking a little fresher.

'Yes. It's nothing. I just got a bit overwhelmed.' She looked up at the woman who was now stepping back towards her table before grabbing the changing bag. 'Thank you,' Maeve said to the helpful stranger, her gaze on the toddler. With that, the woman said a goodbye and grabbed her things. She headed down the towpath, turning her walk into a game with her daughter.

Matty stared sympathetically. 'I know my timing sucks but...' He took a breath and paused. 'I like you and I know things are really bad at the moment but I'm here for you. That's all I wanted to say. I'm such a believer in fate and meeting you on the towpath today after last night, it was meant to be.'

Through her sadness, she let out a laugh. 'That's so corny.'

He shook his head and shyly looked down. 'I know, I know.

I guess I just have a feeling and I don't know, I hope you do too. Last night was silly, it was drunken and we nearly... but we didn't. I'd like to get to know you properly. Maybe we can go out for dinner or a drink.'

She let out a laugh. 'Do you want to know something about me? You might change your mind.'

'I doubt it but go on.' He sat down at their table, his gaze on her as she spoke.

'My sister had a baby.'

'Is the baby okay?'

Maeve nodded. 'Actually Alfie is a toddler now and he's staying with a vicar in Cleevesford, arranged by children's services. I should go and get him, but I can't. I don't know what to do.' She looked down, feeling ashamed of the conflict brewing within. 'Me and Nell weren't close at all. I've barely met Alfie but I cared from afar. I'm not a mother, I mean look at me.'

Matty appeared a little out of his depth, maybe even shocked. He paused and looked down as if all that she'd just said was sinking in. He took a deep breath and looked back at her. 'Maeve, what I see is a woman who's had a huge shock. You will know what to do and when, I promise. Just take some time to let the news sink in. You don't have to be close to someone to care. I also see a kind, lovely, fun and clever woman. You should go and see Alfie.'

'You don't know me.'

'I know what I see. Besides, you don't know me either but I intend to change that. You know I have an IT business. I have four brothers, one sister, and I'm six times an uncle. If you need any advice on kids, I'm your man. Chief uncle babysitter here. They all love me.' He pointed to his face. He then leaned over and placed his hand on hers from across the table. It felt so natural but he was right, she didn't know him but the riskier side of her personality didn't care right now. Maybe Matty was right and them being thrown together at this time was fate. She passed him her phone so that he could pop his number into it.

He checked his smart watch. 'Damn, I have a Zoom meeting soon. No rest for the wicked. I told them I have a day off but do they care? I best dash. Call me later.'

She wasn't a believer in fate. In fact, she didn't believe in anything supernatural, but Matty's timing had been perfect and right now, although she'd only just met him, she had this deep niggle and it was telling her to not let him walk out of her life.

TWENTY

DIARY EXTRACT

Today, I spoke to him and I can't wait to actually see him. He wants me and I've never felt wanted before. I wonder if I can find it in my heart to truly forgive. My heart is leading the way on this.

We have promised each other that we'll start again with a clean slate. It took me so long to reconcile what he did with how I feel about him.

He called today and we spoke about such normal things. He likes watching Dancing on Ice, *he reads autobiographies of comedians and he loves watching* Big Brother. *All normal things. You wouldn't think it from what he's done but everyone deserves a second chance. He's changed. I told him how much I love watching sitcoms and it's silly but I really enjoy sudoku too. He said he loves puzzles.*

Anyway, I've bought him a small gift. I don't know if it would be well received but, in my heart, I feel that evil follows evil. He is no longer evil, he's more misunderstood, I guess. He was abused as a child and that anger followed him through to adulthood. Anyway, just in case evil is following him, I have a small Turkish eye. I got it when I went on one of my many trips.

I'd been walking up the steps to get to Marmaris Castle and some really frail lady pressed it into my palm, telling me it would protect me. She seemed mystical with her hunched back and headscarf. In fact, I could barely see her eyes as the material from her lace veil covered them. I spoke to her nose. As for the Turkish eye, I don't need it. I feel as though it's done its job. I don't need protecting any more. He is not the monster I thought he was. He is kind, gentle, a real family person which is why I'm passing the eye to him. He needs it. He will need protecting from society and trolls.

If I can forgive him, so can they. He is after all my blood, not theirs, so my view of him counts for so much more.

After removing the safety pin that it dangles off so all I have is the plastic eye, I hold it. Finally, I will visit him in prison and it's so small, I'll smuggle it in and pass it to him. Once I'm through security, I can press it into his hand and pass on the protection I've enjoyed for so long onto him. If a person has never been loved, they can't possibly love. I am going to show him that I have his back and that everything will be okay; and I know he won't hurt me.

TWENTY-ONE

Gina headed into the station kitchen to put the kettle on quickly before the briefing. She also hoped to see Trainee DC Kapoor and, as luck would have it, Kapoor was stirring her coffee. 'Would you like one, guv?'

'Yes, please, could I have a green tea though? There's a pack in the cupboard.'

Kapoor raised her brows as she pulled the box out and began to make the drink. 'It's not like you to turn down caffeine.' She smiled.

Gina sighed. 'My head is aching already. I'm trying to be healthier.' She wasn't about to mention her raised cholesterol. After Briggs had spent so long fussing around her during the last case, the last thing she wanted was to be treated like some delicate flower again. The best thing she could do was to say nothing to any of them. Her health was her business and the doctor had told her to improve her lifestyle. It wasn't as if she was about to be admitted to hospital for a triple heart bypass. It was nothing.

'I guess you don't want to see what Mrs O has sent O'Connor in with today. There are eclairs in the incident room.'

Kapoor passed the steaming hot mug with the teabag still in it to Gina.

Gina scrunched her nose up as she sniffed the vapour. She wasn't going to enjoy it. Nothing would ever be as good as her beloved coffee. 'Thanks. I wanted a quick word while we're here. Are you okay attending the post-mortem with me this afternoon? I think it will help with your training.'

'Yes, that sounds good. I mean, it's not good. A PM isn't good as some poor soul had to die. I mean, it sounds educational. Thank you.'

'Great. We'll leave after the briefing.' She pulled her phone from her pocket. The day was already disappearing fast. 'Let's get through the briefing so we can push on.' Gina led the way back to the others. O'Connor, Briggs, PC Smith and PC Ahmed were just finishing their eclairs. Wyre tucked into a meal deal salad and fruit bag. Gina's stomach rumbled. What she wanted was a sugary eclair. What she needed was to be more like Wyre. Kapoor sat and grabbed a cake. It was no good. Gina knew she might not get a chance to eat until the evening and all she'd had was an apple. She grabbed an eclair and a serviette and stood at the head of the room. Kapoor furrowed her brows. Gina shrugged her shoulders and smiled. So much for being healthier. After eating a bite and feeling the dopamine rush, she began to speak. 'This is just a quick catch up. Jacob and I have updated the system with this morning's interviews. As you know, Nell Craven's sister, Maeve, received a worrying hand-delivered letter over the past few days. We don't know the exact date. Would you mind writing on the board, Wyre?'

DC Wyre finished her last mouthful of salad and grabbed a pen. Briggs stepped aside and sat.

'The letter says, "your bitch mum deserves what she got." An officer is going to remain outside her apartment block for now and I've sent the original note to the lab. If we're lucky we might get a fingerprint from it. Because of what has happened to Nell, we need to treat that note as a threat to Maeve. She thinks she might have been followed but there was nothing concrete on that. Someone knows where Maeve lives and given how the leads are panning out, it could be Nell's father. Any news or updates on him?'

Wyre nodded. 'Yes, I've been researching him. After he killed Lynette Craven, Maeve and Nell's mother, he left the scene and it took ten years for police to eventually catch him. No one knows where he went or where he hid, but it's assumed that he moved to another part of the country and used a false identity to work. He was finally caught when Nell and Maeve's grandmother reported seeing him in their back garden. She called the police and he went down after that. That was ten years ago and he got released recently after serving almost ten years.'

'Have you spoken to his probation officer?'

'Yes, apparently Ross Craven was a model prisoner, totally rehabilitated as far as everyone who dealt with him was concerned. He retrained as a chef, worked in the kitchen and never got into trouble. He started drawing and teaching the other prisoners to draw. He'd been deemed low risk to the public. Unfortunately, due to underfunding and lack of staff, when he didn't come back to his hostel and he missed a couple of probation appointments, no one had dealt with it.'

'Do they know of anywhere he might go?'

'No, guv. He told his probation officer he wanted to stay in Cleevesford so that he could rebuild his relationship with his daughter. They mentioned that he'd been applying for jobs. That's all they said really.'

'Make sure all units are looking out for him. Any luck with tracing his phone or has he used any bank cards?'

Wyre shook her head. 'No, it looks like he's lying low.'

Gina pointed to the board. 'How about other leads? Can

anyone confirm if Darrah Kelly was at Cleevesford Manor at the time of the murder? Who followed up on that?'

O'Connor put his cup of coffee on the table. 'Me, guv. I went there this morning and spoke to the general manager. He allowed me to take a look at the CCTV. The rose garden isn't covered by any cameras and, as we already know from a previous case, it's easy to get in and out of the grounds through the woodland at the back.'

Gina knew that would be the case. 'And where is the rose garden in relation to that woodland?'

'Right in front of it. Also, they confirmed that Darrah Kelly gets the bus to work. He doesn't have a car.'

'If you take the path behind Cleevesford Manor there is a bus stop. He could have got home within fifteen minutes.'

O'Connor scrunched his brow as he read his notes. 'I checked the timetables. There was a bus due at eleven forty-five. He could have been home at midday and back on a bus at twelve forty to get back to Cleevesford Manor for one. He was seen on one of the cameras at ten in the morning and another at one thirty. Although there are other staff, he generally works on that section alone. A grounds person said he didn't see Kelly all day as he'd been working around the front.'

Gina sipped her green tea and forced herself to swallow it. 'So, he doesn't have an alibi and it was actually possible that he could have murdered Nell.'

'Yes. We do have one witness, a customer. She went for a walk around the grounds and into the woodland. On her return, she saw a figure walking towards the rose garden. Unfortunately, she didn't take much notice of this person. She only knew what time that was as she was trying to find a place to make a personal phone call, so she was looking for a spot where there were no people. She made the phone call at twelve twenty. We can't confirm the witness saw Kelly.'

'Okay, I think the best plan of action would be to follow up with the bus company, see if they have onboard cameras for that route. That will tell us if Kelly got on the bus. O'Connor, are you okay with doing that?'

He nodded.

Gina glanced at the wall clock. She needed to wrap up the briefing if she and Kapoor were going to make Nell's post-mortem on time. 'What updates do we have on Drake Spool?'

Wyre sighed. 'You'll love this, guv.' She stepped away from the board. 'The substance he was found carrying was caffeine powder. You can literally buy it legally. He was trying to pass it off as coke. The tests confirm it was caffeine.'

'Let me get this right,' Gina continued. 'He was selling caffeine to Nell?'

Wyre nodded. 'Yes. He said she caught him smoking weed and asked if he could get hold of something that would help her to stay awake so he sold her tiny measures of caffeine for an extortionate markup.'

'Did he say why she wanted it?' Gina pictured Nell, worried about cameras being in her house, turfing everything out of her wardrobe, cupboards and drawers. Witnesses had mentioned how tired she looked, how she'd run out of her own house scared.

'No, he didn't know. She saw him on the street on Wednesday the twenty-sixth and asked him to deliver it later that evening.'

'Did he mention seeing anyone else around?'

'Yes, he saw a man, a well-built man standing in the wild-flower meadow just staring in his direction.' Wyre updated the board and timeline. 'It was dark so he couldn't really see much.'

Gina continued. 'What I'm getting here is that Nell was afraid to go to sleep. She was expecting something to happen, she just didn't know when. If it was her father, she was terrified of him and with good cause. I read the case notes relating to Ross Craven. He'd been abusing Lynette Craven for years and there were even concerns raised by the neighbours, but each time the police or social services visited, the whole family looked fine.' Gina shivered at their failings. The authorities shouldn't have left it at that and they all knew it. 'On the day of her murder, Mrs Craven had been out with Nell. Nell was only three and had fallen asleep in her bed. Ross Craven then attacked her for going out. The post-mortem report shows that she had a broken eye socket and that had happened before the fatal blow to the head. His claim that she slipped didn't add up. The investigation showed that her head had been slammed several times into the corner of the worktop. Maeve found her later that day, when she returned from school and ran out of the house screaming and the police were called. Ross Craven was nowhere to be found.'

The room went silent for a few seconds as they all processed the fact that with Ross Craven they were dealing with an extremely violent person. Wyre spoke. 'Do you think that Mrs Craven's broken eye socket has anything to do with Nell's missing eyes?'

Gina sighed. 'I wish I had the answer to that? Maybe I'll know more after Nell's post-mortem. Wyre, could you please look into Abigail Bretton? I've updated the system with her registration number. I need to know if she was anywhere near Nell's place at the time of her murder. We need to check all ANPR records in the area. She and Nell had recently split up. She claims to have been in bed at the time of the murder as she works nights.'

'Yep, I'll get onto that.' Wyre made a note of her task and went back to the board.

Gina continued. 'Lastly, have we managed to obtain Nell's bank records as yet?'

Kapoor shook her head. 'We should have those back this afternoon.'

'Great. As you're coming with me, Jacob, could you look out

for those? We know that when Nell left Abigail she owned a smartphone. When we found her, all she had was a basic phone so we're unable to access any of her online life at the moment. When we get the statements we need to find out who was sending Nell two thousand pounds a month.'

'Could it have been child maintenance, guv?' Kapoor asked.

'I was wondering that. From what Abigail Bretton said, Nell had been trying to find her son's father.' Gina scrunched her brow. 'There had been monthly payments into the account but Nell had only recently started looking for him. Either the money was coming from someone else completely or she was lying to Abigail about looking for Alfie's father. Maybe she'd already found him. We really need to find the person behind the payments rather than guessing at this.'

'Guv.' PC Ahmed held a hand up.

'Yes.'

'I don't know if this is relevant but I've been taking it all in and something happened last week. It may or may not be related to this case.' He glanced over at PC Smith who nodded for him to go on. 'We got called out to the Angel Arms. A man went in enquiring about a job. Elouise, the licensee, had a lunchtime cook's job advertised. After speaking to him, she said he mentioned that he was on probation. He started shouting at her for no reason. She managed to call us but by the time we got there, he was gone. The thing that struck me was she described him as wearing a necklace with a Turkish eye pendant.'

Gina checked her watch, knowing she needed to get going if she was going to make the post-mortem. 'The same type of pendant found dangling from Nell's dog's collar. That's too much of a coincidence.' She thought of Maeve and swallowed. 'I'm going to interview Elouise after the PM.'

TWENTY-TWO

Kapoor started fiddling with the end of her black plait. They both stared through the glass divider as the pathologist began to press his scalpel into Nell's chest, ready to make the Y-incision. Gina knew exactly what came next. There would be videoing, speaking into a recorder, photos, removal of organs and then weighing them all. None of it was pleasant and watching it didn't get better with experience.

'How long does this take, guv?'

Gina shrugged. 'I don't know exactly.' All she knew was that some post-mortems took a lot longer than others. Nails had been clipped; swabs had been taken. Nell's clothing had all been carefully bagged and described, but the worst was to come and that started with the cutting.

As the pathologist continued opening up Nell's chest, Kapoor looked away.

'Are you okay?' Kapoor didn't answer. 'It's always horrible but the first time is awful.'

'I'm okay.' She stood up straight and began observing the pathologist as he continued cutting. 'This is something I need to get used to if I'm going to be able to help solve crimes like you do. I keep reminding myself that I want to do this so I can help to get murderers off the streets. It's not like I've never come across death when working as a PC.'

Gina agreed. 'That's what I tell myself too. Each victim is teeming with evidence and we need to make sure we get everything we can so that when we get the bastard in a courtroom, we nail them. We go through this for them.' She nodded her head in Nell's direction.

After watching for another hour and fifteen minutes, Gina turned to Kapoor. 'I'm really proud of you. That was hard and you're still here.'

Kapoor sighed. 'I'm so relieved I didn't heave, guv.'

'I would have understood if you had but it's normally the smell that catches people out. We've been sheltered behind this glass.' The pathologist began to disrobe from all his protective gear and he pointed to the door. Gina knew what that meant. In a few minutes, he'd be out there, ready to talk to them.

'What happens next?'

'We speak to him and he'll talk us through what they found.' Gina led Kapoor out of the viewing area and back into the corridor. They continued round until they met up with the pathologist who was now wearing a T-shirt and trousers.

'DI Harte, follow me.'

A faint aroma of death and chemicals followed him. Kapoor scrunched her nose.

They turned a corner and went into an office where they all sat, the pathologist had slumped into the big leather chair behind the desk that made a crunching sound as he adjusted his position.

'What can you tell us?' Gina asked while Kapoor opened up a notebook to take down any information that would help their investigation.

'I can confirm that the victim died in situ. The scene confirms that. Lividity had formed in the back, the buttocks and the calves. This tells us that the victim had not been moved.' He looked at Kapoor. 'That's where blood pools in the part of the body closest to the ground. This happens because of gravity and the fact that blood has stopped circulating.'

Gina cleared her throat. 'Can you tell us if her eyes were removed post or ante mortem?'

He opened up his file. 'Post. It's not obvious from looking at the victim but she was hit over the head with a blunt instrument that is consistent with something similar in size to the end of a baseball bat. It may not be a bat but you get the idea. That would have weakened her. Bruises to her chest show that some pressure was then applied.'

'In what sense? Did someone straddle her?' Gina imagined the assailant overpowering Nell.

'Yes, her eyes were removed post-mortem using a serrated knife with no precision at all. This wasn't done carefully. There are no defence wounds but there are pressure marks around the neck. She died by strangulation.'

Gina exhaled and Kapoor stopped writing. They were dealing with a hugely violent individual. One who was capable of killing his wife by hitting her head against a corner of the worktop until she'd died. They needed to bring him in before he hurt anyone else. He was on the run again and desperate people were even more dangerous.

TWENTY-THREE

MAEVE

After a couple of hours of lying on her bed, she'd had a shower before taking a drink out to the police officer who was still guarding her apartment block. He had assured her that when he went off shift, one of his colleagues would take over. If Ross Craven was to come along and try to get to her, they'd catch him. She stared out of her bifold doors, wondering if anyone could climb the wall from the canal. Ross Craven had always been a bit of a lumbering mess, a clumsy oaf. There was no way he'd be able to scale the wall.

Heading back to her sofa, she stared at her laptop screen where she'd been researching the church on Cleevesford High Street, the one that the Reverend Sally Stevens ran. She clicked on a professionally taken photo of the vicar. She didn't look much like a vicar with her long mahogany curls and red streaks. Her trimmed black nails and pale complexion made her look gothic. Her black eyeliner was straight out of the nineties and Maeve guessed her age at around her mid-thirties. Actually, Maeve decided, she was more queen of darkness than queen of godliness. Guilt was gnawing through her as she wondered how Alfie was doing.

Walking through her apartment, she opened the door to her spare room and glanced at the full-mirrored wall that always reflected her sweaty body as she used her rowing machine and treadmill. She imagined what it would look like if it was all gone and turned into a child's bedroom. Closing the door, she headed into her kitchen/diner and imagined a plastic high chair leaning up against the wall. Her muscles tensed up and the words "huge responsibility" kept going through her mind. A wash of panic ran through her as she thought of trying to find a nursery place for Alfie so she could work, how she'd always get called out if he was ill or how she'd never be able to go for after work drinks and to networking events; the very events that had propelled her career to where it was now.

She swallowed, knowing how selfish all her thoughts seemed. Life hadn't been fair to Alfie. His mother had been murdered and that little boy had no one else. She thought of Nell's girlfriend. They hadn't been together that long and Nell had left her. Alfie wasn't her responsibility; he was now Maeve's.

Her door buzzer filled the apartment, making her flinch. She hurried to the wall near the door and snatched the intercom phone. 'Hello.'

'Maeve, it's Matty. I've made you some food and I just wanted to drop it off. I didn't think you'd be up for cooking.'

She buzzed him up and placed the phone back in its cradle. Running through the room like a whirlwind, she threw her clutter into the bedroom, then she opened her front door just as the lift opened. 'Hey.'

He came over to her, wearing a white T-shirt over blue jeans, holding a glass dish covered in foil. 'I hope you don't mind. When I left you abruptly, I couldn't stop thinking about what happened to your sister and your poor nephew. I know it's not much but I made you some food. I don't want to intrude, I thought I'd just leave it with you.' He handed the dish to her which was still warm underneath.

'Thank you, that's really kind.'

'I'll leave you to it, then. You have my number if you need anything.' He went to walk back to the lift.

'Wait.'

He turned around.

'Do you want to come in for a drink.' She raised her brows. 'This is a big dinner for one.' She didn't want him to leave. Being on her own sucked at a time like this. Building up her fashion brand had been her life. She didn't have any real friends in the city and she'd barely had time for them anyway. Most of the people she'd been close to in her early twenties had married and now had children. They didn't have time for her anymore.

'Err, only if you're sure. I know you have a lot to think through and I didn't want to intrude.'

She shook her head. 'You're not intruding.' She opened the door wide and stood aside to let him in.

He smiled and entered. 'You know, I never appreciated how lovely this building was last night. The views are amazing.'

She placed the dish on the coffee table and followed him onto her balcony. 'I love it here. I can't imagine living in a suburb. I'm such a city person.' She swallowed, knowing that if she did have Alfie she'd probably have to sell her wonderful apartment. Then she remembered Toffee, Nell's dog and her heart began to race.

'I live in a nice house in the city. You can still have it all, Maeve. You don't have to compromise.'

'How? I won't be able to do my job, not properly. I don't work thirty-six hours a week and take lunch breaks. And now I feel selfish again. My sister has been murdered and here I am thinking about me. Me, me, me. I am so selfish, I know I am. It's my biggest flaw.' She left him gazing at the canal and went back in, sitting on the sofa.

He followed. 'My sister is a doctor and she has two children. One of my sisters-in-law is a financial director and she has a baby. It's temporary. They grow up and people cope. I'd say my brother helps her but he works on an oil rig. She pretty much holds the fort down herself. She is amazing. You are amazing, Maeve. Besides, you're not selfish. A selfish person wouldn't be sitting here toiling over everything. I can see guilt written all over your face.'

'Seriously, you don't even know me.' She wondered how he could see right inside her.

'I know I don't but I see you, Maeve.' He flashed her that lopsided smile. 'And I see a woman who really needs some food so that she can think about all the big things that are happening in her life right now. She needs to nourish her body and brain so she can go forth and take those big life decisions. It's lentil cottage pie, by the way. I know you had oat milk earlier so I didn't know if you were a vegan, so it's vegan friendly.'

'I'm not. I just like oat milk but thank you, that's so kind. I'll pop it in the oven to warm it up. Take a seat.' As she leaned over, she brushed against her laptop, bringing the screen to life.

He sat on the chair next to the sofa and she saw him looking at her laptop screen. 'What a quirky-looking vicar. It's good you're turning to someone.'

'I'm not turning to her. I'm not even religious. She's the person my nephew is staying with at the moment. The vicar in Cleevesford.'

'I see.' She walked into the kitchen, leaving Matty staring at her screen as she placed the food in the oven. She re-entered with a bottle of white wine and two glasses. 'Wine?'

'Thank you, that would be lovely.' He paused as she poured the drinks. 'The police officer seemed nice. He did quiz me when I said I was visiting you.'

'It's good he's doing his job. They're worried about me, because of what happened to my sister.'

'And you're not worried about me being here?' He rubbed his slightly stubbly chin.

'No, they know who did it. They just need to find him.'

'I won't pry.' He sipped his wine.

'It was Nell's father. We had such a horrible upbringing and Alfie deserves more than me. He needs a fresh start. The less he knows about us, the better. If he lives with me, he'll have a connection to Nell, which means he'll know about his grandfather and he'll find out what happened to his grandmother. He's so young, he might not remember anything he's experienced so far. He could start afresh with someone who will love him and care for him.'

Matty began scrolling on his phone and he passed it to her.

She looked at the huge family line up at a wedding. Children, parents, grandparents, extended family. 'You have a beautiful family. They all look so happy.'

'Yes, and sometimes things are hard. We've had deaths, miscarriages, police arrests; my cousin was convicted of fraud. We've had divorces, drug problems and mental health issues, but we're family. Whatever life throws at us, we get through it. We fight each other's corner. Family is everything to me. You are Alfie's family. I'm not here to guilt you into making the decision to be a part of his life. I will respect whatever you choose but just properly consider how good and competent you are.'

The smell of rosemary began to fill the air as the food cooked. 'I'll think about it.' She closed her laptop and for a second, she had a feeling she didn't recognise. She felt the connection between her and Alfie and it was like she was missing a part of herself. Her family. He was all she had. Maybe she needed to contact the vicar. Scrap the maybe. She grabbed her phone and decided now was the time to make the call.

TWENTY-FOUR

After pulling up in the Angel Arms car park, Gina watched a group of drunken customers laughing and joking at the wooden tables. She could almost kill for a cold lager.

Kapoor unclipped her seat belt and checked her phone for messages. 'There's an update, guv.'

'What is it?'

'It's from Jacob and he's heading over to take a proper look around Nell Craven's flat. He said he'll meet us there in about half an hour if we can make it but not to worry if we can't, as he has Wyre and a couple of PCs assisting. Do you think we'll make it?'

'It depends on what happens here.' Ideally, she wanted to be there to look through Nell's things and finding a diary that hadn't been destroyed would be a bonus, but she didn't know what this lead might bring with it to follow up on. Jacob was capable and if he found anything, he'd let her know straight away. 'Let's go and see what Elouise can tell us about Ross and take it from there.'

They headed through the crowd of drinkers as the sun beat down on the garden. Cigarette butts had been scattered on the covered patio slabs. Gina didn't envy Elouise. She worked hard to keep the drinkers' pub running smoothly. As she entered, she skirted around the pool table and stopped at the bar. The smell of hops filled the air, along with a sickly-sweet aroma from the spilled dark spirit on the bar. A young woman in jeans and pumps ran over with a cloth to clean up the spillage. Gina glanced back to see a group of older men sitting in a booth playing dominoes as Fleetwood Mac played in the background.

'What can I get you?' The woman threw the cloth behind the bar.

'We've come to speak to Elouise. Is she here?'

'She's upstairs. Who shall I say is asking for her?'

'Gina from Cleevesford Police.' Elouise knew who she was. They had talked many times and Elouise had always been helpful with past cases.

The woman left them to go up the flight of stairs behind the bar.

'Do you just want me to take notes, guv?'

'Yes and no. The notes are important, but if you think of anything to ask that you feel I've missed, do speak up.'

Kapoor smiled and nodded. The woman came back with Elouise following her closely. She tottered in wearing a pair of pink open-toed Mary Jane shoes and a coral sundress. With her dyed black hair piled up in a vintage twist, she smiled. 'Gina, come through.'

As they entered Elouise's office, Gina dodged the wavering pink helium-filled balloons.

'Sorry about that. I'm a bit short of space. I have a new great-niece so I'm off out in a while. How can I help you?' Elouise pulled out a compact and swiped her red lipstick over her lips as she waited for Gina to answer.

Gina sat opposite Elouise and Kapoor sat next to Gina ready with her notepad. 'We wanted to talk to you about Ross Craven.'

'Oh him. Yes, he came in last Monday, that's the twenty-fourth of June, and asked about the job I have advertised for a lunchtime cook. I've never wanted to do food but needs must. People aren't quite drinking as much now so I thought, what the hell, the business comes first and if I have to do food, then so be it.'

'I know you've already spoken to one of our officers but can you talk me through what happened?'

She nodded. 'Ross came in when the pub opened at midday and ordered a pint, then he introduced himself and asked me about the job. I told him I would need a CV so that I could see what he'd done before and check his references. With that I explained how important references were as the new cook would have keyholder duties to come in before opening to prep. That's when he began to explain that he'd been in prison and he'd gained his qualifications there. It was just me and him at that point. Mondays are normally quiet so I work them alone and no customers had arrived either. I was more than happy to still consider him for the job but I wasn't about to give anything away, not before letting the job ad run its course. There may have been more applicants and really I wanted someone with a bit more experience, preferably of working in a pub as I knew I'd need them to occasionally cover a shift at the bar.'

'What happened after that?'

'He took his drink and sat down for about an hour. After another couple of drinks, he came up to the bar and just stared at me. His friendly face had turned into a frown, then he went on about how I wouldn't give him a chance and that he'd done his time and it wasn't murder. He kept saying that he'd killed her by accident. I didn't even ask what he'd done time for. Then he threw his glass at me. I dodged it and it hit the mirror under the optics. By then he was shouting and kicking the chairs. I locked myself in my private quarters and called the police. That's when the PC turned up and took my statement. I'm used

to dealing with drunken people and sometimes they're aggres-
sive, but I couldn't talk him down at all. Your officer took the
CCTV. You can just see us in one of the frames and there's
some blurred video of him throwing a chair after I locked myself
behind the door.'

Gina watched as Elouise took a deep breath.

'I was talking to some of my regulars about him this week, as
you do.'

'And did anyone else mention him?'

Elouise nodded. 'Yes. They mentioned him coming in on
another occasion. It was one lunchtime. He came with a
woman.'

'Do you know when this was?'

'I didn't but I decided to take a look through my CCTV. It
was on Sunday the twenty-third of June. I wasn't working that
shift but I have a clear still of the footage. He came in with a
woman.' She clicked a few buttons on her keyboard and turned
her computer screen around so that Gina and Kapoor could
see it.

'Do you know who she is?' Gina asked. The man definitely
looked like Ross Craven. The woman had a long black plait that
fell forward over one arm and she was sitting at the table,
hunched over.

'Yes, her name is Biba, I think it's short for Habiba. She
works at the supermarket across the way and she lives local. She
has a daughter who used to do a Saturday shift for me before
she started uni. Her name is Saira.' Elouise paused. 'There's
more to this than someone behaving aggressively when drunk,
isn't there?'

Gina nodded. 'As you might have seen, there has been a
press release regarding a murder yesterday morning of a young
woman.'

Elouise's eyes widened. 'Did he do it?'

'We just need to locate him to question him, that's all. Any help you can give to us would be much appreciated.' Gina punched a quick message to O'Connor asking him to call the supermarket and see if he could set up an interview with Habiba.

'There is one other thing. Later that same day, I think I saw him, I mean the back of him after working the evening shift. I can't confirm it was definitely him but when he came in to ask about the job, I was sure I'd seen him before and I guess it was more of a build and gait thing. I saw the back of a man that night when I was locking up on the Sunday, about midnight, and I'm almost certain it was him. He was wearing the same large black hoodie that we can see on the screen and the CCTV your PC took away, and he had the same dark hair and the way he lumbers is quite distinctive.'

'So, you saw someone who looked like him around midnight. Tell me about that?'

Elouise furrowed her perfectly shaped dark brows. 'He was walking in the direction of the church. The weird thing was, he was with a young woman and they were arguing. She shouted something but I couldn't hear what, then she pushed him and it looked like he threw something at her, something small. He then shouted back; she took whatever it was before running. He didn't run after her so I saw no need to intervene or call the police.'

Gina felt her heart rate begin to pick up. 'What did the woman look like?'

'Dark clothing.' She sighed. 'It was too far away and they weren't exactly underneath a street lamp. She was a little shorter than the man. When she leaned forward, I could see that she had longish hair as it passed her shoulders.'

Nell had hair that passed her shoulders. 'Thank you. That's really helpful.'

Kapoor began to scrunch her eyes. 'May I just zoom in a little on this frame?'

Gina's phone beeped. It was a message from O'Connor.

Contacted the supermarket and spoke to Habiba. She lives just behind where she works and she's heading home now. I'll send her address in a separate message. She said it was okay to head over anytime this evening.

They weren't going to make the search of Nell's flat. Right now, they needed to head straight to Habiba's place, see what she knew about Ross Craven.

Elouise nudged the keyboard and mouse towards Kapoor.

Gina watched as Kapoor made the image larger and stared. 'What do you see?'

'Does that look like a necklace to you?'

Gina nodded. Then she saw what Kapoor had seen. While Ross Craven had been sitting in the bar earlier on the Sunday at the Angel with Habiba, he was wearing a cord necklace and Gina could just see the hint of blue that was almost tucked under his T-shirt. It was a Turkish eye pendant, the same type that had been attached to Toffee's collar.

TWENTY-FIVE

SALLY

Sally held Alfie's tiny hand and walked him around the graveyard. Toffee and Jerry jumped at each other playfully as they yapped and tore back and forth through the bushes and undergrowth. While speaking to Maeve on the phone, Sally had sensed her apprehension which was why she'd asked Maeve to come and stay for a few days. She had a small annex attached to the far side of the vicarage and it was rarely used. Maeve could stay there and maybe she'd have a chance of getting to know her nephew. She'd called the social worker and he agreed that in the long run it would be ideal for Alfie to be placed with her pending a home visit and checks. All Sally wanted to do was help Alfie and this was the best way. She glanced at Toffee. He was a delightful little dog. She hoped that Maeve would want Toffee too because that dog had been loyally close to Alfie since he arrived.

'Right, let's go and check your aunt's quarters, shall we?' She called the dogs over. They followed her to the annex and she unlocked the door. The small studio wasn't much to look at but it was clean and functional. Simple and basic with a single bed at one end, a wooden cross on the wall above it and a Bible resting on the bedside table. The small kitchenette had a kettle, toaster and a microwave. Sally had made sure there was some bread, butter, milk, tea and coffee for Maeve. The telly worked and it was able to connect to Netflix and the small sofa just about fit in the room. She checked the wet room and it too was all clean and ready to use. 'Perfect.'

Alfie sat on the doormat yawning as the dogs waited for her to leave the annex. She leaned over and scooped the sleepy toddler up. It had been another long day for him.

'Ollolow,' the boy said.

Sally furrowed her brows. 'Ollolow. What is ollolow?'

The boy laughed and grabbed her hair. She had no idea what he meant. She checked her watch. It was almost six thirty and Maeve would be arriving soon. She headed back to the house, the evening sun casting the last of its rays across the one end of the house, all signs of last night's thunder now gone.

'Ah, Sally.' Reverend Langham almost made her jump as he appeared from alongside the house, just as she was about to step inside. 'I'm off now, but I'll be back tomorrow lunchtime to supervise the AA meeting. I'll leave the counsellor to it but I'll make sure he has all that he needs. You have a wedding booked on Saturday and then there's Sunday service. Do you want me to prepare to take those, just in case?'

'That would be much appreciated, thank you.'

'You're welcome. Hope you and this little man manage to get some rest.' The reverend pulled a funny face and Alfie laughed again.

'Drive safely, Ernie, and see you in the morning.'

With that, he'd left. She stepped into her kitchen and both dogs thundered through, running excitedly up and down the hallway. She walked over to the fridge with Alfie and went to grab the apple juice but it wasn't there. She checked the fridge doors, the salad tray and she even checked the freezer to see if she'd absent-mindedly popped it in there, but it was nowhere to be seen.

'Olllolloloo,' Alfie said as he began chewing his fist and grinning.

'I can't find the apple juice, mate,' she said to him as she shrugged. That's when she saw that the bin lid was slightly sticking up. She pressed the pedal to open it and there was the empty juice container. She must have drunk it earlier and forgotten. It had been hot. She glanced at the sink and saw an empty beaker waiting to be washed up. Picking it up, she sniffed. It smelled of apple. She was tired, so tired. It seemed obvious now. She must have given it to Alfie earlier. She'd chased after the toddler all day trying to keep him safe and it was catching up with her and she'd barely slept. Every little movement Alfie had made in the night had set her on alert. She'd checked on him several times, worried that he might need her, that he might try to escape from the cot and hurt himself or that he might choke on something.

The knock on the front door made her flinch. The little dogs gathered there and yapped. Hurrying through with Alfie still in her arms, she checked the spyhole and exhaled. Knowing it was safe, she removed the chain and opened the door. 'You must be Maeve?'

The woman nodded. 'And you must be Sally. Thank you for letting me come over and stay with you.' Despite what had happened, Maeve looked amazing. Her athleisure wear was pristine and fitted to her toned figure. The only giveaway to her family tragedy was smudgy make-up. 'And this must be Alfie?' Maeve's gaze fixed on him.

The dogs gathered around Maeve's ankles. Sally called them into the kitchen and closed the door. 'Would you like to hold him?'

'Err, I'm okay. He looks comfortable and I don't want to

upset him.' She stepped inside, wheeling her tiny case behind her.

'I'm so sorry for your loss.' Alfie began to fight his tiredness and fidgeted in Sally's arms. She put him down and he staggered sleepily into the living room. Peering in, she saw he was safe as he stood at the window, patting it and babbling to himself.

'Nell and I weren't close and now I wish we had been. I stuffed up. I should have been there for her.' Maeve swallowed. 'I always tried to be there for her from afar but I should have got to know Alfie. I should have babysat, listened to her and been a sister but instead I blamed her for our mother's murder and all the time I should have been blaming him.' Everything was spilling out of Maeve, like she'd held back until that point.

'Him?'

'Nell's father. He's just got out of prison and now this. Not content with taking our mother, he's taken Nell. I'm so scared. I never thought I'd say that but I am. I was okay earlier but the more I think about things, the more fearful I get. Then there was the horrible note someone hand delivered to me saying that my mum deserved what she got and I don't know what came over me. I even managed to ignore that until I found out Nell had been murdered. Only Nell's father could have written that.' Maeve bowed her head and held back her tears.

Sally placed a hand on her shoulder. 'Well, I'm glad you're here, Maeve. You can stay as long as you need.'

She took a couple of deep breaths. 'What's Alfie like? I mean, you've had a chance to get to know him.'

'He's a lovely and clever little boy. Honestly, he's an absolute delight. Once you get to know him, you'll see that too. He loves cuddles, toy trains, scrambled eggs, honey on toast, and he loves his dog, Toffee, too.'

'Yes, Nell had a dog.'

Sally pointed to the chihuahua. 'That's Toffee. He's so good with Alfie.' She hoped Maeve would see that the two of them should be kept together.

Maeve smiled and then peered into the living room, looking unsure about stepping in. 'I can see Nell in him, and he has our mother's fluffy hair.' She turned back to Sally, frowning. 'I've never even looked after a child before, let alone a toddler. I won't know what to do.'

'That's okay. We can work through that together. I'll help you. It's not hard. He just needs love right now. The rest will come, I promise you. He is so adorable.' Sally meant every word. She would keep Alfie in a heartbeat if she had the chance. She'd love nothing more than to smother him with love.

Maeve turned and held on to the doorframe as Alfie banged his hands on the window. 'Man, man.' She stepped in and kneeled beside him as she looked out.

Sally's heart began to thrum. She was sure that Alfie was saying man. She glanced out of the window and once again, she couldn't see anyone. Ernie had already left and the place looked deserted.

'Man.' He turned around, looking up and smiling at Maeve before popping his knuckle in his mouth. She bent over and lifted him up.

What should have been a heart-warming moment with Maeve smiling and holding her nephew had left Sally with the jitters. She placed her shaking hands down by her sides, trying hard not to ruin their moment. Maeve looked like she hadn't really heard what Alfie had been saying as she took him to the settee and began telling him that she was Aunt Maeve.

Sally remained at the window. Had he said mum? It sounded so much like man. And then there was the apple juice. She still couldn't remember giving it to Alfie in the beaker. While out with the dogs she'd left the back door unlocked. 'I'll be back in a moment.' Leaving Maeve with Alfie, she ran upstairs, checking each room in turn. There was no one in the house. She was safe. She picked up the teddy bear in Alfie's cot and cuddled it as she walked back onto the landing and checked the upstairs window. Her own fear was getting the better of her.

Man, man, man. That's all she could think. That word was almost shouting in her head. She offered up a silent prayer and took a deep breath before heading back down. There was no one in her house and there was no one outside the vicarage. They were all safe, weren't they?

TWENTY-SIX

Gina knocked on the door of the mid-terraced house. A hanging basket full of plastic plants swung in the slight breeze. Greyness formed in the sky above. Kapoor smiled at her, eager to be working with Gina today.

'Hello,' the woman said as she opened the door. 'You must be from Cleevesford Police?'

Gina held her identification up. 'I'm DI Harte and this is Trainee DC Kapoor. May we come in?'

Just like in the CCTV, Habiba wore her hair in a single long plait that fell over a shoulder and across her chest. Her sharp navy-blue trousers and crisp white shirt made her look professional. Her name tag stated she was the assistant manager of the supermarket. The woman barely came up to Gina's shoulders in height.

'Er, yes. You'll have to excuse the mess. I've just got home.'

'Of course.' Gina smiled.

'Can we talk in the lounge?'

'That would be lovely,' Gina replied. Kapoor sat in the armchair in front of the window, Gina sat next to a pile of clean washing on the sofa. The flowery scent tickled her nostrils.

Habiba pulled out a pouffe and sat on it. 'How can I help you?'

Gina waited for Kapoor to grab her pen and head up her notebook. 'Can I take your full name please?'

'Is this about Ross?'

'Yes. I'll explain more in a moment.'

'Of course. Habiba Bal.'

'Ms Bal, were you at the Angel Arms on the twenty-third of June?'

She scrunched her brow as she thought back. 'Yes, that was a Sunday. I was there for an hour or two at lunchtime.'

'You were with Ross Craven, is that correct?'

Habiba's eyes widened. 'Yes.' She paused. 'I was going to call you, the police I mean. I haven't seen him since Sunday. He normally answers his phone. I wondered if something had happened.'

'How do you know Ross Craven?'

Habiba pursed her lips and placed her hands together and began to pick the skin alongside her nails. 'We go back a long way.'

'It would really help us if you start at the beginning. How do you know Mr Craven?' Gina tilted her head and smiled, hoping to put Habiba at ease.

'I met him about twenty years ago when I was managing a shop at a caravan park in Evesham. He'd booked one of the rental vans for a couple of months which seemed a long time. He told me he'd been a bit down on his luck and didn't have anywhere to live. We connected instantly; I know that sounds cheesy. He was fun and we had a laugh.' She hesitated, then continued. 'We'd go out drinking together and I fell for him. Before I knew it, he'd moved into my flat. I didn't know him as Ross until recently. He told me his name was Rod Cross and that he worked as a builder. He always came home with cash. I should have suspected him at the time, as surviving on cash jobs is odd but I was young, in love and naïve. I didn't overthink it. Soon after meeting, I found out I was pregnant and we had Saira. She wasn't planned but we were happy and in love. After that, I found myself constantly busy with parenting and I could tell we were drifting apart. At first, he slept on the sofa because Saira kept waking up crying and he was tired at work, but he never came back into our bed. I don't really know what went wrong but I felt like we had a relationship of convenience. We barely spoke but we decided to stay together for Saira. Then, one day when she'd just turned nine, he called me out the blue to say that he wasn't coming home, ever. I was angry and upset but I picked up the pieces and got on with my life. By then, I'd been promoted at work so I threw myself into that.'

Gina knew that Ross Craven had been arrested about then. 'And when did you hear from him next?' Gina took in the orange walls and bright abstract elephant painting that hung above the fireplace as Habiba continued.

'He was outside my work about three weeks ago, I can't remember the date. He found me through my social media posts. That's when he confessed that he'd been arrested on the day he called me to tell me he was leaving us. He said it was to protect me and Saira from the attention that would have come our way and that minutes before his arrest he'd thrown the phone he'd been using over a fence. Anyway, when we were speaking, that's when it all came out. He told me his name wasn't Rod, it was Ross, and that the murder he'd been imprisoned for was an accident. It's like something clicked. That's why back then he had nothing but cash jobs. He could never be on a system as Rod Cross didn't exist and, unknowingly, I helped him to hide for years. While he was telling me all this, I didn't know what to believe and I've been so confused. He said all he wanted was to see some photos of Saira so I let him come to my house. Then, he said he was desperate for somewhere to stay and if I didn't help him, he'd be on the streets. At the end of the day, he's still Saira's father so I said he could have her room for a few days until he sorted out somewhere to stay. That's when we were at the pub together. I didn't want to go to the pub with him but Rod,' – she scrunched her brow – 'I mean Ross, he can be quite insistent.' Habiba began to tremble. 'His temper got worse over those few days. He kept saying that no one would give him a chance being an ex-con, and he kept shouting and ranting. At times he scared me. I then regretted letting him stay at my house. Once again, I'd been naïve. I asked him to leave but he wouldn't go. He said he had some business to attend to in Cleevesford and that he'd be gone in a few days. I thought I just had to bide a bit of time for an easy life. I used to hear him roaring with anger in Saira's room. He'd hit the walls and punch the door.'

'That must have been upsetting.' Gina gave Habiba a moment. 'Did he mention his plans to you?'

She shook her head. 'No, he was distant and either out or in Saira's room most of the time. I didn't want to ask him anything in case he started shouting again. He always seemed to be out at odd hours. That made me angry too as he'd go out the back door and leave it unlocked. I can't remember the times he came and went so there's no point asking.' She frowned. 'He mentioned having another daughter who was born before Saira. That was a shocker. I mean who has a daughter and fails to tell his pregnant new girlfriend? Again, that's the first I'd ever heard about him having a child before he met me. He was such a liar! He said he wanted to reconnect with her. Do you know who she is? Maybe she's seen him or he might be with her?'

Gina sat forward a little. 'There was a press release earlier. A young woman was found murdered in Cleevesford.'

'We've been talking about that all day at work.' Habiba opened her mouth and paused as realisation hit her. 'Was it her? Was she his daughter?'

'I'm sorry to say, but yes.'

Habiba began to inhale and exhale sharply. 'I googled him a couple of days ago, that's why I was going to call you. Why the hell did I believe anything he said?' She began playing with the end of her plait.

'We're going to find him and we're going to get to the bottom of all this.'

'It all makes sense now. He killed that poor woman, then he went on the run and he played me for a stupid idiot for ten years so that I could hide him. Then as soon as he was released, he killed that poor girl, and now he's on the run again. He knows how to hide. You'll never catch him. There will be some poor woman who's falling for his lies right now while he gives her a fake name and a sob story.' She let out a little sob and held a hand to her mouth for a moment. 'Am I safe? Is my daughter safe?'

'Does he know where your daughter is?'

She shrugged. 'He knows she's in Spain. She's studying modern languages. She's in Madrid on an exchange programme for another week. What about me? Will he hurt me?'

Gina agreed that Habiba would need some sort of protection. Ross Craven had been convicted of killing his ex and now he was their main suspect in the murder of Nell. 'I'm going to arrange for a PC to come to your house later, if that's okay. I'd like you to have a panic alarm fitted and we'll arrange for another officer to be stationed outside at all times for now. I'm sorry, I know this is hard for you but your safety has to come first.'

'Thank you.'

'Does he have a key?'

'No, thank goodness. I never gave him one. That's why he used the back door.'

'What was he wearing when you saw him last?'

Habiba stopped picking her skin. 'He wore basically the same kind of clothes every day. Dark jeans, a charcoal-grey hoodie over a T-shirt. He had a necklace on. It was a Turkish eye pendant threaded through a shoelace leather necklace. He's a large guy, broad and he has a bad back which makes him lumber a little as he walks.'

'Thank you.' Gina thought back to the stranger that one of Nell's neighbours had described and the dark top matched. 'In the meantime, if you hear from him, or see him, can you call me straight away? Here's my number.'

Habiba nodded and took the card that Gina handed to her. 'He's left some things here.'

'Can I see them?'

The woman went upstairs and brought a pile of clothes down with her. She dropped the two hoodies and a couple of navy-blue T-shirts, underpants and socks on the settee next to Gina.

Gina pulled out several large evidence bags from her bag and snapped on some gloves. She carefully placed each item in a separate bag after checking them and completing the forms that went with the bags.

'His coat is missing. Wait.' Habiba ran out of the room and left through the back door. 'Here, he must have left it on the back of the garden chair.'

Gina took the coat from her. As she slid her hand into one of the pockets she felt something long and hard. That's when she pulled out the serrated knife.

TWENTY-SEVEN

Gina yawned as she stood at the head of the incident room. Jacob, O'Connor and Briggs were tucking into the chip shop chips, bags opened out in the middle of the table. Gina leaned in and ate a handful swiftly as Wyre came in and sat. As Gina stood straight a sharp pain flashed across her chest. She lay a hand over it.

'Everything okay?' Briggs stopped eating. Gina knew she'd told him to give her some space but she could tell he was genuinely concerned.

'Yes.' She dropped her hand to her side. 'Just indigestion from these chips.' She pulled an antacid from her pocket and began chewing the chalky tablet. The pain hadn't gone but it wasn't sharp anymore. She checked her phone to see if she'd had another message but nothing had come through. She needed to try and call the number again later.

Kapoor came in last with several cans of pop and placed them in the middle of the table before sitting.

Briggs stood. 'Right, we're all here now. Gina, go ahead and let us know how you and Kapoor have got on today.'

She took a deep breath and started. 'PC Smith has arranged for a panic alarm to be fitted at Habiba Bal's house and uniform will be stationed outside. We are hoping that Ross Craven returns to Ms Bal's house so we can pick him up. As for Craven, Elouise went through the CCTV with us. He was at the Angel on Sunday the twenty-third of June. We can see that he was wearing the Turkish eye pendant attached to a cord around his neck. Given that we found Nell's dog with the same pendant attached to its collar, more suspicion is being cast on Mr Craven. And now we have the knife, which Kapoor and I dropped off at the lab with his clothes before coming back here. The coat was one that was left in Habiba Bal's garden and she confirmed it belonged to Ross Craven. One of the forensics team is taking a look to see if that knife could have been used to remove Nell's eyes.'

O'Connor threw the chip he was holding down on the chip paper.

Gina continued. 'On Sunday the twenty-third, when Elouise was closing the pub up for the night, she saw someone who looked like Ross Craven arguing with a young woman. We need to bear in mind that it could have been Nell.' Gina glanced down at the notes that Kapoor had taken. 'Habiba Bal is forty-nine and very short, I'd say around five feet tall so she doesn't match the description of that woman. Jacob, how did the search of Nell's flat go?'

He exhaled. 'We didn't find much out of the ordinary apart from what you saw on the day. All the cupboards being empty and the clothes piled up on the bed and food all over the worktop was about as odd as it got. Although, we found a slight cut in her mattress and when we delved deeper, we found Alfie's birth certificate.'

'Was the father's name mentioned on it?'

'No. It was blank.'

Gina continued. 'I've updated the system with the information I have from the post-mortem. Have you all had a chance to look?'

'I haven't,' Jacob said. Gina knew that he'd been busy at Nell's flat.

'I'll give you a speedy summary.' Gina picked up her note-book. 'Nell's eyes were removed post-mortem. The trauma to her body is showing that she was hit over the head with a blunt instrument that would have weakened her. Bruises to her chest were recorded, one possibility is that they were caused by someone straddling her. Her eyes were removed using a serrated knife and they weren't removed carefully. She was most likely unconscious during this attack as no defence wounds were found. Pressure marks around the neck tell us she died by strangulation.'

The whole room went quiet.

Wyre breathed out. 'So, the PM shows that she was hit, then straddled, strangled and then the killer removed her eyes.'

Gina nodded. 'Which is why we need Ross Craven in an interview room. Have all units on alert.'

TWENTY-EIGHT

SALLY

Friday, 5 July

It had been a lovely evening with Maeve. Sally knew that the woman was warming to the idea of having Alfie in her life. They'd talked until nearly midnight about parenting and how hard yet rewarding it could be. Maeve had bathed him and he'd even cuddled her. She'd started off playing with his toys and then she progressed to holding him and speaking softly as he'd fallen asleep in the cot. Then Maeve had retired to the annex to get some sleep, leaving Sally alone with Alfie.

Sally gazed at him with nothing but the light of the moon to pick out the smooth shape of his little button nose and soft forehead. His chest rose up and down. She wondered what he was dreaming about and a twinge of sadness hit her. He was probably missing Nell. Leaning in, she stroked his soft hair and pulled the sheet up a little so that it reached his neck. It had been a hot day but with night came a chill in the air, especially in her big old house. The joists had started to creak as they'd cooled down. Ordinarily, she never thought about them, but since she'd seen Nell's body, her heart hummed and she felt a bit nervy.

Toffee came over and sniffed at her ankles before heading back to the large cable knit blanket she'd folded up on the floor. The little dog seemed to want to be close to Alfie, so she'd allowed him to stay in the room with the boy.

Jerry snuffled in the hallway and began whimpering as he ran down the stairs. Her dog had been unsettled for a while but she knew that he wanted to be in the same room as Toffee. Toffee then jumped off the blanket and followed, then he too began crying and barking. Sally closed the bedroom door, not wanting to wake Alfie. She hurried down in her nightshirt and went into the living room. Opening a curtain slightly, she looked out. That's when she saw Maeve standing outside the back door of the church in her pyjamas and trainers.

As Sally opened the front door, the dogs skipped out, barking. 'Maeve, what are you doing?' She wondered how Maeve had managed to open the back door to the church.

'I heard banging noises. Then I went back to sleep for a short while and I thought I heard a door slamming. When I came out this door was open and I wondered if it was you. I thought I'd see if everything was okay.'

That's when Sally realised that Maeve hadn't opened the door and it was silly to think she had. Why would Maeve want to go into the church at one in the morning? They'd been broken in to. She wondered if the perp was still inside. 'Maeve, can you go into the vicarage and look after Alfie while I check this out? It looks like we've had a break-in.' It wouldn't be the first time. Thieves had taken some lead off the lower part of the building above her office only a month ago so this was nothing unusual. This time she was going to catch them at it. 'Can you take the dogs with you?'

'Yes, will you be okay? If there's someone still in there, come back out and we can wait for the police.' Maeve called Jerry and Toffee over and grabbed one collar in each hand.

Sally nodded. 'Yes, I'll be fine, honestly. Can you call the police? The thieves are probably long gone now but you never know.'

Maeve nodded and hurried back into the house with the dogs.

Without touching the main door, Sally stepped inside. She could see that the door had been forced open with a crowbar, damaging the lock. Security had been a big issue but the funds were never there to get it sorted. It was the same story with the roof and the heating system. She stepped into the dark corridor, the torch on her phone lighting the way. She knew that the police might want to check the light switches and door handles for prints so she needed to make sure she didn't touch a thing. 'Hello,' she called out.

There was no answer. Her office door was ajar. Running towards it, she peered into the room and noticed that nothing had been messed up. She left the office and could see that all the cupboard doors were closed and this time, she did remember locking them earlier. She pushed open the toilet doors with her bottom. No one was hiding there. She hurried through to the nave. Being alone with the sound of an owl hooting outside sent a shiver through her. A stack of parish magazines had been thrown to the floor and all the Bibles turfed off the stand. The flowers that one of the parishioner's had lovingly arranged lay in a pool of water amongst cracked glass.

Her gaze travelled across the rows of pews. If someone was in the church, hiding, they could easily crouch between them. 'Hello, please I don't want any trouble. Just come out so we can talk.'

One step after another, she crept up the aisle checking each row in turn but there was no sign of anyone. Then she reached the pulpit. She glanced behind a huge wooden chair, heart pounding as she realised that no one was hiding there either. That's when she noticed that the solid silver candlesticks were missing. They normally adorned the altar and she knew they'd been there earlier, unless Ernie put them away in a cupboard. No, the cupboards were definitely locked. She couldn't imagine that he would have. It had to be thieves.

Then the huge wooden door to the vestibule clattered. She left the altar and ran towards it. It was ever so slightly ajar. Now she knew that the thief had come in through the back and had left through the front, probably when she called out.

Stepping outside, she glanced each way and could still see no one. Her legs began to weaken and her fingers trembled. She took a couple of deep breaths. The thief was gone. She was safe.

As she turned to go back through the church, a blinding pain caught the side of her head just before she fell onto the hard floor. There had been an intruder in the church all along, watching and listening as she searched for them. The last thing she saw was the glint of the candlestick as her attacker brought it down again.

TWENTY-NINE

DIARY EXTRACT

I can't express how upset I am. I came home and I cried for hours. That's more than I've ever cried. I mean, he abandoned me and him coming out of prison was meant to be a new start, and he promised that we were going to do so much together. He had apparently been so sorry about all that I'd missed out on. Sorry, sorry, sorry. His words are empty. All he wanted was company and I gave him that while he was inside. I filled a hole in his pitiful life and in return he filled the hole in mine. I thought we needed each other.

I keep going over everything again and again in my head. He'd been so hard to get hold of since coming out of prison so when he called me up to ask me to meet him, I had to say yes, despite it being so late and me being so upset with him. It's in my nature to give people second chances.

I'd stood there for ages waiting in the bus stop on the high street for him to arrive and then he didn't even say sorry for being late. He was even wearing the Turkish eye that I gave him on a cord around his neck.

The things he said still reach into my soul and twist my innards. I literally feel sick thinking about it all. To top it off, the woman who works at the pub was staring at us while she was locking up. For a second, I thought she might come over to see if everything was okay but I didn't give her the chance.

Anyway, Diary, I ran all the way home. One minute I've been angry, the next I've felt like a scared child again with only my trusty silly diaries again. They were his idea. He kept giving them to me as gifts and look at me now, I write in them all the time. I'm writing in one now and I don't even know why. What is all this for? It was for him. He didn't want to miss any of my life but he couldn't be with me so I made a promise to him to KEEP DOING THIS. Keeping this silly diary.

I've paced and paced until my feet ached. That's when I stared out and saw him outside my kitchen window but when I opened the door, he'd gone.

I gave him something which he threw back at me. That stung. Maybe I shouldn't have said what I said but he had to hear it. I thought I was the one in control of all this but I'm not. It's him. It's creepy that he was outside my kitchen window. I'm now hugging a cushion, as if that'll help.

There's a noise coming from the kitchen...

THIRTY

KARINA

She did up the buttons on her dress and laughed. Her gran would have called this the walk of shame but no one cared about things like that anymore. She giggled to herself as she ducked behind the houses and past the community centre. Ouch, her heels pinched and the black lacy bodysuit under her yellow tailored shorts didn't look like office wear. A woman jogged past her and gave her a knowing smile. Was it that obvious? Of course it was. She made an attempt to flatten her wiry red hair down but it just pinged back out.

Karina checked her watch. Her mum would wake up to her alarm soon. She had aimed to get home before seven in the morning and sneak back into bed. It was ridiculous really. She was nineteen and could do what she liked as far as the law was concerned, but her mum was strict. If she told Mummy that she'd spent the night with a hot man who busked for a living and lived in a damp bedsit, she'd freak. Her sister would then think it was hilarious and use it to score points. Her mum was such a snob. If she then found out she'd been dating him for three months, all hell would break loose. Maybe she'd have to move out and live with him in his bedsit. That wouldn't be so bad.

She needed to get a move on. Maybe taking a short cut wouldn't hurt. Watcher's Way, as nicknamed by the locals, was rumoured to be a dogging area and everyone she knew joked about it but what did she care. There would be no doggers out at this time of day and she wasn't even sure she believed the rumours anyway. She tottered past the brook and headed towards the most avoided car park in Cleevesford. Her feet were throbbing now. Only a few more minutes and she could take her shoes off and go to bed.

A crunch came from behind her. She turned around to see who was there but all she could see was a thicket with trolleys tangled in it. That and an old pushchair and several bags of rubbish. Suddenly she felt vulnerable in the shoes. There was no way she could run from danger in them. If she took them off her feet would be torn to shreds by the gravel and broken bits of glass.

After pausing for a few seconds, she continued edging the car park. That's when she heard another crunch. Heart pounding, she turned and stared into the messy heap for longer this time. Was the noise even coming from that direction? She wasn't sure. She glanced around the whole car park.

Her heart nearly flew from her mouth as Arlo jumped out from behind a bin, laughing. 'Had you there.' His long wavy dark hair and stubble made her want to sink into him again.

She playfully slapped him. 'You scared the life out of me.'

His mouth downturned and she was struggling to look angry as she stared into his blue eyes. 'I've written a song for you.'

'Well in that case you're forgiven. Why are you out here following me around a doggers' car park like some creepo?'

He held up her phone. 'You left this on my bed. I thought you'd need it to call me later.' He laughed again.

She snatched her phone from him.

'I was going to give it to you ages ago but watching you walk in those shoes was way too funny. I could carry you the rest of the way.'

He went to pick her up. She laughed and dodged him. 'You know my mum would go mad.' He placed his arms around her and she welcomed his embrace. Her tongue met his and they stepped back slightly, close to where the rubbish heap was. 'Arlo, I have to get back. My mum will be awake soon.'

He stood back a little. 'Promise me you'll meet me later. I love you, Karina.'

He'd never said those words to her before. She'd remember this day forever. Maybe in many years to come she'd share this story with their grandchildren. Inwardly, she wanted to do a little happy dance and punch the air. Should she say it back? Before she had the chance, he smiled and waved as he jumped over the rubbish and into the dense growth, obviously taking an even quicker route back to his bedsit. 'I love you, too,' she shouted, hoping that he heard.

Smiling, she continued across the car park until she heard Arlo shrieking some words she couldn't make out.

Tottering over the rubbish heap, she saw him standing amongst a carpet of stingers, staring ahead. She couldn't quite see what he was looking at.

'Don't come any closer, Karina.' He dry-retched. 'You don't want to see it. Call the police, now. Tell them we've found a body.'

THIRTY-ONE

Gina stepped out of the shower and immediately caught the shrill ringing of her phone. She narrowly missed tripping over her cat, Ebony, as she grabbed it. The cat scarpered down the stairs. 'Hello.'

'Gina,' Briggs said. 'We have an emergency and I need you to attend a scene right now. I'll call Jacob in a minute too. He can meet you there.'

'What's happened?'

'Another body has been found and, once again, the victim's eyes have been removed. It looks like our murderer has struck again. I'll send you the exact location in a message but it's the car park on Rookstone Road, also known as Watcher's Way.' Gina shivered as drops of cold water meandered down her bare body. Watcher's Way once again alluded to eyes. She wondered if the killer had chosen it for that reason. 'Do we know who the victim is?'

'No, not yet. The young man who found the body didn't say too much, he was too busy retching. Apparently, the body is in a really bad state. I've called Bernard and his team are already on their way.'

'I'll head there now.'

'Great. There is something else. Just to keep you in the loop, I thought I'd let you know that the church was broken into last night. The thief took a couple of candlesticks and hit Sally over the head with one as they ran off.'

'Poor Sally. How is she?'

'She got checked over at Cleevesford General but from what I've heard, she's back at the vicarage now.'

'Is Alfie okay? Did he go with her?' Gina wondered who'd looked after the little boy.

'Yes, he's okay and Nell's half-sister, Maeve, came to Sally's last night. She was the one who called the police to say that Sally had gone into the church to see what had happened. A PC on the nightshift went over to the hospital to take a statement from Sally and a small forensics team was called in to see if the perp had left anything behind. It looked like the back door was forced open and they left out of the front.'

'Thanks for letting me know. Right, I best head over to Watcher's Way. I'll see Sally later.'

As she ended the call, her phone beeped again. It was another message from the unknown person.

I bet you'd love to call me. Thing is, I don't want to chat. Not yet. I want to keep the mystery going because we all love a bit of mystery in our lives, don't we? Haha, I have a line for you. Do you come here often? Don't worry, it's not a chat-up line. When I saw you coming out of the Angel Arms yesterday, it just felt so apt. Nice pub, at least it was a nice pub once, a proper drinkers' pub. But I guess all good things must come to an end. Is your life good at the moment, Gina? Oh, happy anniversary, by the way.

Happy anniversary. What the hell did that mean? It wasn't her wedding anniversary and it wasn't the anniversary of

Terry's death. What did July the fifth mean to her? The harder she thought, the more frustrated she got. It meant nothing to her at all. Her knuckles went white as she gripped her phone.

She tried to think back to when she and Kapoor left the Angel yesterday, and she didn't remember seeing anyone at all. Someone was toying with her, but who? Reading between the lines, the messenger was trying to tell her that her good life must come to an end. And what did they have to do with the Angel Arms? She opened her bedroom curtains and stared out. All she could see was a country road and fields. Time was passing and she needed to attend the murder scene.

Twenty minutes later, Gina was out of the door, hair still damp and she'd thrown on some clothes in a hurry. As she arrived at the car park she saw Bernard's forensics van and two others pulled up at the back end of the car park. An ambulance and two police cars were beside them. PC Ahmed had already marked out the outer cordon and he was just working on the inner cordon. PC Smith stood dutifully at the boundary, ready to keep the public out and maintain a log of who came and went. A blue tent had been partly erected amongst the undergrowth and trees. Gina waved and caught Bernard's attention. He waved back and began walking over in his crime scene suit. A CSI walked around with a camera, taking photos, while another began placing the stepping plates on the ground. Gina passed the rubbish pile and met him outside the inner cordon. PC Smith acknowledged her as she walked past him a little so she could speak to Bernard across the police tape. 'I know you haven't been here long but can you tell me anything?'

He re-tucked his beard back into his beard cover. 'You're right, I haven't been here long but what I do know is the victim has two missing eyes and it looks like they've been removed with a serrated knife. This time, there are several blows to the skull and the cranium is actually broken. This may well have killed him but we can't be sure until we've done the post-mortem.'

'Can you describe him?'

'Male in his mid to late fifties. Broad shouldered, brown hair speckled with grey, beard, wearing a dark-grey hoodie and a navy T-shirt. Dark jeans. One of his trainers had come off. He has size thirteen feet. A wallet was found close by.'

Gina knew who the man was immediately. 'And?'

'He has a bank card with the name Ross Craven on it.'

She let out a long breath. Ross Craven wasn't their murderer, in fact he was another victim. First, they had Nell's body and now Ross's. 'Do you have any indication of when he was killed?'

'As you know I can't be too precise but I'd go with around three to four days ago, taking the weather into consideration too. His body is bloated which means internal decomposition has started to take place. It's not a pretty sight back there.'

Her imagination was already conjuring up an image of what she was about to see and a part of her wanted to be back at home in bed. 'He was murdered first,' she mumbled. 'He is victim number one.'

'Yes, it appears so.'

Gina took a moment to re-jiggle the timeline in her head. 'Is he wearing a necklace?'

'Not that I saw.'

'Is there any sign of strangulation?'

Bernard shook his head. 'Not that I could see, but then again the body is in such a bad way and he's covered in dried up blood. I could get in for a closer look but I don't want to tamper before we've taken all our samples.'

'Was he brought here?'

'No, he definitely died here. There are no drag marks amongst the stingers or undergrowth and he's a hefty man. It would have taken more than one person to move him.'

'Can I see him?'

'If you step on the plates, I can take you over. Tog up.'

She grabbed a crime scene suit pack and began pulling it up over her thin trousers and short-sleeved shirt. PC Smith held the crime scene log out for her as she passed him. She thanked him, took the pen and signed.

'You need to brace yourself for this. The poor lad who found the body is still being treated for shock. His girlfriend is with him but she didn't see or go near the body.'

She took a couple of deep breaths and pulled her face mask on, knowing that it wouldn't block the putrid odour. As her flat comfy shoes clanked on the plates behind Bernard's her stomach began to knot at what she was about to see. A body left out in nature for five days, during a hot month, was going to be the stuff nightmares were made of. On reaching the now fully erected tent, the CSIs stepped aside to let her see. She peered through the opening. Ross Craven's face was bloated to extremes, distorting the features she'd seen on the photo they had of him. Foam had gathered around his mouth and the crack to his head revealed more than she wanted to see. She had to briefly look away to regain her composure. No longer able to hold her breath, she drank in the scent of rot, like fruit and bad meat mixed together and her stomach clenched as she caught sight of all the maggots. She stepped out of the tent and Bernard gave her some space to take it in and breathe. She had confirmed it was Ross Craven and she couldn't see his necklace. Formal identification would be made later but there was no doubt in her mind who the corpse belonged to.

'Are you okay?'

Gina nodded. She was far from okay but she had a job to do and she was going to do it before the killer had the opportunity to strike again. She batted one of the many flies away from her face.

'Scenes like this are particularly hard. Do you need me to check anything in there for you?'

She shook her head. 'No, I think I have what I need for now, but thank you for offering.' She spotted Jacob walking over to PC Smith and she waved.

'I'll email you later with the photos.'

'Thanks, Bernard. That would be great.' She left him to his work. While trudging back, the tip of a stinger caught her ankle. After signing out, she hurried over to Jacob, removed her face mask and bent over to take a few deep breaths, enjoying the clean woodland air.

'Was it that bad, guv? You're looking a bit green,' Jacob asked.

She stood up straight. 'That and worse. I haven't seen one that bad for a long time. Eyes removed, head bashed in several times, maggots, bloating. It's Ross Craven.'

'And he's bloated?' Jacob furrowed his brow. Gina knew he'd just worked out who died first between Ross and Nell. 'Are you sure it's him?'

'Yes, it's Ross Craven and he was murdered before Nell. I guess it's back to the drawing board.' She turned back to watch the forensics team at work. 'You don't need to go and see that. Can you message the station? Someone needs to tell his probation officer and Habiba Bal.'

'Yes, I'll do that now.' He tapped away on his phone.

'Is the man who found him still in the ambulance?'

'Yes, but it should be okay to speak to him now.'

'Great. We'll get that done then we can get back to the station.' She popped her crime scene suit into the bag next to the forensics van. 'I'll just send Briggs a quick message too.'

After filling Briggs in, she went to follow Jacob towards the ambulance.

'Gina,' Bernard called out, carrying a camera in his hand. 'Wait, we found something.'

'I'll handle this interview, guv. You go,' Jacob said as he continued walking towards the ambulance.

She hurried back over to the cordon.

Bernard held out the camera and showed her the screen. She moved slightly to avoid the glare of the morning sun. 'Where was this?'

'On that tree, just behind the tent.' He pointed at the CSI standing next to it.

Someone had carved an eye on the bark. The removed eyes, Watcher's Way, the Turkish eye and now a carved eye; it all meant something and she had to find out what before anyone else got killed. Her phone beeped. As she read the message from O'Connor, her jaw almost dropped.

> *We are holding an emergency briefing as soon as you are back. Abigail Bretton's car was caught by a speed camera close to the murder scene on the morning of Nell's murder.*

THIRTY-TWO

MAEVE

As Maeve finished pouring Sally a cup of tea, her phone beeped. She glanced at the WhatsApp message.

Matty: Just thought I'd see how you were doing this morning? I know yesterday was worrying you.

They'd messaged the previous evening and she'd really appreciated his support. She and Alfie had been getting on well and against what she ever thought of herself, she'd began to imagine her future with Alfie in it. She sent a quick reply.

Maeve: So much has happened since we messaged last night, you just wouldn't believe it.

Matty: How about a drink? I'm passing through Cleevesford to see my sister in Wixford and you're staying at the vicarage, aren't you? Do you want to meet somewhere?

Maeve: Yes, it's on the high street. Give me five. I'll get back to you.

She really did need to get out of the vicarage for a short while but it would only be right to see if Sally could manage on her own given that she had a head injury.

Maeve dropped a chunk of lemon into the cup and followed that with a sprig of fresh mint picked from the plant on the windowsill, just as Sally had requested. She grabbed a packet of chocolate biscuits from the cupboard and took them both to Sally. 'How are you feeling?'

'Not too bad now. I'm more upset than anything.' Sally shrugged. 'Thank you for the tea. Did the police tell you when forensics would be here as I've already had to postpone today's appointments at the church?'

Maeve had spoken to the police last night while Sally was being treated at the hospital and she had been told that someone would come but no one had turned up yet. 'They only said it would be today. They didn't say what time that would be.'

Sally smiled. 'Thank you for being here and looking after Alfie. How did you both get on last night while I was having my head sewn up?'

'He slept like a little log.' She paused. 'I couldn't help but check on him every five minutes to the point of being obsessive.'

'I know what you mean. You can't help but worry. Thank you for walking the dogs too.'

The dressing on Sally's head reached from her left brow underneath her black fringe.

'That's okay. They were no problem at all and Alfie enjoyed the walk. I'm glad I could help.' She paused. 'Do you think the break-in had anything to do with what happened to Nell?'

Sally frowned. 'I doubt it. We get broken into a lot. We had only just replaced the candlesticks after the last break-in.' She let out a slight laugh. 'I'm tempted to get purple plastic ones next with battery flames.' Then she sighed and sipped her tea. 'That was a joke.'

Lying next to Sally on the settee, Alfie began to stir from his nap. Maeve stepped over to him, kneeled down and stroked his forehead. 'Hello, little man.'

He laughed and reached out for her face and stroked her cheek back before yawning and giggling. 'Would you mind if I pop out in a bit? My friend is passing through and he asked if I wanted to have a drink with him.' It felt odd asking if she was allowed out but she knew that Sally would have to look after Alfie on her own and that she wasn't feeling brilliant. Alfie now felt like her responsibility. Her heart started to race. This would be her life forever more. She couldn't just pop out anywhere. She'd have to take a humungous bag full of things for Alfie. She'd seen those struggling parents, toddlers having tantrums on the floors of shops, while the flustered parents lugged bags full of luggage around. And if she wanted to go out alone... what do people do? Maybe she could get an au pair or someone to help, or a babysitter. Do they need qualifications, DRB checks, first aid training? She gasped and came back to the present.

'Of course I don't mind. Anytime,' Sally replied. 'You're welcome to come and go as you please and last night was a worry for you too. A bit of time out will do you good.'

'I know and you've been very kind letting me come here to get to know Alfie.'

'We'll be fine, won't we?' Sally allowed Alfie to climb on her lap, despite the pain Maeve could see she was in. 'We have Netflix and I'm sure I can find something for us to watch.'

'Thank you again. I really appreciate everything you're doing for me, for us.'

'You're welcome. As I said, anytime. I've grown fond of this little one.'

Maeve left Sally with Alfie and went into the kitchen. Jerry and Toffee were sleeping together in the large dog bed. She sent Matty a WhatsApp message.

Maeve: I'd love to meet up for a drink. I passed a pub when I drove here, on the high street. It's called the Angel Arms. Do you want to meet there?

Matty: Sounds good. I know that pub well. I can be there in about half an hour. I'm just grabbing some bits from the shop for my sister's kids. They'll wonder what happened if Uncle Matty turns up without treats – haha.

Maeve: Half an hour sounds perfect. See you there!

She called to Sally. 'I'll be back in a bit,' and she left out of the back door and headed towards the annex.

She opened the annex door and went in. A breeze whipped from one end of the room to the other, like a powerful vacuum. She closed the kitchen window and hurried past the bed to the far window and closed that too. Her clothes were still neatly lain over the back of a chair, just as she'd left them. Grabbing her floor-length halter-neck summer dress in deep jewel colours, one of her company's own designs, she slipped off her shorts and T-shirt and fed the dress over her head. She matched the dress up to her leather Carvela sandals.

A wash of guilt went through her as she checked out her reflection in the full-length wardrobe mirror. How could she stand there, excited to meet up with Matty, when Nell had been murdered and Sally had been attacked? She exhaled. It had been a long time since she'd liked a man. Her career had always come first but Matty seemed different. She had only properly known him for a couple of days, but he'd been there for her in a way that no one else had. That had to mean something.

Again, her thoughts went back to Sally. Should she really leave her alone? She bit her bottom lip. Sally said she'd be okay and it wasn't for long. While she was out, she'd pick up some ingredients and make Sally a nice meal later as another way of saying thank you. Then, she was going to sort her life out and plan how she was going to look after Alfie and work out what she was going to do with Toffee. She quickly sent an email to her assistant, telling her to hold the fort for a few days. Her assistant instantly called. 'Hello, everything okay?' she asked.

'Yes,' she replied.

'The police called and asked where you were on Wednesday morning and lunchtime,' her assistant said.

'I was in meetings all day Wednesday.'

'That's what I told them. Didn't you pop out? It wasn't in your diary but I'm sure you had to do something and I couldn't remember when the police asked so I thought I'd check with you and call them back if needs be.'

'I didn't go anywhere. As you said I was there all day, like my diary says.'

'Oh, okay.' Her assistant paused. 'I won't bother you again. If you need anything, just call. Otherwise, everything is in hand. We're sorting out some of the production issues and everything is looking fine.'

'That's wonderful. Thank you.' She ended the call.

As she turned to grab her Gucci sunglasses from the bedside table, she realised they weren't there. She opened the drawers and they were empty. Running around to the other side of the bed, she checked the other bedside table and it was empty apart from the Bible she'd popped in the top drawer.

After letting out a long slow breath, she wondered if someone had come in through the window to steal them or maybe earlier when she'd been walking outside with Alfie, had Sally popped into the annex. Why would Sally want her sunglasses? Her phone pinged.

Matty: I've got us a booth by the window. See you soon. X

If she hadn't lost her sunglasses, she'd be sitting there

wondering if the kiss at the end of his message meant anything. She had to forget the sunglasses and she needed to put some make-up on, and fast. After no sleep, she was well aware that she looked like the walking dead. A bit of mascara and blusher would fix things. She ran into the bathroom and stopped dead with a grimace. Her dark glasses stood out on the white toilet seat. She couldn't remember leaving them there but she must have done. Glancing behind her, she could see she was alone. After applying a bit of make-up, she picked them up and put them on.

As she locked the door and left, she went to walk around the building, passing the church to reach the car park. A forensics van pulled up and a woman stepped out. She said hello as she headed to the vicarage.

Maeve pulled her keys from her little bag and pressed the central locking button. As she went to grab the door handle, she stopped just shy of stepping onto the dead crow on the tarmac. Had someone left that for her to see?

THIRTY-THREE

Gina hurried into the station with Jacob, the weird message still on her mind. As she reached the incident room, Briggs was standing at the head of the table. Wyre passed cans of cola to O'Connor and PC Ahmed. Kapoor sat in front of a laptop and tapped away as she updated to the system. Without wasting a moment, Gina gave everyone a speedy summary of what Bernard had said at the murder scene. 'Right, tell me about Abigail Bretton.'

Wyre tapped her nails on the edge of the desk. 'On the morning of Nell's murder, Abigail's car was caught speeding on the main road that feeds into Hay Loft Lane and then it was later caught on an ANPR camera. Her return wasn't flagged up on ANPR, which means she went a different way back. We know that her car was close to Nell Craven's flat at eleven in the morning on the day Nell was murdered. We also have a photo of the driver from the speeding camera.' Wyre pointed to the printed-out photo that was being passed around the table.

O'Connor passed it to Gina. She could make out that the woman behind the wheel was Abigail Bretton. 'She lied to us. We need to bring her in. Have we verified Darrah Kelly's whereabouts on the day of Nell's murder with the bus company?'

'I'm waiting for an email, guv,' O'Connor said. 'They're sending me the footage that covers the bus he would have taken to get from Cleevesford Manor back to his flat. I'll let you know when I have it.'

Nick, the desk sergeant, walked through the door. 'Guv, there's a woman in reception. She said she needs to speak to you urgently. Her name is Kira Fellows.'

'Could you please tell her I'm on my way?'

Nick nodded and left.

'I'll be back in a minute.' She left the team talking about the case and discussing how they should proceed with Abigail. As she entered reception, she saw Kira sitting on a plastic chair wearing a sundress, her little boy straddling her knee while eating a piece of apple. 'Kira, come through.' Kira pushed her buggy one-handed, baby bag in it and her son on her hip. She took them to the family room and gestured for them to sit on the couch. 'How can I help you?'

'I found something and thought you should see it. When Nell and I were sitting outside my flat a couple of weeks ago, we took some selfies of us and the kids on my phone. I didn't look at them at the time but earlier this morning, I was at home missing Nell and I went through them. Look at this one.'

Kira passed Gina her phone. Nell and Kira both held their children and stood in front of Kira's hanging basket. Between the two women's heads, Gina could see Nell's flat across the road and standing staring in their direction was a woman.

'This was taken on another day.' Kira took her phone, scrolled through a few photos and showed Gina another. 'This is me, obviously. I was going out with some friends and waiting for a taxi. I took a selfie to post in our WhatsApp group and again, check out the background.'

Gina took the phone from her again and zoomed in. The

same woman was standing by Nell's back garden, leaning up to look over the fence. Gina could tell it was Abigail Bretton. 'Have you seen this woman around at other times?'

'No, I don't think so.'

'Can you forward these photos to me?'

Kira took her phone back and selected the photos. Gina read her number out and a few seconds later, her phone pinged with the message. 'Thank you for bringing these in.'

The little boy began to fidget and started to cry. 'I best get going as his dad is picking him up at lunchtime.'

'We may be in touch to speak about these photos.'

'That's no problem. You know where I live and you have my number. Pop by or call at any time. Do you know what will happen with Nell? Will there be a funeral soon or anything like that?'

Gina knew that Nell's body hadn't been released yet and when it eventually was, she'd be discussing it with Maeve first. 'I don't have any information as yet. Her next of kin will be informed when we know.'

'Thanks, anyway. I guess I'll wait to hear something.' The woman stood. She flung her baby bag over her shoulder and popped her son in the buggy. Her face reddened with the heat. Just as they went to leave the room, Kira stopped and turned to Gina. 'What if all this time I thought Nell was scared of a man and she was really scared of a woman? What if this woman murdered her? I mean, what was she doing looking over Nell's fence? That's so creepy.' Kira's hands were shaking slightly. 'Do you think you'll find her?'

'We know who she is.'

'Really? Who is she? Do I need to worry because as you can see, she was looking at my flat in one of those photos? She knows where I live and she could see I was hanging out with Nell. If she's some crazy stalker she might try to hurt me, and I have a child to think of.'

'I can appreciate that you're worried. If you see anyone or hear anything suspicious, please do call us immediately. I'll let the team know what you've told me.' Gina was hoping to pick Abigail up by close of day.

'Thank you.' She walked Kira back through reception and watched her head out of the sliding doors.

Back in the incident room, everyone hushed as Gina entered and showed them the photos. 'These photos, and the fact that Abigail Bretton's car was in the area not long before Nell's murder, has well and truly put her in the frame. I'm making the decision that we arrest her, see what she has to say for herself. Nell and Abigail had recently split up. Nell had moved out and Abigail lied to us about her whereabouts. It looks like Abigail was watching Nell. Could jealousy be her motive? Had she seen Nell enjoying herself with Kira?' Gina pondered on that thought.

'What about Ross Craven's murder? What could her motive for killing him be?' Kapoor asked.

'Good question,' Gina replied, 'and I don't have a theory on that as yet. He was killed first and Darrah Kelly claims to have encountered someone matching Ross Craven's description by Nell's flat in the early hours of Sunday the thirtieth. Maybe in some warped way she killed him to protect Nell, if she saw him by Nell's. She could have followed him and killed him but that would make Watcher's Way too much of a coincidence. The missing eyes mean something and Watcher's Way ties into them.' She paused and tried to work it out but couldn't. 'We need Abigail Bretton. Let's arrest her on suspicion of Nell's murder and take it from there. We'll have twenty-four hours to investigate and, during that time, we can search her house and question her.' She looked at Jacob. 'Gather a team. Let's find out why Abigail lied to us. I want to be outside her house within the hour.'

THIRTY-FOUR

MAEVE

Matty placed the large glass of elderflower cordial down in front of her. She watched as the fizzy bubbles jumped on the surface of the drink, her mind obsessing over the dead crow. She'd reluctantly stepped over it, trying not to look but its image kept burning through her mind.

'Is it the dead crow, Maeve? You look really worried.'

She took a sip of her drink through the paper straw and stirred the drink with it. 'There's more. Last night after we were messaging, I'd just fallen asleep and I heard a noise. It stopped so I went back to sleep, then I heard another noise, like a bang, so I went out to explore.' She placed her sunglasses down on the mahogany table.

'You went out there alone?'

She raised her eyebrows. 'Yes. I wasn't worried. I just thought it was Sally out with the dogs but I felt the need to check, just in case something had happened. She did tell me that kids sometimes lurk around in the graveyard, daring each other to do silly things like summon up spirits to scare each other. When I stepped outside, I couldn't see anyone around the back. The graveyard was empty. Then I thought I heard something coming from around the front of the vicarage, which is closer to the church. I walked around and saw that the back door was open. That's when Sally ran out. She thought it might have been a burglar and then I could see that someone had broken the back door to gain entry. Anyway, cutting a long story short, Sally went to check. Someone hit her over the head with one of the church candlesticks and they ran off. Basically, the church got robbed. Sally spent half the night in A&E waiting to have stitches in her head, while I looked after Alfie and the dogs.' She allowed her gaze to wander to his lightly tanned arms. That's when she spotted the graze just above his wrist. 'What happened?' She pointed to it.

'Oh, that. It's nothing. I was carrying a couple of shopping bags up to my house and I leaned against my porch while trying to fish the key out of my pocket. I caught the wall, that's all. It doesn't hurt one bit.'

'So, you're off to see your sister. Are you doing anything nice this afternoon?'

'Only taking the little ones for a walk by the river. We'll probably stop at a pub and have a spot of lunch.'

'It's so lovely that you make time for them. I bet they adore you.' She wondered if he could tell that she was starting to fall for him. He was kind, good-looking but not big-headed with it. She almost wanted to reach out and touch his hand. What had almost begun as a one-night stand was beginning to feel special.

'I think at heart I'm a family man, I've just never met the right person to start a family with.'

'Me neither. I thought I'd never want a family and I'm still not sure but losing Nell has really shaken me up. There has to be more to life. I have my company that I've built up from the ground and it virtually runs without me. I've achieved what I set out to do and, until now, I didn't think I wanted anything else, but I think I do now.' She thought of Alfie again but this time she pictured herself in a house with Matty, being in love and happy. For a second she dared to wonder what it would be like to actually grow a child inside her. She sat up straight. Her stupid hormones were pulling her in all directions. She was grieving and Matty was being kind and her guilty feelings was sending her silly.

'What do you want?'

She shrugged. 'I can't answer that question until I've found it.'

'Do you think you might have found it?' He placed his hand on hers, sending a tingle through her.

'I think I'm confused. I've lost my sister and I wish I'd visited her or tried to spend more time with her.' If Maeve thought too hard about her failings right now, she knew she'd start to cry and she didn't want to cry in front of Matty. 'I need to change the subject for a bit.'

'Of course. Tell me what the wacky vicar is like.' He moved his hand.

'She's really kind. I like her.' Maeve sipped her drink again and crunched on what was left of a tiny ice cube. 'What did you get the kids?'

He frowned. 'What did I get?'

'You know, you were at the shop doing your uncle Matty duties and getting the kids a gift.'

'Oh that. I got them some sweets for later.'

A couple of men in workwear entered and sat at the bar. Maeve picked up her sunglasses and placed them on her head. 'I best get back soon. I shouldn't leave Sally on her own for too long, not after last night, and she'll probably need me to entertain Alfie for a bit.'

'Well, it was great seeing you. Can I see you again soon?'

She smiled. 'I'd like that a lot.'

He leaned in and kissed her gently on the lips. 'I'll call you later, okay?'

She nodded and stood. They both walked out to the car

park and the sun dazzled Maeve's eyes. He followed her to her car and then he gently lifted her sunglasses back onto her head. 'I just wanted to look into your eyes again. You are so beautiful, Maeve.'

She laughed. 'Is that one of your regular lines?'

'Okay, okay. That sounded cheesy, I know. But I mean it. When I look at you, all I want to do is get to know you better and peel back those deep layers that make up the Maeve I see in front of me.' He kissed her again before she got into her car.

She waved as she pulled out of the car park. Normally such a cheesy chat-up line would turn her off, but right now she loved that Matty had wanted to stare into her eyes for longer than felt right. It was intense and extremely sexy. As for what he meant by peeling back her deep layers, she had no idea, but she would leave her windows open for him. No one had ever really looked at her, not like he had, and it felt special, so special.

THIRTY-FIVE

As far as Gina was concerned, when approaching Abigail Bretton, she could be dealing with a double murderer. She placed a finger between her stab vest and her clothing underneath to try to relieve the tightness that was making her chest ache. A flash of pain shot through her as she hunched over slightly. Jacob frowned as she flinched again. PC Ahmed stood behind her, ready to use the battering ram should they need it, but Gina had hoped not to give the neighbours a scene. From what she'd seen of the nurse, she didn't think Abigail would run for it or try to fight them.

'You can step back,' she said to PC Ahmed. 'I think we'll be okay.' She knocked at the door and waited. O'Connor and Wyre were positioned by the back garden, just in case she did try to slip out of the back.

No one answered.

Gina banged again, harder this time, and called out, 'Police, open up.' Again, no one came to the door. Abigail's car was parked on the drive and the curtains were closed. Gina bent over and peered through the letter box but all she could see was the dark hallway and stairs. She turned back to Kapoor who was standing at the end of the path. 'Can you call the hospital where she works, see if she is there now? Maybe she got a lift to work. We have to check.'

Kapoor nodded and took her phone out.

Just as Gina was about to knock again, a girl who looked to be about twenty came out of the house next door and stared at them all. 'Are you looking for Abbie?' She stretched her pyjama top down over her shorts, almost covering up her midriff.

Gina walked across the drive, nodding to Jacob to stay put. 'I'm DI Harte from Cleevesford Police. Have you seen her today?'

'I said hello to her maybe three hours ago. As she left her house I was letting our cat in.'

'Did she say where she was going?'

'No, but she did say something about a lift and going on a trip. She had a rucksack with her and someone in a dark car picked her up at the end of the road. She asked me if I'd water her plants. I normally water them when she goes on holiday. Has something happened?'

Gina furrowed her brows. It looked like Abigail had already escaped them, knowing her lie would catch up with her. Kapoor called her over. 'Excuse me one moment.' She walked over to Kapoor. 'What do you have?'

'Abigail called her ward manager this morning saying that she'd had a bereavement in the family and needed to take compassionate leave.'

'Damn, all we know is she left approximately three hours ago and got picked up by someone in a dark car. I'm just going to speak to the neighbour.' She turned to Jacob.

Gina crossed the drive again in front of Abigail's car and went back to the neighbour. 'Can we speak inside for a moment?' She'd noticed that a few passing people had stopped to watch what they were doing.

'Of course.'

Gina gestured for Jacob to follow her and for PC Ahmed and Kapoor to stay put for now. She followed the young woman into the kitchen.

'Do you want a drink?' she asked.

'No, thank you.' Jacob shook his head too. Gina continued. 'Can I take your name?'

'Thalia Pappas.' She brushed away her large bouncy dark curls that had fallen over her face. 'I live here with my parents but they're in Greece visiting my grandpa so it's just me.'

'How did Miss Bretton seem when you saw her?'

'She seemed a bit rushed. Maybe flustered. I heard about Nell on the "What's Up Cleevesford" Facebook page. It's terrible news. I wanted to say how sorry I was to Abigail but she didn't stick around long enough. I guessed that was why she was going away for a bit. I tried to call her as I was worried but her phone was dead.'

Gina leaned on the breakfast bar, next to a wooden stool, and Jacob began taking notes. 'How well did you know Nell Craven?'

'Not well at all. She barely spoke to me. Her little boy was cute, I used to wave at him and smile if I saw her coming or going. I'm finding it hard to believe what happened to Nell. That poor kid.' Thalia bit her bottom lip. 'Can I speak candidly. I mean, there are things I want to say but I don't want to get anyone into trouble.'

Gina raised her brows. 'Please do.'

'When Nell first moved in with Abigail, Nell used to say hi when we passed but I got the impression she was always looking over her shoulder. Then one day, when I tried to ask how she was, she looked back at Abigail's house and suddenly stopped talking to me and went in. I think Abigail was jealous of me and there was no reason to be. I was just being neighbourly, not hitting on Nell. After that, Nell never spoke to me again. She avoided eye contact with me when we passed but the weird thing is, Abigail spoke to me like nothing had changed. I still watered the plants if they had to go anywhere and she still chatted to my parents on the drive. It was just Nell's behaviour that changed.'

Gina was sensing that Nell had become trapped in an abusive relationship with Abigail. She remembered Abigail mentioning the money that Nell was receiving in her account and she wondered if that had sparked Nell's exit from their relationship. Nell had money, she left when Abigail wasn't at home and she knew that Nell had met up with Abigail recently for a day out with Alfie. Gina knew that coercively controlling relationships were complicated and maybe Nell was considering getting back with Abigail. 'Did you ever hear anything coming from next door?'

Thalia slowly blew out a breath. 'There was always a lot of shouting and I would then hear Alfie cry. It sounded like things were being thrown around. I was in bed one night and I'd just fallen asleep and they started. The walls are pretty thin here so it's not like I could avoid hearing them. I'd mostly hear Abigail shouting and Nell crying.'

'Did you hear what they were saying?'

'I'm sure Abigail was shouting about some messages and I heard Nell crying that Abigail had broken her phone, then Toffee's barks got louder so I couldn't catch what else was said that night. I think the words lying and cheating were brandished but I really couldn't see that Nell was cheating on Abigail. She was so meek, and plain, I guess. She never dressed up or did her hair and she always swamped herself up in an oversized hoodie and jeans. I did see something bizarre about a week ago.'

'What was that?'

'I could smell smoke coming in through my bedroom window. When I looked out, Abigail had lit the barbecue and was throwing a load of notebooks onto it.'

Gina wondered if Abigail had been trying to destroy Nell's diaries, the same diaries that Abigail had told them that Nell had burned. 'Is there anything else you can tell us?'

She looked away. 'I did see Abigail talking to a man. It was out the back and it looked like he was shouting at her in quite a threatening way. Again, I was in my bedroom and I heard a bit of what was being said. Abigail was telling him to fuck off.' Thalia blushed slightly, then continued. 'Those were her words, by the way. Then she slammed the back gate in his face.'

'Can you describe the man?'

'Broad, large, aged fifty to sixty, beard, black hoodie. He walked a bit funny, like he ached. That's all I really have.'

Gina knew it had to be Ross Craven and that argument could be considered a motive for his murder. She tried to reframe the information they now had. Maybe Ross Craven knew that Nell was being abused and maybe he and Nell were in contact, somehow. If he knew, maybe he took it upon himself to tell Abigail what he thought of her. 'What day was this?'

'I don't know. Last week, later in the week. I really can't remember and it sounds too important to guess.'

'Do you mind going to Cleevesford Police Station to make a formal statement?'

'Of course not. My online lectures start in half an hour and they finish at three thirty. I'll drive over then. Cleevesford, did you say?'

'Yes, and thank you.' They were going into Abigail's house next and she knew it would be so much easier with a key. 'You said you water Abigail's plants?'

'That's right.'

'You must have a key.'

She nodded. 'I can't just give it to you. That would feel wrong.'

Gina pulled out the warrant. 'We will be gaining access to the house. We'd rather not have to break the door down.'

The girl took a key from a drawer and passed it to Gina.

'Thank you.' Gina gave Thalia her card. 'If you see or hear from Miss Bretton, could you please call me immediately?'

'Will do. Did she kill Nell?'

'I can't discuss the case at the minute as we're still investigating. We just need to speak to Miss Bretton but please don't approach her yourself if you see her.'

'Okay.'

Gina thanked her again for the key and she and Jacob left Thalia's house. She turned to Kapoor. 'Make sure all units are on alert for her.' Kapoor grabbed her phone.

O'Connor and Wyre had returned from around the back. They all pulled on gloves and shoe covers before Gina placed the key in the lock.

THIRTY-SIX

Gina stepped into Abigail Bretton's house first. With all curtains and blinds closed, the house was in darkness. 'O'Connor, Wyre, can you check out the kitchen and this room? See if there's any paperwork lying around that might tell us where she's gone. We are also looking for a serrated knife, and I hate to say it but we are looking for Nell and Ross's eyes. In fact, anything to do with eyes, flag it up. Check the washing machine and the back garden too. Our assailant would have got bloody. Bag up anything from the washing machine filter and I even want someone checking out the pipework, just in case she has tried to wash away traces of evidence. Nell lived here for a few months but, as far as we know, Ross Craven never has so if his DNA turns up, flag it. Jacob?'

He raised his eyebrows.

'We'll check upstairs.' She left the room, leaving Wyre and O'Connor to search downstairs while she started ascending the stairs. As she reached the top, she saw into a very sterile white bathroom. The stainless-steel taps literally bounced light across the room. There was very little bathroom clutter. The only thing that stood out was a couple of yellow rubber ducks on the window ledge. She inhaled. 'It smells like bleach in here.' She opened the medicine cabinet and spotted a packet of Sertraline, medication used to treat depression or panic attacks. Gina had taken them herself in the past for a short while. She glanced at the label. 'These were Nell's tablets.'

'The bedroom doors are closed.' Jacob stepped back out onto the landing and Gina followed. He opened the first door.

A king-size bed had been pushed against the opposite wall and the room was spacious. Again, the curtains were closed and the bed had been left unmade. 'Jacob, do you want to check out the fitted wardrobes? I'll take a look in the bedside tables and under the bed.'

'Will do.' He slid the wardrobe open to reveal neatly hung-up clothes and Abigail's uniforms.

Gina slid open the bedside table on the rumpled side of the bed and found a few pairs of underpants and a couple of bras. Underneath was a packet of paracetamol and a packet of mints. She kneeled down and checked under the bed, again there was nothing of interest. After pushing everything out of the way, checking behind and under the furniture, Gina found nothing. 'I'm going to head into the other room. Are you okay finishing up with the wardrobe?'

He nodded and continued checking seams and pockets of clothing.

Gina stepped back out onto the landing and spotted a loft hatch. They'd take a look there later but first she pressed the handle to the second bedroom and pushed it open. At the far end, under the window were a few baby items piled up. An old baby walker crowned several bags of plastic toys and bags of clothing. Gina guessed that those were the items Alfie had no longer needed so Nell had left them behind. She turned on the bedroom light. Opening the curtains would have been easier but she thought it best to leave the house as it was. An old writing bureau sat against the opposite wall next to a wardrobe and a set of drawers. Gina opened the drawers in turn and they were all empty. She turned to the bureau and pulled the front hatch down to reveal little shelves where ink bottles would have been stored. It had been cleared out.

'Nothing in the wardrobe,' Jacob said as he entered. 'The whole place seems super tidy. Maybe she did a pre-holiday clean or she was trying to erase evidence. From what the neighbour said, she burned Nell's diaries so we have a case for the latter.'

Gina turned to the window and saw a handprint on the glass. It had been left on the catch. Gina walked over and pushed it open. That's when she saw a piece of paper slotted into a sandwich bag that had got caught on the roof of the pitched frontage. She leaned out, not quite being able to reach far enough to grab it. Jacob swapped places with her and reached out. 'Got it.'

Gina pulled the small torn piece of paper from the bag. 'The message says, "Help me. Please someone help me. I don't want to be locked in this room. I want my baby boy. I am so scared she'll hurt me."' She pulled her phone from her pocket and took a photo. 'Damn. What had Abigail been doing to Nell?'

Gina felt herself shaking slightly. She placed her hands by her sides before Jacob noticed. The pain still hung in her chest but it was okay as long as she didn't move too much. She gently breathed in and out before leaving the room. She glanced up, then down. How had she not seen the slide locks at the top and the bottom of the door? There was also a keyhole. For a moment, she pictured Nell being dragged into the room and locked in. How long did Abigail leave her there and where was Alfie? Was he with her? She could never ask Nell those questions. Gina wondered how Abigail had found out where Nell had moved to and she kept thinking of their day out with Alfie. Abigail had probably made so many promises to change and

Nell had probably told her where she lived. A flashback to her past stopped her in her tracks. Terry used to lock her in the shed and he once shut her in the cupboard on their landing with all the towels. She understood Nell's fear. At the time, Gina thought she might die. Heart racing, she gasped.

'Are you okay, guv?'

She inhaled and exhaled. 'Yes, it's hot in here. What we need to do is to find Abigail Bretton. She called her mother when we spoke to her. We need to find out if her mother lives local and start with her.'

'Guv,' Wyre called. 'We've found something.'

She hurried down the stairs. 'What?'

'A phone number on a piece of paper. I just googled it. They hire camper vans out.'

'That's where Abigail has gone. O'Connor?'

'Yes, guv.'

'Can you call the camper van company? See if Abigail Bretton or someone matching her description has been in to hire a van? If so, we need the registration of the one they're using and then we can get all units on the lookout for them? Wyre?'

'Yes.'

'Can you call Bernard? I want the plumbing and the loft checked and there's evidence upstairs that is pointing to Abigail locking Nell in the second bedroom.'

THIRTY-SEVEN

SALLY

'Ollolo,' Alfie babbled as the dogs jumped at the window.

Sally woke to the sun beating through the living room window. 'Alfie.' Her heart rate went from slow to rapid in a matter of seconds. He was fine and now he too was awake. The little boy picked sleep from the corner of his eyes. 'Toffee, Jerry, stop it. There's no one there.' The dogs began to play bite each other before chasing about in the hallway.

She glanced at Alfie, taking in his kinked hair and the lines on the one side of his face where he'd lain. As soon as he'd nodded off on the settee, she'd lain the other side, head on a cushion, cradling him with her legs. The events of the night had finally caught up with her. She checked her phone. It was gone lunchtime and she knew the little man would be hungry. 'You want a jammy sandwich, Alfie?'

'Jammy.' He began to awkwardly climb over her legs. She reached over and lifted him onto the floor before he hurt himself.

After a huge yawn, Sally followed him through to the kitchen.

'Olloll, olllolo.'

'What are you saying?' Sally said with a smile as she bent down to face Alfie.

He placed his finger on the dressing on her head. 'Ouch.'

'Yes, ouch,' she said. She reached in the fridge for the jam and then the bread bin for the bread and began making the sandwich. She handed him a quarter and he began to eat.

She glanced out at the graveyard, staring for anything that might seem out of place but it was a beautiful summer's day. She spotted a couple of women walking dogs near the shrubbery at the back and a man was laying flowers at another grave. Someone knocked at her front door. She hurried to answer it, fighting to get through the dogs. Checking through the spyhole, she could see it was Maeve. Opening up, she let Maeve in and smiled. 'Did you see your friend?'

'Yes, thank you. I've also just seen the crime scene person. She told me that she'd finished up and you could now use the church. She said she rang your bell about fifteen minutes ago but there was no answer.'

Sally frowned. She had slept deeply, even the dogs hadn't woken her from her nap.

'She gave me this.' Maeve handed her a card with the CSI's details on it. 'She said they'd be in touch.'

'I best call the stand-in vicar, tell him that we can resume business. Are you okay looking after Alfie while I go over and lock up?'

'Of course. I'm sure we'll be fine. I've just got to pop next door to get changed but I'll take him to the annex with me.'

'Okay.'

Alfie grabbed the end of Maeve's dress with his jammy fingers and giggled. Maeve leaned down and picked him up, laughing as she grabbed some kitchen roll to wipe his hands. 'I guess I need to get used to this, don't I?' she said to Alfie.

Warmth flooded through Sally. Maeve was growing to love him, and that was just what Alfie needed. Toffee whined at her

feet for attention but Maeve ignored him and left the kitchen to
go to the annex. Sally still hoped that Maeve would fall for
Toffee, too. The little chihuahua tilted its head and whined.

Sally popped her Crocs on and left through the front door,
following the path all the way to the back of the church. The
emergency locksmith had done a great job. She tried the new
key and it fit like a glove. As she walked through the back,
passing her office and the toilets, her heart began to pound so
hard she felt like it might burst from her chest. It saddened her
that someone had attacked her in her safe place. She'd never
once been scared to be in church. She traced the dressing on her
head as she tried to remember anything but just like she'd told
the police officer at the hospital, she hadn't seen her attacker. As
she entered the nave she stopped, whereas normally she'd have
walked in confidently. The church had always been a sanctuary
for her and other people. Sanctuary was one of the main reasons
she'd decided to become a vicar. She wanted people to feel
loved and safe when they spent time in church. After growing
up in care and being passed from pillar to post, she knew she
had to help other people and it started with offering them a safe
place to be. She started off as a nursery teacher, then she
became a foster carer, then she became a vicar. The church was
her home but Sally no longer felt safe in it.

She pushed open the heavy wooden main doors and
flinched as she saw Kira standing there, crying. After regaining
her composure, Sally stood aside. 'Kira. Come in.'

'Can I light a candle for Nell?'

'Of course. We can light a candle together.' Sally's church
didn't have an area for candle lighting. It was more of a catholic
tradition but she wanted to make Kira welcome. She led the
crying woman to the altar where the stick candles had been
discarded by the burglar. She reached into a drawer at the back
and pulled out a dish. After striking a match to light the longest
candle, she allowed the wax to liberally drip. With her other

hand, she passed Kira one of the nearly used candles before nudging the matches towards her. Kira pulled out a match and struck it, the smell of sulphur dioxide filling the air. She placed her candle into the half-set wax. Sally bowed her head and prayed with Kira. She prayed for Alfie and Nell. The horror of seeing Nell's body flashed through her mind again. Again, her sanctuary threatened.

She inwardly gasped and Kira opened her eyes and made the sign of the cross. 'Thank you.' Kira took a couple of deep breaths and wiped her eyes. 'I didn't know where to go or what to do. My son has just gone to stay with his dad and I feel so lost and alone.'

'Do you want to talk about it?'

Kira nodded and headed towards the front pew. 'I just miss her. Nell and I hadn't been friends that long. I started messaging her because we were both in a parenting forum on Facebook. Reading between the lines, I guessed she was trying to escape an abusive relationship, so I helped her. I told her of a flat that was available and before I knew it, she'd moved in. I live opposite her. I knew about the flat because we share the same landlord and I got shown her flat too. Of course, Nell was quite a closed book, not like me. I'm a talker, Nell was the opposite.' She began to rub her eyes. 'I should have known her messages were being read. Whoever she was with found out where she was going. Even ditching her phone hadn't saved her. They found her and they killed her. I shouldn't have interfered. If I hadn't messaged her, she'd still be alive.' Kira's sobs echoed through the church.

'Kira, none of this is your fault. You tried to help Nell. You did nothing but be a good friend.'

'Do you think God forgives me?'

'God would never blame you. You don't need forgiveness for helping someone.'

Kira leaned into Sally's chest and sobbed. Sally placed a

caring arm around her and let her cry until she was empty of tears. 'I think Nell was trying to hide something.'

Sally bit her bottom lip, wondering if she should share with Kira her own suspicions of why Nell had been lurking around the back of the church on the morning she was murdered, but Sally hadn't found anything except the leather bracelet. 'What do you think she might have been hiding?'

'I don't know. Nell was scared, that's all I know, and she came here. I told her coming here would help. She had something and she was going to show me later that day but she never got to show it to me. I guess the police will get to the bottom of everything.' Kira paused. 'I took some photos on my phone. I saw a woman watching Nell and I think she might have been watching me too. I now think she killed Nell.'

That's the first Sally had heard about a different suspect. Maeve had been certain that Nell's father had killed her.

'Can I use your toilet?'

'Yes, just head to the back and turn right.'

Sally sat in front of the burning candle; brows furrowed. A few minutes later, Kira came back with a wad of toilet roll, blowing her nose. She stopped and glanced back. 'I had this strange feeling back there.'

'What do you mean?'

Kira shivered. 'Sometimes I feel things and I can't explain them. It's like there's someone present but there's no one there. I felt this dark pain in my heart and...' Kira began to shake. 'I need to get out of here.'

'Kira, you've lost a good friend—'

Scooting past her, Kira hurried towards the main door. 'Thank you for listening and for the candle.' She kept looking back and forth.

'You're always welcome, Kira. Are you okay? We can carry on talking outside if you'd like.'

Kira shook her head and rushed outside.

As Sally left the cool church, the sun pounded. The crows flocked around a pile of old-looking bread and oats that someone had dumped on the grass in a pile.

Kira let out a piercing scream, sending Sally's heart rate into overdrive.

'What is it?' Sally called.

She pointed at the dead crow. Sally ran over and scared the birds away. 'It's a sign. I believe in signs. It's a harbinger of death. That feeling I had, it was trying to tell me something.'

Sally didn't necessarily believe that the crow was a harbinger of death but she could see that Kira did, and she was terrified. What lay on the ground was simply a dead bird and she'd seen many dead birds on the grounds over the years. Sally decided to offer her some comforting words to ease her anxiety. 'Sometimes they symbolise the end of bad things and the beginning of new and better things. A new era in a person's life. Hope.'

Kira shook her head over and over again. 'No, I don't believe you. It's death. It's coming for me. It's coming for you. It has already come for Nell and I can tell it's not satisfied. I can feel it reaching inside me.' A wash of fear filled her face. She glanced around the grounds before staring at Sally for a few seconds, then she ran.

'Kira, Kira,' Sally called, but Kira had already gone. Sally glanced at the crow and shivered. What worried her most was the woman Kira had mentioned. If Nell's father hadn't killed her, then who had?

She called Reverend Ernie. Now the church was open for use again, he could continue with her work, for now. She needed to protect Maeve and Alfie. No one could know they were staying with her. She was, after all, their sanctuary.

THIRTY-EIGHT

Gina chugged from a can of lemonade as they went through what they'd found out at Abigail Bretton's house. 'O'Connor, any luck with the camper van hire company?'

'Yes, guv. I've just been speaking on the phone with a man called Jaxon Cound and he confirmed that someone matching Abigail's description came in this morning with a woman to collect a camper van. The woman who booked the van is called Shirley Bretton. He said she was fifty-six years old and the younger woman called her Mum.'

Gina updated the board as they spoke. Jacob, Wyre and Kapoor listened intensely. Briggs was heading the press release so now the public would know about the body they'd found. She needed to tell Maeve as soon as possible. She needed to know that it wasn't Nell's father who'd killed her.

'All units have been alerted. Now we have the registration, I'm hoping we can pick them up fast. There's something else we need to talk about, something that has really thrown the investigation.' As soon as Gina had left the search at Abigail Bretton's house she'd received an email from Bernard. 'The knife's serration patterns match up to the knife that was used to cut out both Nell and Ross's eyes and it was the one found in Ross's coat pocket. Let me run through this for you. That knife was first used to remove Ross's eyes. It was then used to do the same to Nell, then it appeared in Ross's coat pocket in Habiba Bal's garden. We have also confirmed that there are two different blood types on the knife and no fingerprints at all. Whoever killed them, wiped it clean of their own prints or wore gloves, but they left the blood. This also shows that the killer either knows about Ross's other daughter, Saira, or the killer followed him to where he lived.'

'Are we treating Habiba Bal as a suspect?' Wyre asked.

'Not at the moment but we don't want to close that avenue off completely. We should check to see if she was working at the supermarket at the time Nell was murdered. However, if the killer planted that coat back in her garden, they know where she lives so I want to up the protection. Keep an officer outside her house at all times. Can you organise that?'

Wyre nodded.

'Until we find Abigail Bretton, we stay on high alert. Any news on the bus footage, O'Connor?'

He glanced at his phone. 'It's just pinged through now.' He ran over to the desktop in the corner and opened the email from the bus company with the footage attached. He began to watch and fast forward. 'I can't see Darrah Kelly on the bus, guv. In fact, I can't see him on either bus he could have got on.'

'Okay, thanks for following up on that. So, he didn't catch the bus and he still hasn't got an alibi for the time Nell was murdered.'

Nick came in from the front desk. 'Guv, I have Kira Fellows in reception for you again. She's in a right state.'

'Thank you. Can you take her through to the family room, please? I'm on my way.' She addressed the room. 'Can someone chase up Nell's bank statements. We need to know who was sending her two thousand pounds a month.'

As the team turned back to their work, Gina and Jacob left to speak to Kira.

Gina nudged the door to the family room open and immediately felt like she'd walked through a hot wall. She opened the window at the back and took a seat next to Jacob. Kira had been biting her nails and one of them had bled onto her pale-blue shorts. Gina nudged the box of tissues towards her. 'Kira, what's happened?'

'I, err, it sounds silly but I keep feeling like Nell is all around me, like she's trying to tell me something. I can't sleep and when I eat, I just feel sick. Those photos I gave you...'

'Yes.' Gina hoped that Kira had something more concrete to offer them than a feeling, but she remained patient. Kira had lost a good friend.

'I found another photo. After giving you those two, I went through everything I had and I remember taking a few on my iPad one day as I was sitting outside in the sun and I was using it to apply for a job...' She furrowed her brows as if she'd lost track of where she was.

'So, you took some photos on your iPad?'

Jacob stopped writing as they waited for Kira to continue.

'Yes.' She stared at Gina to the point that Gina almost wanted to look away, then she continued speaking. 'I sent these to my phone this morning as I wanted to file them on my phone later, then I popped to the church to light a candle and when I left, I looked at the photos and I saw this.' She thrust the phone into Gina's hands.

Gina squinted. All she saw was Kira's son standing outside their front door with a plastic car in his hands.

'Pinch the photo to zoom in.'

Gina pinched and as the background got bigger, she saw

Abigail Bretton again. Not only was Abigail standing by Nell's back garden gate, she was leaning over and passing something to Darrah. 'It's the strange woman who's been hanging around. Darrah knows her. What if they are in it together?'

'Can you send this photo to me?'

Gina waited a moment while Kira sent it to her and her phone beeped. 'Thank you. What day was this photo taken?'

'My iPad told me it was the eighteenth of June. It's the same day that Darrah was looking after Toffee while Nell went out for the day. Also, it was taken just after ten in the morning.'

Gina thought back to Darrah's interview. He'd got a little tipsy at Nell's and after taking the dog out, he'd then gone up to his flat with Toffee to sleep it off. He'd also left Nell's door unlocked by accident. Had it been an accident or had he intentionally left Nell's door open for some reason? 'Thank you for bringing this in.'

A short while later, they'd got all they could from Kira and she left.

Gina headed back to the interview room with Jacob and filled the team in on what had been said.

'Guv,' O'Connor said. 'I've got an update on the bank statements. The money in Nell's account had come from Maeve.'

'Maeve?'

'That's right. She's been paying it into Nell's account since Alfie was born.'

'I wonder why she didn't say anything. I need to speak to Maeve anyway before the news about Ross Craven gets out. I'll head over to the vicarage now with Jacob. Do we have any ANPR updates on the camper van?'

Wyre nodded. 'We do. It was driven down the Cleevesford Bypass at eleven this morning, but that's all we have.'

'I think she's still in the area. Either that or she's managed to stick to the tiniest of roads that have no cameras on them. Can you check all the campsites that she could have reached? If I'm right, I think there are only two.'

'Yes, I'll get onto that.'

'And now, what I want to know is why Darrah didn't tell us about him speaking to Abigail on the day Nell asked him to look after Toffee. He's hiding something so I want him brought in. This pair are now as suspicious as hell. Find Darrah Kelly.'

THIRTY-NINE

DIARY EXTRACT

Ross Craven, you never told me about your other daughter and that upsets me more. You thought I'd never find out but I followed you. I hate the fact that I went in through the back door and snooped around the house when no one was in, but at least it gave me the answers I needed.

I don't know why I'm addressing you in my diary, but I guess that's what I need to do right now.

Here's what I know. I know your other daughter lives in Cleevesford. I also live in Cleevesford. It's only temporary until I sort out what I want in life. What I don't know is why you keep coming to my place at odd and weird times. You don't knock or show yourself since we argued, and I knew you were angry about the things I said, but they needed saying and I don't regret a single word. Since then, I feel you everywhere. It's like you can't keep away from me.

You are the shadows I catch out of the corner of my eye. You are the faint sound in the breeze I hear for just a second and you are the musky scent that hangs in the air. Those prickles I feel creeping across the back of my neck, they're you too. I feel like you're everywhere and that fills me with anxiety.

First you want me in your life and then you remind me that I'm not as good as her and I never will be. You will never love me as much, you said so yourself. I still feel used, by the way. As your rock and the person who listened when you needed someone, I'm totally bereft. It really was all about you. You go about hurting people, walking all over them and leaving them, and there's no getting away from the fact that you are a killer. I was the only one who promised to stand by you, despite how you turned my life upside down all those years ago. Forgiveness had been a long journey but I made that journey for you, for my father, but I don't trust that you're the man you say you are.

I know you keep a knife in your pocket. What for? You're on probation. I bet that would get you into a lot of trouble if I were to tell your probation officer or the police. Is someone after you? Maybe I shouldn't have thrown that in your face when we spoke. Are you scared? Or are you dangerous? Should I be scared?

My mind is running wild. You've been in prison and I know that must have been hard.

You are my dad and I know you killed my mum. I know you're "rehabilitated" but what the hell does that mean? Have you just said all the words a panel expected you to say? I bet that's all you did. You're a man who knows how to say the right thing at the right time regardless of whether you mean it. I have been so stupid to trust you!

My back door just slammed.

I'm back, Diary. I checked and there was no one there. All that lingered was the scent of body odour this time. I wished I had the money to live somewhere safer but I don't. You've actually come into my home and right now, I'm shaking. I've locked the door and shut all the curtains and blinds. Was it you? I didn't see you. Maybe it wasn't. If not, then who was there?

FORTY

MAEVE

Maeve sat on a plastic garden chair, legs stretched out, eyes closed, as the sun's rays kissed her pale face. Alfie had happily gone back to the vicarage when Sally had returned from the church. All she could think of now was the future. Planning Nell's funeral would be hard and she wasn't looking forward to discussing Nell with Alfie. He was young but earlier, when he was saying Mum, she'd almost cried. Then she thought of Matty. How life could take such a turn was beyond her. She wondered how he was getting on with his sister and her children. She pictured him happily walking along a canal to a cosy pub and she imagined her and Alfie slotting into his life. She took a deep breath and almost wanted to slap herself. Allowing her thoughts to run away with her like that was ridiculous.

'Maeve.' She almost fell off the old flimsy chair.

'Huh.' She'd almost been asleep just then, but DI Harte and DS Driscoll were blocking the sun out.

'There have been some developments in the case. May we sit down?' DI Harte asked as they grabbed another two plastic chairs from the stack of four.

'Of course. What's happened? Have you found him?' She hoped they'd found Ross Craven, the man behind all of this.

'We have.'

'I hope he'll never see the light of day again after what he did.' DI Harte paused, leaving Maeve to wonder if she'd guessed right. They had to have caught him by now. She needed to get back to her life and Alfie and Sally did too. They couldn't all hide at the vicarage forever.

'Ross Craven was found dead this morning. He's been murdered. A press release has gone out but his name hasn't been revealed yet.'

'What? Are you saying he killed Nell, then someone killed him? You said murder didn't you, not suicide?'

'It's even more complicated. We haven't released full details as yet but he was murdered before Nell. He didn't murder Nell. He couldn't have murdered her.'

Maeve sat rigidly and paused as she let the news sink in. 'But... I don't understand. Who killed Nell?'

'We don't know at the moment but we are exploring other avenues as we speak. We found something out during our investigations. You were paying two thousand pounds per month into Nell's back account.'

Should she have mentioned that to the police before? She had a cast-iron alibi as she'd been in meetings with lots of other people at the time. Her assistant had confirmed that. 'You're looking at me like that makes me suspicious.'

'I don't mean to,' the detective said. 'I did wonder why you didn't mention it when we spoke to you.'

'To be honest, it was the last thing on my mind when you told me Nell had been murdered and I'm only just thinking about it now you've brought it up.'

The DI slumped back in the creaky chair, while her colleague wiped a film of perspiration from his brow. 'Why were you transferring two thousand pounds a month to Nell? I have to ask as a part of the investigation.'

Maeve thought back to when Nell came to see her, telling her she was pregnant. Nell didn't know how she was going to cope. It had been too late to consider her options looking at the size of Nell's belly. She remembered seeing the life inside Nell moving through the material in her leggings and thinking that Nell had blown it all now. She had tried to keep their contact to a minimum but she couldn't blame or hate that innocent life growing inside her half-sister. 'Nell told me she was pregnant and when I say told me, I could see for myself. She didn't own her own home or have a secure tenancy, and she'd existed on agency jobs, flitting from one thing to another, before swanning off on long holidays with the proceeds.' She paused, not wanting to continue having a go at Nell. Nell had been Nell. She'd been young, irresponsible even, but she was also dead. 'We spoke about it. I remember asking her about work and she said that the agency she'd been working for hadn't given her any more contracts since she'd announced her pregnancy. As I said, Nell had nothing apart from an ugly room in some shared house. It was no place to bring a baby up. I remember her nipping to use my loo and leaving her phone on my coffee table. I slipped out her bank card and took a photo of her account number and sort code. I really didn't want her to know it was me giving her the money. If she knew, she'd have just told me she didn't want it. Although irresponsible, Nell was quite proud and didn't take help easily, which is why I sent her the money every month.'

'Did she ever mention the money to you?'

'I spoke to her on the phone and she said she was doing okay for money and I didn't say anything. For whatever reason, she chose never to question why she was receiving the money and I never told her. I wanted Alfie to have some security. I know I'm not exactly Mother Nature but I couldn't bear him to go without, and I know that benefits don't stretch to much. We were brought up by our nan on a shoestring after Mum, and I didn't want that for my nephew. I've set up a trust fund for him and everything. I might not look like I care, but I do.' And she did. She cared for Alfie more than she ever thought possible. The trust fund she'd set up was for his future, for university or to pursue his business dreams. She had money and no one to share it with and they had needed it.

'It did confuse us a little. We wondered if she was receiving money from his father. We thought Nell might have found him.'

Maeve shook her head. 'She'll never find him. Sorry to disappoint you but it was just me sending money. In hindsight, I know I should have said something. Again, I'm sorry.'

DI Harte waited for her colleague to catch up on his note-taking.

'Where does that leave us, Sally and me? I thought Ross had killed Nell. The murderer is still out there.'

'But no one knows where you are. We've asked Sally to refrain from her duties and she has done that.'

'How about Nell's ex?'

'We're looking for her as we speak.'

'You think it's her?'

'Again, it's just another line of enquiry.'

She could tell that DI Harte was holding something back. She'd scrutinised people in the boardroom on many occasions and reading body language was like second nature to her. She knew that Nell's ex was more than an average line of enquiry.

'Have you told anyone where you're staying?'

'No,' Maeve replied. She'd mentioned to her personal assistant that she needed some time out. She never had to give reasons or explain anything.

The DI looked like she was reading a message on her phone. 'We're going to organise for a family liaison officer to be with you and Sally. Is there any way you can stay in the main house rather than on your own in the annex?'

The police were going overboard now. If no one knew where they were, why did they need a police officer to stay with them? Maeve didn't want to be under Sally's feet and she doubted Sally would want her there every minute of the day either. Then she remembered from watching crime programmes on the television, FLOs were sometimes assigned to keep an eye on the families they were with. Maybe they suspected her of being involved, or maybe they thought she might be working with someone else.

The DI continued after reading another message. 'The family liaison officer is called Ellyn and she'll be with you later this evening. Always ask for identification and if you are remotely worried, you can call the station to check on anyone who comes to the house claiming to be from the police.'

'I will and thank you.'

The DI and the DS stood. 'We're just going to update Sally. Is there anything else we can help you with?'

Maeve shook her head. 'I have your number.' She watched as they both knocked on Sally's back door. The dogs barked and they entered the kitchen, leaving Maeve alone again, with just the squawking birds to listen to. She watched as a lone crow flapped around in circles for a minute before toppling. Standing, she walked over the graves and saw it twitch before going still. Another dead crow.

Despite the warmth from the sun, she felt like fingers were creeping up her back. Was death following her around? She couldn't breathe. It was as if her throat was closing up. She had to get away from the hideous graves and the dead birds. As she turned back to run to the annex, she let out a yell as she was grabbed at the waist. She went to scream but a hand reached for her mouth. She could see DI Harte's back through the kitchen window but it was no good. DI Harte wasn't looking.

FORTY-ONE

Nicely refreshed after a cup of Sally's tea, Gina sat in the passenger seat of Jacob's car as he pulled into the Angel Arms. She was satisfied that Sally was okay with the arrangements for the FLO to be with them and she agreed that Maeve should stay at the vicarage.

'There he is, guv.' He unclipped his seat belt. Darrah Kelly leaned back on one of the pub benches, laughing with three men wearing vests and yellow jackets. As he leaned back, his pint sloshed over the top of the glass and splashed his T-shirt.

The team had called Cleevesford Manor and Darrah Kelly hadn't been to work that day and then they'd tried the Angel, the second likeliest place that Darrah might be, and they'd struck gold.

'O'Connor said Elouise knows we're coming so all is squared with her.' Gina knew she didn't have to ask Elouise, the licensee, but she wanted to maintain their good relationship and she'd do all she could not to cause a scene. 'Let's go and have a word. If he won't come in voluntarily, we're going to have to arrest him on suspicion of Nell's murder. As it stands, he has no alibi and we have the photo of him talking to Abigail Bretton, so we know that they know each other. Has backup arrived?'

Jacob checked his messages. 'Yes, PC Ahmed has parked the van out the front and he has another officer with him, just in case Kelly kicks off or makes a run for it.'

'Let's go.' Gina stepped out of the car.

Darrah grimaced as he saw her and Jacob approaching, then he hiccupped.

'Mr Kelly, may we have a word?'

'Really?' he asked. 'I've just finished work and you want a word now. I told you; I don't know anything else.' He drank what was left in his glass and slammed it on the table. The other three men looked slightly sheepish and supped their pints.

She knew he was lying. He hadn't been to work today. What other lies had he been telling? 'New evidence has come to light and we need to speak to you at the station.'

He shooed away a wasp that hovered above his glass. 'I don't want to come to the station. I'm not under arrest and I've already told you everything I know.'

Gina glanced at the other men. 'Could you gentlemen please give us a moment?'

Not wanting any trouble, they stood up and the last one stroked his beard. 'Darrah, mate, we'll just go inside. It's getting a bit hot out here anyway and the wasps are a bit of a pain. We'll see you in a minute.'

As soon as the men left, Darrah spoke. 'Okay, what is it?'

'We know you haven't been to work today as we were hoping to find you there.'

'So, you're spying on me...' His eyes were half-closed as the sun dazzled him.

'No, we were looking for you. Like I said, some new evidence has come to light and we need to speak to you at the station.'

'What new evidence?'

'We can discuss it at the station.'

'What if I don't want to go to the station and what if I don't want to talk to you again. All I did was kindly look after my neighbour's dog and do a bit of plumbing, and now this happens. I won't be kind next time. I'll tell whoever wants me to help to go do one, so I will.'

'If you won't come voluntarily, I'll have no option but to arrest you and I really don't think you want to make a scene.'

'For what?'

'The murder of Nell Craven. Your alibi doesn't stack up.'

He laughed. 'What the bloody hell! You're serious, aren't you?' Darrah glanced at the lane at the back of the beer garden.

'It's no use running.'

'What? I wasn't going to run. Look at me. I'd fall in a ditch.' He paused and nodded to the three empty pint glasses in front of him. 'Okay, I'll come. Of course I will. I don't want any trouble and it's not about me, it's about poor Nell. I'm innocent so do what you will with me. You'll soon see that whatever evidence you have is nothing to do with me because I didn't do anything and I wouldn't do anything and I'm not a bad man. I'm a nice man. I help people.' Darrah was waffling and Gina wasn't looking forward to interviewing him. In fact, she'd give it an hour and make sure he had a couple of cups of coffee first. He stood. 'Okay, let's do this. I'm volunteering so no I don't need handcuffs, okay?'

Elouise stood at the back door of the pub and nodded gratefully to Gina, thankful that there was no trouble.

As he went to stand, he suddenly looked completely sober and bolted like a hare towards the lane.

'Dammit!' Gina yelled as she caught PC Ahmed heading her way. She darted after him, eager to not let him slip through her fingers and Jacob followed. From the lane, he ducked in between some bushes onto a field. Gina hurried after him, jumping over a dried-up brook. Just as he tried to escape through a dense thicket, Gina reached out and grabbed the back of his T-shirt, yanking him back. PC Ahmed and Jacob caught up and before she had a chance to say a thing, Jacob had arrested him on suspicion of Nell's murder and PC Ahmed had him handcuffed. He'd now be taking a trip in the back of the van after doing the walk of shame past the Angel Arms. He definitely had more to hide than he was letting on and Gina was going to take great pleasure in questioning him.

A sharp pain running from the front of Gina's chest through to her back almost took her breath away. She fell to the ground and gasped.

'Guv.' Jacob ran over.

She breathed in and out, trying to will the pain away and then the messages flashed through her mind again and her breathlessness blended in with the panic. *Get a grip,* she thought, as she calmed herself down. No way was she going for a check-up when she had Darrah Kelly to interview and if she carried on like this, someone would insist she did. It was nothing and she hated the way Jacob was looking at her. 'I just tripped and winded myself, that was all. I'm okay now. We need to get back, okay?'

'Are you sure?'

'Yes.' She stood up and forced a smile. As soon as the case was over, she'd make an appointment to see her doctor for her stupid indigestion. As Jacob turned his back to her and walked up the lane toward her car, she slipped an antacid from the foil wrapper and chewed on it. She flinched as the pain shot through her upper arm this time.

FORTY-TWO

As Jacob introduced Darrah for the tape, Gina took a sip of peppermint tea in the hope that it would calm her pains down. The duty solicitor placed her black satchel down on the floor and she whispered to Kelly behind a cupped hand and a mass of curly black hair. He nodded and raised his brows before smiling at Gina.

'Darrah Kelly, you've been arrested on suspicion of murdering Nell Craven on the third of July,' Gina said. 'Now tell me what really happened on that day.'

'It's not what you think.'

'So, explain yourself.' The normal neutral expression she tried to maintain was being compromised right now, she was fast losing patience with people like Darrah. She'd seen what was on his phone, now things were about to really open up, but she needed him to talk.

The solicitor nodded. 'I left Cleevesford Manor at around eleven forty-five and I walked through the woodland to the road. I passed the bus stop and carried on walking until I reached the garage where I bought two cans of Stella. I drank them in the woods before going back to work.' He ran his hands

through his sweaty hair. 'I didn't want the managers at the
manor to know as I'm on a final warning for drinking on the job.
That's why I lied to you. I'm sorry, really, I am.' He sighed. 'I
have a drink problem and I'm trying to get help. I booked today
off as I was going to start attending the AA meetings at the
church but it was cancelled. When I got there, the reverend
took my number and said she'd message me later with the new
time and date. All this with Nell has set me back and I went on
a bender. Today was going to be my last drink ever. Please don't
tell the manor. I really need my job, so I do. Surely God loves a
trier and I really am trying in life. I hope you can see that.'

Gina despaired at the number of times people lied over next
to nothing. 'It would have made our job easier had you told the
truth in the first place.' Gina knew the garage that Darrah was
speaking of and they'd check out his real alibi this time. She felt
her fists tensing under the table. All that wasted time spent
trying to find out if Darrah had been eating lunch in the rose
garden made her blood boil. But there was more and she was
getting to that. What she didn't feel was any sympathy for him.

'I'm sorry.' With puffed cheeks, he slowly blew out a breath.
'Was that it, can I go now?'

'Mr Kelly, an arrest on suspicion of murder is serious. We
need to check your alibi and we also need to ask you a few more
questions.'

'Okay.' His solicitor made a note.

'Why did you run away from us at the Angel Arms earlier?'

'I knew you'd probably checked out my alibi and find out I'd
lied. I panicked.' His solicitor placed her pen on the table and
began to whisper again.

'It's okay, I don't want to go no comment. I didn't do it,' he
said, before looking back at Gina and Jacob. 'It was a stupid
impulsive thing to do and I'm sorry. I also knew it was only a
matter of time before you found out that me and Nell knew
each other before she moved into the flat. When I saw her

moving in, my jaw almost dropped to the floor. I thought I'd never see her again. Not that I expected to see her again, ever.'

Gina wasn't expecting that revelation at all. She was expecting to have to tease it out of him. 'How do you know, Nell?'

'I thought my eyes were deceiving me at first as it had been over two years. We met in a club in Birmingham one night and after that we met up a few more times. When I saw her moving in, I did a double take. I'd never forget that face as we had such a laugh.'

'Did you and Nell have a relationship?'

He shook his head and his eyes widened. 'No, it was nothing like that. We weren't looking for love, if you know what I mean. We just went out, had a good time and that was it.'

Gina thought about the Turkish eye that had been attached to Toffee's collar. 'What do you know about the Turkish eye?'

He scrunched his brows and shrugged. 'Am I meant to know what that is? Is that when a Turkish woman gives you the eye?'

Gina ignored his question. 'Did you and Nell sleep together?'

'I think so.'

'You think?' Gina needed more clarification than that.

'We probably did. We got wasted a few times and sometimes when I drink a lot, I can't remember much that happened. I know we shared a bed. I know Nell wasn't upset with me over anything, which was all that mattered. Okay?'

'How did your relationship end?'

'As I said, we just met up and got wasted a few times over the course of about a week. Nell didn't call me back so I assumed our casual thing was over and I moved on with my life. I'm not into harassing women to stay in contact with me if they're not interested and I gathered by Nell's silence that she wasn't interested in going out with me again. Although, she did get upset because I vomited on her favourite coat, which is why I thought she hadn't called. I never saw her again after that until she moved in underneath me.'

Gina nodded to Jacob and he slipped the photo from the brown paper file and passed it to her. 'I'm showing Mr Kelly a photo that was taken on the morning of eighteenth of June. It's a photo of Abigail Bretton passing something to Mr Kelly over the fence of his and Nell Craven's shared garden.' Kira's son's face had been blurred to preserve their anonymity. 'You told us that you walked to the patch of grass with the dog in the morning, then you were in Miss Craven's flat until lunchtime, then you took the dog up to your flat, after which you slept all day.'

'That's correct.'

'But in this photo you're in yours and Miss Craven's shared garden that morning. You didn't mention seeing anyone else or being in the garden.'

He scrunched his brow. His solicitor butted in. 'I need to talk to my client.'

'It's okay, it's okay,' he said, his Northern Irish accent getting thicker as his worry grew.

The solicitor rolled her eyes and leaned back.

'Tell me what was happening in this photo?'

He sighed. 'I lost Toffee, okay. I know I told you I took Toffee out for a wee on the grass but what I didn't say was that his lead wasn't clipped onto his collar correctly and the pesky thing escaped me. Before I knew it, he'd darted across the meadow and into the trees. The woman in the photo was outside Nell's. She said she was Nell's friend but she didn't say who she was. I didn't ask for her name. Anyway, she helped me to find Toffee. We both followed the dog into the woods and finally we found him in the clearing, sniffing and peeing up a tree.'

It had become obvious that Abigail hadn't met Nell for a picnic at Stratford-upon-Avon that day. Gina wondered if Nell had offered to meet her there, not wanting her to know where she'd moved to and when she got there, Abigail had stood her up. She pictured Nell trying to make the most of it on her own with Alfie and having that picnic regardless. She then knew that Abigail had been to the clearing in the woods. She'd have known it was the perfect place to tie Toffee up. Just far enough away so the neighbours wouldn't hear him barking.

Darrah continued. 'When we caught the dog, I carried him back and Abbie held the lead. I put him in the garden, locked the gate and she passed me the lead over the fence.'

'And was Miss Craven's door still unlocked?'

'Yes, it was on the latch then and it stayed on the latch until she returned because, as you know, I forgot to take it off the latch.'

Gina had another line of questioning and this was going to make him squirm. On booking him in, they took his phone and the messages told her there was still more to uncover. 'You and Nell argued when she got back later that day.'

'I told you we had. I left her door on the latch, for heaven's sake. I'd have argued with me too if I was her. It was no big deal.'

'Except it was. Yes, she wasn't happy that you'd left the door on the latch all day, but she was also unhappy that you'd been harassing her to let you take a paternity test to see if Alfie was your son. We've seen the messages on your phone.'

He leaned back. 'I'm not saying another word.'

His solicitor agreed.

'Do you know this man?' She passed him a photo of Ross Craven. He had described Ross Craven picking up his keys and giving them back to him on the thirtieth of June, only a short while before Ross had been murdered. The timing of Ross's death fitted that time, making Darrah a firm suspect.

Darrah stared at his solicitor and she made a zip motion across her lips.

Gina cleared her throat, taking no pleasure in reading one of the messages that he'd sent to Nell. 'In the message you sent to Nell Craven on the eighteenth of June, the day you looked after her dog, you replied with a serious threat after she refused the test.'

He shrugged. 'I was drunk. It was stupid. I didn't do it.'

The threat made Gina's skin crawl. She wanted to scratch so badly. Was the message nothing more than a drunken mistake? She looked at him and he stared deep within her before turning away. 'Let me read that message out. "You fucking bitch, I'll kill you."'

FORTY-THREE

MAEVE

Maeve took deep breaths, trying to calm her nerves. 'You scared the shit out of me.'

'I didn't mean to. I was just going to walk over and see what you were up to. I even called you from the annex but you didn't reply, then I saw you staring at the birds.'

'Then I crashed into you.' She rubbed her arm, sure there would be a bruise coming up soon. He was more solid than he realised.

'I'm sorry for grabbing you. I was trying to prevent the crash but I was too late. And you screamed and I was just trying to hush you, sorry. Did I hurt you?'

'No, you just made me jump.' She furrowed her brow. 'How did you know I was here, at the annex?'

'Well, I knew you were staying here and when I walked around, I saw you.' He looked back. 'Is that the annex?' He pointed to the garden chairs outside the small building tagged on to the end of the vicarage.

'Yes, but no one is meant to know I'm here. Come with me.' She led him into the annex after checking that Sally hadn't seen her and she closed the door behind them.

'Well, this place is basic.' He made the sign of the cross and laughed.

'I know, but it's safe and Sally is nice. It's only for a few days, at least I hope it is.' A part of her didn't want to leave as she'd have to step into some big adult parent shoes. If she left, did she take Alfie with her there and then, and what was she meant to do when they got back to her apartment? She didn't have a cot, or a high chair, or even any childcare organised. Her heart began to pound at the thought.

'Where's Alfie?'

'He's with Sally.'

'That's a shame, I hoped to meet him.'

She raised her brows. 'Is that why you came?'

He pressed his lips together, sat on her single bed and smiled for a moment. 'No, I came to see you. I missed you. While walking with my sister, all I could think about was you and I can't explain it. We barely know each other but I've never felt like this before. There. I'm wearing my heart on my sleeve.'

She went to speak but nothing came out. This was ridiculous. She barely knew Matty. Was her sudden neediness for him because Nell had been killed and she needed someone to lean on? No, she didn't think so. It was more than that. Her skin tingled when he spoke and her body craved him, not in the same way it did when she'd dragged him back to her apartment a few nights ago, it felt deeper. As her mind toiled with how much she'd let Nell down, she reminded herself that she didn't ask for any of this. She still deserved to be happy.

He held out a hand and led her closer to him. He placed his hands on her hips and pulled again until she'd straddled him and placed her arms around the back of his neck. His mouth met hers and before she knew it, his hand reached up her dress, unclipping her strapless bra as she pressed herself into his hardness. He stood, lifting her, and then lay her down on the bed, then he slipped her underpants off before their lips locked again. Just as she felt his weight upon her, there was a bang on the door. He went to speak but she pressed a hand over his mouth and whispered in his ear. 'Hide in the bathroom and don't come out until I say.'

He silently laughed and nodded. She stood, pulled her dangling bra from the top of her dress and hid it under the quilt, before slipping her underpants back on. 'Coming.' She peered through the window and saw Sally standing there holding Alfie's hand. She opened the door. 'I'm really sorry, I fell asleep.'

'That's okay, lovely. I wondered if you could have Alfie for a bit. I spoke to the DI and she said that you should move into the vicarage for the time being.'

'Yes, is that okay with you, Sally? Only I don't want to get under your feet.'

'You definitely won't. I think we'll be better off together until this is sorted. Anyway, we have a police officer coming to stay with us too, I guess she'll get under both our feet. I just have to attend to something at the church now that the forensics officer has finished up there and Alfie wants to watch cartoons.'

'I'll just pack up my things and head over in a moment, is that okay?'

'Of course. I've got to dash but I won't be long. Twenty minutes, tops.' With that, Sally walked off, leaving Alfie with her.

Damn, she still had Matty hidden away in the bathroom. 'Alfie, come and sit on the bed while I get ready.'

He toddled over and reached up, not quite able to get there on his own. She lifted him and sat him against the pillows, then she found some cartoons on Netflix. It was awkward, she knew, but she hoped Alfie wouldn't take any notice when she let Matty out. He began giggling and pointing at a purple monster on the screen. She opened the bathroom door and Matty was standing there. They'd have to pick up where they left off another time. Getting carried away like that with Matty had been stupid. Right now, she had to take care of her nephew.

'Sorry,' she said in a hushed voice.

He burst into laughter. 'It's okay. I actually feel like a teenager again,' he replied, in a loud whisper.

She leaned in and kissed him, just out of Alfie's view. 'Me too and I can't wait to continue what we started but you have to go before I get into trouble. We have a family liaison officer coming soon and you can't be here.'

His Adam's apple bobbed as he swallowed. 'Is everything okay? I thought you were safe here.'

'I am, well I think I am. They thought my stepdad killed Nell but he was found murdered today.' It finally hit her. Although she felt nothing for Ross Craven, it made her shudder to think that Nell's murderer was still out there. No one knew where she and Alfie were staying. She had to remember that. They were safe at the vicarage.

'Do you want me to stay? I can hide out here if you think it might be good to have someone else around.'

'No, we'll be fine. As I said, the FLO will be here soon to keep guard.'

'Then I'm leaving, but only if you promise to message me later, Maeve Craven. I'll be worrying like mad.'

No one had ever said her name quite like he had.

'And I can't wait to meet the little man one day. Can I say hi to him, now?'

She shook her head. 'Best not confuse him. Right, out of here before Sally gets back.' She playfully slapped his arm and tears pricked her eyes. The toughest woman in the boardroom was softening and it felt alien to her. Overwhelmed with guilt at being so happy was horrible. Maeve took a deep breath and fanned her eyes with her hands.

He passed her a small wad of toilet roll. 'Everything will be okay. I'll look out for you, now.' Again, the intense eye contact he made with her made her tingle. If she hadn't been so taken with him it would be creepy, but Matty wasn't creepy. He was lovely. He crept out of the bathroom and Alfie yelled out, 'Man, man.' Then he laughed.

FORTY-FOUR

As they neared the station, Gina's phone beeped with a couple of messages. Jacob continued driving with the air conditioning on full blast. It was getting stickier as the day went on.

'Jacob, go all the way around the island.'

'What?' He indicated right and did a U-turn, heading back the way they came.

'We have to get to Kira Fellows's flat. She's just called in saying she's seen Abigail Bretton.'

Jacob kept his focus in the impeding rush hour traffic as Gina grabbed her phone and pressed the number for the despatch. 'I'll call for backup. I don't want to lose her.' After making the call, Gina nervously sat back as Jacob drove down several more roads. Finally, she could see Kira's flat. A message flashed up on her phone. 'PC Ahmed has a few officers at the ready to search Darrah Kelly's flat so we can go there next.' She paused and frowned. 'I've just read the updates. The garage that Darrah said he went to at lunchtime doesn't have working CCTV at the moment but the manager can't remember serving any customers matching Darrah's description on that day.'

'So, there is a possibility that Darrah and Abigail have been working together.'

'We can't rule it out.' As he pulled up outside Kira's flat, she saw her staring into the meadow. Gina hurried out of the car.

'She ran towards the trees. I'd just got back from doing a bit of shopping when I saw her.' Kira pointed across the meadow.

'Right, we'll go after her. Update the team and tell them where we're heading,' she said to Jacob. 'Kira, what was she wearing?'

'Err, skinny dark jeans and a pale-pink vest top.'

'Did she see you?'

'Yes. I saw her over there, leaning on the lamppost outside my flat. I recognised her straight away and I think she knew who I was because she just stared at me. It was weird and I didn't know what to do. I asked her why she was watching Nell's flat and what she was doing here. She didn't reply so I said I was calling the police. Then she ran.'

'Right, let's go.' Gina jogged across the meadow and through a couple of trees until she reached the clearing where Toffee had been tied to a tree.

Jacob stopped next to her, both of them listening out for any sign of Abigail. 'How long since we got the call in your car?'

She pulled her phone out. While wiping his brow with the back of his sun-kissed arm, Jacob waited as Gina opened up her call log. His short-sleeved shirt had untucked from his light trousers. 'It was almost fifteen minutes ago,' she said.

'We've lost her, haven't we? With a fifteen-minute head start, she could be anywhere now.' Jacob sighed.

'Think. Where could the camper van be parked? She had to get here somehow and we know she doesn't have her car and the camper van hasn't triggered any ANPR cameras. She can't have gone back to get her car as we've been watching her house.' Gina started to run. 'I know where she might be. There are no

ANPR cameras on the route I think she might have taken and it's not too far from Watcher's Way.'

She kept on running, charging through stingers and shrubs, until she reached the car park that ramblers and dog walkers used, but there was no camper van parked up. There were only two cars and a man was just about to get into one of them with his panting husky. 'Excuse me.' Gina held her identification up. 'Cleevesford Police. Have you seen a camper van parked up here?'

'No, sorry. I got here about half an hour ago and I've stayed quite close to my car with the dog. I haven't seen anyone come or go. That car over there was here when I arrived.'

She glanced at the small, blue electric car.

'I did bump into a woman in the woods, she was putting elderflowers into a straw basket. It might be her car.'

'Thank you. Have you seen anyone else hanging around?'

'No, it's always quiet here. No one tends to venture from the estates as you need to cut through a lot of trees and there are no footpaths through all this, but my dog gets excited by all the undergrowth. She loves ducking and diving in it.'

Gina knew that much. The surrounding woodland was classed as a nature reserve. It was boggy in parts and the nettle and stinger carpets were off-putting for most people. 'What did the woman look like?'

'I guess she might be in her fifties. She's wearing a broad-brimmed sun hat with a blue ribbon tied around it, trousers and a long-sleeved T-shirt. I did say hello, but she ignored me.'

'Where was she?'

He pointed ahead. 'Keep going straight ahead and if she's still there, you'll see her.'

'Thanks again.' Gina turned to Jacob. 'Let everyone know where we're heading. She fits the age of Abigail Bretton's mother. We don't have a description as yet.'

Jacob made a call to the others as Gina moved branches and

brambles out of the way. She spotted the straw hat in the distance. 'Excuse me, Cleevesford Police. Can we have a word?'

The woman began to run in the opposite direction.

'Police, stop!'

There was no way Gina was going to let the woman get away. Her basket got caught on a low-hanging branch. As she turned, Gina first saw the woman's sunscreen-covered nose. 'Sorry, I'm so sorry.' She eased her basket from the branch. 'I didn't know I had to ask for permission to forage here. It's only a few elderflowers to make a cordial with.'

'What's your name?'

'Sherry Proctor.'

Gina sighed. The woman in front of her looked more like she was in her mid-sixties at least. She wasn't Abigail Bretton's mother. 'It's not related to foraging. Can we speak with you for a moment? I'm DI Harte and this is DS Driscoll.'

She nodded and walked over to them. 'Okay.' She frowned at them suspiciously, then slumped her shoulders. 'Shall we head back to the car park?'

Grateful to get out of the tangled undergrowth, Gina nodded. 'That would be great.' After stepping back into the car park, Gina turned to the woman who was placing the basket on the back seat of her car. 'Have you seen anyone else around while you've been here?'

She shook her head. 'No. Only a man with a dog.'

'Have you seen a camper van?'

'Yes. I saw one that had been painted like the Mystery Machine from *Scooby-Doo*. There were five teenagers in it. They seemed to just be leaving when I arrived.'

Deflated, Gina thanked the woman and hurried back towards Kira's flat with Jacob. 'I took a gamble that she came this way and it didn't pay off. All I know is we're not looking for the Mystery Machine.'

'Uniform has all other routes covered. If they're trying to

drive away from here, we'll pick them up. If Abigail Bretton is on foot, that might be harder. The perimeter is huge. A dog team has been called. You never know.'

'You never know.' Abigail Bretton had slipped through their fingers. 'Why would she come back? What is there to come back for?'

Jacob scrunched his brows as they crossed the meadow. 'Alfie. Do you think she is looking for him?'

'I don't know but I'm glad Ellyn is going to be staying with Sally and Maeve tonight. I don't like this one bit. I'm just thinking about the eyes. The removal of the eyes would mean that the victim couldn't see any more, in effect, they're blind. I know they're dead but is it that they didn't see something? Were they blind to something? Then there's the eye on the dog and Watcher's Way. Is the killer telling us they're always watching?'

'Do you think Abigail Bretton wanted to be seen today?'

'I don't know. I think she's good at hiding.' She glanced at Darrah Kelly's flat. PC Ahmed was getting out of his police car and a police van pulled up behind him. Several neighbours were out on the street, watching what was going on.

'Guv, you have to see this.' PC Smith called her over towards the lamppost outside Kira's flat. She ignored what was going on at Darrah Kelly's place for now. PC Ahmed had it under control. They knew what they were looking for.

She followed PC Smith and glanced at the really simple line drawing of an eye on the post, drawn in what looked like permanent marker. She turned to Jacob. 'She wanted to be seen alright.' Gina hurried over to Kira, who was nervously biting her nails at her doorstep.

'Did you find her?'

Gina shook her head. 'I don't think it's a good idea for you and your son to stay here tonight. Is there anywhere else you can go, just for a short while?'

Kira nodded. 'I'm on my own. My son is staying with his

father for a few days. When I told him what had happened, we were both worried and thought it was for the best. I found a cheap holiday let so I'm heading there when you've gone. There's no way I want to be here alone until you've found her. Do you think she's working with Nell's father? Could they be trying to scare me now? I mean, have you even caught him yet?'

Gina was aware that Ross Craven's name hadn't been released along with news of his murder, but Maeve had now been told so it would be soon. 'Mr Craven's body was found this morning. He didn't kill Nell.'

'Wait, no way...' She scrunched her brow. 'I thought...'

'I can't discuss the case further as it's an ongoing investigation but I'm glad you're not staying here tonight.'

'Why are the police at Darrah's? Is it because of the photo I sent you?'

'Again, I can't discuss the case right now, but thank you for the photo. Can I have the address of where you're going?'

'Yes, it's Sunshine Barn on Henley Avenue.' Despite it being so warm, she shivered. 'Shit, it was like the dead walked through me then.' She took a breath. 'Do you think I'll be okay there?'

'Please don't tell anyone where you're going. You also have my number. Any worries at all, call myself or nine-nine-nine immediately.'

'Why did she come back here?'

Gina didn't want to say what she was theorising in her head. Abigail Bretton was trying to tell Kira that she sees her and she made that clear by drawing the eye on the lamppost. Abigail Bretton knew that Kira helped Nell to escape her abuse. Gina managed to deduce that Abigail was jealous and had been reading Nell's messages. She would have known everything, even where Nell had moved to. Abigail now blamed Kira for everything that had gone wrong in her life. Gina knew that was only a theory and until they could find Abigail, it was all she had.

'She blames me, doesn't she? She is going to kill me, and if it definitely wasn't Nell's dad, it has to be Darrah who's working with her. You don't have to say anything. I can see it with my own eyes and my instincts are normally spot on. I have a bit of a sixth sense. It's them. It has to be.'

Kira had been seen and Gina couldn't help but think that Kira was right and that she might be next. They had Darrah in custody but they were nowhere near catching Abigail.

FORTY-FIVE

MAEVE

Hurrying back from the toilet, Maeve kneeled down beside the settee where Alfie was still enjoying his afternoon nap. She stroked the dogs who now both lay on the floor beside him as if offering him some protection. Maeve removed the stuffy cushions she'd surrounded him with while she'd been out of the room, hoping that his sticky head would now cool down. Toffee kept nudging her under the arm so that she'd cuddle him. 'I guess you're missing your mummy too.' She stroked his short fur and he whined. She wondered how hard it would be to rehome the little chihuahua.

Alfie began to stir and a stench hit her nostrils. He needed changing. Damn. Maeve had never changed a nappy in her life. She knew that Sally had been taking him upstairs in the room he'd been sleeping in when she changed him. It was happening, whether she liked it or not. She exhaled as she picked him up. Her mind flitted to toilet training and she pictured herself trailing after him with a plastic potty, hoping that he'd eventually work out what to do before he drenched all her carpets. Had Nell already started training him? 'Come on, mate, let's do this.'

She headed upstairs, nudging the door open. The cot bed had been neatly made with Alfie's teddy at the foot. She opened the wardrobe and saw the plastic changing mat with all the supplies at the bottom of it. After lying Alfie down on the carpet, she placed the mat on the floor and scrunched her brow as she tried to work out what to do with the nappy. It made sense. It wasn't rocket science. She pulled out a scented nappy sack and the baby wipes in readiness. As she pulled his shorts off, he giggled and all through the change, even though Maeve had heaved a couple of times, he'd still laughed. She stuck the new nappy on and sat him up. 'There we go. Aunty Maeve did it and she didn't throw up. What an achievement.' She grabbed a few more baby wipes and cleaned her hands, then she followed that with a squirt of gel. That would have to do until she had a wash in a minute.

'Teddy.' He pointed at the bear.

'You want this?' She picked it up and smiled. As her hands reached around the bear, she felt two hard lumps on the back of its head. She turned the bear around and saw two stuck on plastic googly eyes and she laughed with Alfie. 'A bear with eyes in the back of its head.'

'Ololllo lollo.'

'Ollo lollo to you too.' She had no idea what he meant but he was funny. She removed the eyes and gave him the teddy. Although funny she did worry that he'd try to pull them off and choke on them. She'd have a word with Sally later. Although, the woman had been through enough over the past twenty-four hours. She was probably suffering with concussion. Maeve shouldn't have left her alone when she met Matty.

The back door slammed.

'Hello.' Maeve picked Alfie up. The dogs ran to the back door, barking. 'Sally,' she called as she hurried down, but there was no one there. As she headed into the living room, calling the dogs to follow, she heard a loud bang on the kitchen window. She placed Alfie on the floor and ran back into the kitchen with the dogs. A bloody smear graced the centre of the window. She gently opened the kitchen door and peered at the graveyard. There was no one around. The only thing out of place was the dead bird on the garden tiles under the window. Another dead crow. She glanced down, wondering if it had flown into the window, killing itself in the process. Heart banging away, she ran back into the kitchen and locked the door. The birds were really freaking her out. Her phone beeped.

Matty: I can't wait to see you again, to properly see all of you. Xxxxxx

There was a loud bang on the front door. She crept towards it and opened it, leaving the chain in place. A woman in her early thirties with hair tied up in a messy bun piled on the top of her head, stood there and smiled. She pulled her identification out of her bag and held it up. 'Hello, you must be Maeve. I'm Ellyn, the family liaison officer.'

Maeve had never felt so grateful to see someone from the police in her whole life. She breathed a sigh of relief. No one would dare try to hurt them with a police officer in the building.

FORTY-SIX

Gina hurried over to Darrah's flat. The late afternoon sun had now given way to a couple of clouds but the sticky close air remained. She held back a yawn. It already felt like she'd had two days in one with the amount of running around they'd done. The officer standing guard at the entrance to the garden was speaking to Elaine and Reg Hampton, the couple who had looked after Alfie and Sally on the day of Nell's murder. 'Is it Darrah? Did he kill Nell?' Elaine waited for Gina to answer, her hair sticking out of the edges of a bath towel. 'Even if you don't answer me, it doesn't matter. Why would you be searching his flat? I told you he was a weirdo, and he's always drunk,' she said to Reg as she tightened her bathrobe.

'Love, let's go in. I told you, you never really know someone even when you think you do. They wouldn't be here if he wasn't a suspect. Come on, we should let the police do their jobs without the likes of all of us hanging around making things harder.' Gina agreed with him. The loitering crowds were generally being a nuisance. Not one of them looked as if they had anything to say that could help and she wished people wouldn't film them all the time and post speculative comments all over social media. She watched as officers spoke to them in the hope that someone saw Abigail hanging around. As it stood, they had yet to charge Darrah Kelly but social media would probably have him hung, drawn and quartered before she even got back to the station.

Elaine shook her head. 'I'm not going in, Reg. I want to see if they find anything. You go back home.'

Reg shook his head and sighed before leaving Elaine tapping away on her phone and gossiping with a woman who rocked a baby in her arms.

Gina popped on her boot covers and gloves and went up the stairs with Jacob close behind. She heard PC Ahmed discussing the search with the officers as he walked out to the hallway.

'Shaf.'

PC Ahmed turned to see her. 'Guv. We've made a start.'

'That's great. I know you haven't been here long but have you found anything?'

'Not yet. There's a fair bit to get through. It's a small place but every cupboard is cluttered. I opened a kitchen cupboard and a sandwich maker nearly knocked me out. Then I literally waded through a million packets of out-of-date food.'

Gina stepped into the living room, the same damp room that she'd first spoken to Darrah Kelly in. The curtains were still drawn and the mouldy scent made her recoil. A stack of empty lager cans next to the sofa had been crushed and half a bottle of vodka was leaning against a cushion. Two officers were on their knees checking around the back of the settee. She backed up to give them some space as one of them slid it away from the wall and she almost stepped on Jacob's foot. The kitchen was as lively.

Her phone rang. 'O'Connor.'

'Guv. Great news.' She stood in the dark hallway. 'The camper van has passed an ANPR camera near Stratford-upon-Avon. Several police cars have been despatched but there are at least five routes without ANPR that Shirley and Abigail Bretton could have taken. Uniform is hoping to block them off. They're closing in on them but it could still take a while. I thought you'd want to know.'

'Great. That's brilliant and, yes, I'm glad you called.' Gina tried to picture all the back routes that Abigail Bretton's mother would had to have driven through to avoid so much ANPR. Her stomach churned with hunger and that in turn was making her nauseous. She felt a slight bit of acid at the back of her throat. She pulled the antacids from her pocket and quickly popped another into her mouth. 'Can you head over and be there to make the arrest should it all go well?'

'I'm on it now.' He ended the call and Gina turned back to Jacob.

'Good news, guv?' he asked.

'We have a hit on the ANPR. We're finally closing in on Abigail Bretton.'

Jacob smiled. 'We'll have this case wrapped up by the end of the day.'

'I love your optimism.' They still didn't have Abigail at the station.

She nudged open the door to the poky bathroom. No one had started to search that yet. She opened the rusty medicine cabinet and the only items on the shelves were half a tube of toothpaste, a bar of cracked soap and a disposable razor. No one had screamed that they had found any blood-soaked clothes or anything else that might be evidence of Darrah Kelly's guilt. They needed so much more if they were going to prove he killed Nell and Ross Craven. All they had so far was a man who'd lied, a man with no alibi, and some threatening texts. Forensics results would take ages. She stared down at the urine-stained loo and the yellow splattered mat that circled the toilet base. The smell of vomit hung in the air. After peering behind the curtain of the dry shower tray, she concluded that there wasn't much to find and if there was, it would be in the pipework, which would be checked later.

'Guv.' PC Ahmed came into the bathroom as another officer ran out of the door heaving. 'You have to see what we've found in the fridge.'

After bracing herself, she followed him. As they reached the kitchen a PC held up a plastic lunch box in outstretched arms as if she didn't want the contents anywhere near her. All she could see was polythene covering some slightly pink and pale balls in a tightly tied up bag and they were sloshing in some white liquid. Swallowing her nausea down, she looked back at Shaf to avoid staring at the ugly mess behind the plastic.

Shaf swallowed and spoke. 'I think we've found the eyes.'

FORTY-SEVEN

Gina headed through the main reception after passing through a mob of reporters, all waiting for Briggs to deliver his next briefing. Each one of them wanted to know the identity of the man they had in custody and the man who had been murdered. Neither of which had been released. She quickly checked the 'What's Up Cleevesford' Facebook page and just as she refreshed, a photo of Darrah Kelly's flat surrounded by police came up. Not only that, the original poster, Elaine Hampton, had given his name and mentioned Nell, too. Then came the comments.

> **Elaine:** I always thought he was a strange one but to think that I've been living next door but one to a murderer. #NoSmokeWithoutFire

> **DeeDee:** Caught him in my garden having a piss or maybe he was watching me. Who knows? The man is always out of it and he's creepy. If Nell hadn't let him into her life, she'd still be here now. She was too nice for her own good. Bless her. RIP, Nell!

Kira: Murdering scum. He was always hanging around her and staring at her like some psycho stalker. He didn't do it alone but I can't say anything yet or I might get into trouble!!! RIP Nell. Always in my thoughts. XXX

DeeDee: So sorry for your loss, Kira. I know you two were close.

Kira: #Heartbroken mate. I even let him help me when I moved in. Feeling sick at that now.

With anger flaring up inside her, Gina closed the app. She hoped that Kira didn't get tempted to release Abigail Bretton's name. They didn't need vigilantes getting involved and they didn't need Abigail being more evasive than she already was. They simply needed to find her and bring her in.

'There are goodies on the table,' Kapoor said as she hurried into the incident room and grabbed a giant cookie. 'News about Darrah's arrest is out of the bag, too.'

'I know, I just saw. It doesn't take long for word to spread. Could have done without that.' She turned to Kapoor. 'I know the search has been wrapped up but can you make sure we have some officers in unmarked cars watching Kira Fellows's flat just in case Abigail comes back?'

Kapoor nodded and began sending a message.

Briggs paced by the window, looking down at the reporters in the car park. He nodded as she entered. Jacob came in with a tray that jangled with glasses of water and he placed it on the table. Gina grabbed one and swigged down the liquid and her stomach screamed again for food. Despite knowing that she'd get indigestion again, she snatched a cookie and began to eat it, enjoying the sugariness that was now waking her up, ready for the night ahead. Wyre was already sitting, waiting for the update.

Gina's phone rang. 'Bernard.'

Everyone stopped talking and listened. 'Gina, we've taken a look in the box.'

'And?'

'It's not what you think it is.'

'What is it?'

'I'm sorry to say, it's sweetbreads soaking in milk. They were slightly off.'

She almost wanted to kick the chair in front of her, instead she allowed her shoulders to drop. 'Thanks for letting me know.' She ended the call. It had felt like they'd been so close but, in fact, they were getting further away from solving the case. All they had was Abigail Bretton now.

'What is it?' Briggs asked.

'Sweetbreads. Not eyes. Who the hell eats sweetbreads? He was soaking them in milk, in the bloody fridge.'

Briggs slowly blew out a breath. 'He still doesn't have an alibi. Who was checking that out?'

'Me.' Wyre checked her emails on her phone and smiled. 'We've just this second had an update, sir. I'm just reading an email from the garage. One of their employees has just arrived to start the evening shift. The same colleague also turned up yesterday around midday and served Darrah Kelly.' She carried on reading the email and summarising what it said. 'They looked over their records at that time and they can confirm that a four pack of lager was sold. Also, the employee's boyfriend dropped her off. He then backed into one of the parking spaces so he could send a few messages and emails and his dashcam was still recording.' Wyre clicked on the attached video. They all huddled around the front of the table to watch the clear footage that showed Darrah approaching the door of the garage at twelve thirty-five on the day that Nell was murdered.

'The time needs verifying by Garth in digital forensics but it

looks like Darrah has his alibi for Nell's murder. After it's
confirmed, we're going to have to let him go. He can't have
killed Nell and we have nothing on him for Ross Craven's
murder, either.'

Everyone looked deflated. Kapoor had even left half a
cookie on the table. Gina spared a thought for Darrah and his
name being released on social media. He wouldn't be able to go
back home, for now, not without being hounded by the neighbours and the press. 'Right, I know we've had a couple of
setbacks, but we need to keep up the momentum. There is a
double murderer out there and I don't think they are going to
stop at Nell and Ross Craven. Which brings us back to Abigail
Bretton. Where are we with her? Has anyone spoken to
O'Connor?'

Wyre put down the small box of salad she was picking at to
answer her phone. 'He's calling now.' She placed it to her ear
and nodded a few times, while scrawling notes on her pad, then
she ended the call.

'What did he say?' Gina was desperate to know.

'He said they're closing in on the camper van. They've
narrowed it down to two possible routes they could have taken.
There is a campsite on one of them. The camper van that
Abigail Bretton's mother has been driving hasn't activated any
other ANPR cameras and it's looking likely that by process of
elimination, they are there. It's called Avon Camp Site as it's
right on the river.' Wyre's phone beeped. 'I have another update
from O'Connor.' She read the message. 'They've found the van.
Do you want them to make the arrest?'

Gina nodded. 'Yes.'

They all waited for Wyre to tap out the message, then they
anxiously waited for his reply. Her phone rang and she
answered. 'O'Connor, what's happening now?' She looked up
at Gina. 'They're knocking.' Another minute or two passed and

Wyre leaned back in her chair and puffed out a long breath. 'There's no one in the camper van.'

Gina clenched her fists. 'We're heading over there. Jacob, let's go. When they come back we need to be there, waiting.'

FORTY-EIGHT

Darkness was starting to fall and Gina sat in Jacob's car with the windows rolled down, watching the camper van as clouds gathered above. A warm breeze circled the car as it whipped up a little. The police cars had discreetly parked out of sight with the cooperation of the site manager, while they all waited for Abigail and Shirley to return to the camper van. She checked her watch. 'We've been sitting here for an hour now and no one has seen either of them.' She sighed, knowing that they were wasting time. O'Connor had returned to the station to help with enquiries back there.

Jacob opened a packet of mini sausage rolls and he began to eat one, depositing flaky pastry all over his lap and in the footwell of his car. 'Want one?' He offered her the pack.

'No, I'm good, thanks.'

'How's your indigestion?'

She fidgeted slightly to see how bad the pain was. 'A bit better, which is why I daren't eat a sausage roll. I ate a cookie back at the station, that was enough. So far, so good.' She wasn't good. That was a lie. The deep pain in her chest had lingered all day but it wasn't sharp, not like it had been. As long as she refused the sausage roll, she'd be fine. 'I could murder a drink though but that'll have to wait.'

'Same.' He paused. 'Where do you think they've gone? There is a pub that you can walk to. I know officers checked it out and they weren't there. There's literally nothing else around here but farms and the river.'

She knew that officers had also discreetly checked some of the walking routes. Abigail and Shirley Bretton had moved around like ghosts. After checking her phone to see if her messenger had sent anything else, she pressed Sally's number.

The woman answered after a few rings. 'Gina, how are things going?'

'They're still going,' she replied. 'How are you feeling now?'

'Oh yes. My head is a bit sore and I've slept a lot today, but I think things are improving. At least Maeve is here to help with Alfie.'

'And how is Maeve?'

'Worried. We both are but Ellyn, the FLO, has been really nice. I feel safer with her here, so thank you for sending her to be with us.'

'I'm glad she's there. I was hoping to pop by this evening but I'm caught up in a stakeout. I'll visit tomorrow, though.'

'It's always lovely to see you and I hope your stakeout goes well. I can't get Nell out of my head. Whoever did that to her is extremely dangerous. Take care. Okay?'

'Thanks, Sally. I will. Any problems, call me. You take care too.' Gina ended the call.

'Everything okay at the vicarage?' Jacob munched the last bit of sausage roll in his mouth and brushed the crumbs off his lap onto his car mat.

'Yes. Ellyn is with them so at least they're okay. We just need the Brettons to turn up now.' A family in a caravan came out and began lighting a barbecue. 'Great, when the Brettons get back we now have an audience.'

Gina's phone rang again. 'Hello.'

'DI Harte.'

'Speaking. Who is this?'

Gina listened to the caller clear her throat and swallow. 'It's Habiba Bal.'

'Are you okay? Is the officer still outside your house?'

'Yes, and I am okay, thank you. I'm calling because I thought you should know something.'

Gina scrunched her brow. 'I'm with DS Driscoll so I'm placing your call on loudspeaker. Has something happened?'

'It's my daughter, Saira.'

'The one who's in Spain?'

'Yes. She's not in Spain. In fact, she's been staying in Birmingham for the last month and she didn't tell me. I'm not very happy. I paid for her to study in Spain and she left early to spend a few weeks with some boy who she met on a beach. Anyway, you're not interested in my daughter's lack of commitment to her study but I am worried about her. I found out when I called her to break the news about her dad. That's when she told me that she'd been writing to him in prison recently, until he left. She kept that from me and I can't tell you how upset I am. He didn't even tell me she was writing to him, but I guess he knew I'd be angry at both of them for keeping me in the dark. I don't even know how she knew he was in prison but that's another story. She's obviously distraught that he's been killed. My main worry right now is that Ross's other daughter was murdered. Could the murderer go for Saira next? I'm worried sick. I wish she was still in Spain.'

'Where is she staying?'

'She's coming home. She should be back later this evening.'

'Good,' Gina replied. 'The officer will stay positioned outside your house. It'll be good that you and Saira are together.'

'Thank you.'

'If you hear anything else, please call me.'

'Will do. Oh, Saira's trying to call me now. I have to go.'
Habiba ended the call and Gina's phone rang again.

The officer positioned at the site entrance spoke and Gina
relayed what he had said to Jacob. 'An Uber has just dropped
a woman off at reception. The woman is heading this way
now.'

'Only one woman?'

'Yes.' They waited for what seemed like forever but Gina
checked her watch. It had only been three minutes.

A heavy-set woman eventually ambled down the road
carrying a shopping bag. She glanced at Gina and Jacob, said
hello to the family who were popping sausages onto a metal tray
ready to barbecue and she pulled a key from her pocket.

Gina got out of the car. 'Mrs Bretton?'

The woman scrunched her brow, her face a blotchy red.
She pulled her errant bra strap up and popped it back on her
shoulder. 'Yes, and who are you?'

'I'm DI Harte and this is DS Driscoll. We're looking for
your daughter, Abigail Bretton.'

'Er...' She placed the key into the lock of the camper van. 'I
guess you should come in and take a seat.'

Gina sat at the table at the end of the van, the one that obviously collapsed into a bed. Three holdalls were piled up in the
corner.

'I saw her earlier. She said she'd be here this evening for
dinner but I haven't heard from her since. I've tried calling her
but she hasn't been answering. Has something happened?'

Gina cleared her throat. 'We need to speak to her in
connection with the murder of Nell Craven. Do you know
where she is?'

Shirley Bretton let out a snigger. 'You're serious, aren't you?'

Gina nodded.

Shirley stared at them, as if she was trying to process what
Gina had just said. 'No, you've got this wrong. I know Abigail

has a bit of a temper and goodness, she and Nell had a bit of a turbulent relationship, but murder?'

'When did you last see her?'

'I picked her up this morning around eight. She knew I was hiring the van as I camp regularly, and she said she had a few days off due to compassionate leave. She asked if she could come with me on my little tour. She was upset about Nell and I thought it would be good for her to come away with me. After I picked her up, we'd barely got down the road and she said she needed to do something first, so I let her out. She said she'd get the bus later to this campsite and meet me here. I got worried about midday so I called her again. She hasn't answered all day. That's all I know and now I'm even more worried because you've turned up.' The woman ruffled her damp blonde hair.

'Did she say where she was going?'

'No, but she said she had to see someone and it couldn't wait. She told me she loved me, which was odd. She never says anything like that normally.'

Gina needed to try to work out where Abigail had gone or who she'd gone to see. 'Tell me a little about Abigail and Nell.'

'Well, in my opinion, they met and moved in together far too fast. My daughter is and always has been impulsive. She loves wholly and deeply. She fell for Nell and wanted nothing more than to have this cute little family with Nell and Alfie. Then the arguments started.'

'Arguments?' Gina knew that Abigail's neighbour had mentioned that she and Nell had argued.

'Yes, Abigail is normally a closed book but she was really upset. She said that she read Nell's messages. Nell was trying to contact her son's father. Of course, Abigail being Abigail kept going through Nell's phone. She always was jealous, even of her friends when she was younger. Anyway, that's irrelevant. Abigail also thought that Nell might be seeing someone else and was planning to leave her. It played with her head. As I said, she loves deeply and she found out that Nell was telling so many lies. I said she'd rushed into things. I mean, they'd barely dated before Nell moved into her house.'

'Do you know who Abigail suspected Nell of having an affair with?'

'No, just a woman. She had a child too.' Gina knew that Abigail had jealousy issues and she already knew that she had a problem with Kira as she'd scared the woman at her flat earlier that day.

'Did Abigail mention Alfie's father's name, the man who Nell was trying to contact?'

'No, but she did say that they met abroad but he was now living in the UK. Nell told Abigail that she'd met him in Turkey. He'd been doing some work at the hotel where Nell had stayed.'

'Doing some work?'

'Yes. I don't know what work, just that he was there to fix things.'

Gina felt a jolt of adrenaline run through her. Abigail knew about Ross Craven. She was seen arguing with a man matching Ross's description by her house. She knew about Alfie's dad and that Nell and he met in Turkey and she was angry and jealous of Nell communicating with him and Kira. Gina remembered the Turkish eye. They'd found their link.

'Did Abigail mention anyone else when it came to Nell? It doesn't matter how irrelevant you think this information could be. We really need to find her.'

'Please don't go too hard on Abigail. Whatever you might be thinking right now, you're wrong.'

'What do you think we are thinking?'

'You think Abigail could have hurt Nell. She just wouldn't.'

Gina pressed her lips together as she thought about what to say, but it had to be said. 'We have evidence to show that

Abigail was locking Nell in her spare room at times. I think there was more to their relationship than you know about.'

'No, that can't be true. Nell was probably making it up. That's ridiculous. My daughter isn't like that. She isn't...' It was as if the penny had dropped. Shirley frowned.

'This has happened before, hasn't it? The abuse.' Gina wondered if pushing Shirley a little might help or hinder.

Shirley looked into her lap and shook her head. 'Only once. Her ex was going to leave her so she locked her in the bedroom. I went around and told Abigail how ridiculous she was being and that you couldn't do that to people. Her ex left and never said anything. I spoke to Abigail about this and I thought it wouldn't happen again. I don't know what to do.'

'This is not on you,' Gina replied.

'It is. I left her when she was a child.' She swallowed her tears back. 'I had a breakdown when she was six and went into hospital. With no one to care for her, she ended up in temporary foster care until I got better. She's scared of being left, that's all. As I said, she's sensitive. She loves deeply. I know Abigail has done wrong but right now, wherever she is, she's very vulnerable and she needs help. There is something else.' She paused. 'I don't know why I'm telling you this but I'm actually her aunt. Her mother died when she was a baby. It was an accident. I adopted Abigail.' Shirley paused and her jaw wobbled as she fought the emotional pain she was holding back. 'And I failed them both.'

'You did not fail them. Bringing up a child is hard.' Gina sympathetically tilted her head. 'Is there anything else you can think of?'

Shirley wiped the tears pricking in the corners of her eyes. 'There was another girl. She mentioned that Nell had been in some sort of contact with someone called Saira who lived in Spain and I think they were also going to meet up. Abigail guessed that Saira was someone Nell had met on one of her wild holidays before she had Alfie. I remember the girl's name as Abigail has a cousin called Sarah and it sounds similar.'

'That's really helpful, thank you.' Gina's heart began to pound. She left Jacob talking to Shirley in the camper van and went outside to call O'Connor. She needed to fill the team in before they headed back to Cleevesford.

'Can either you or Wyre head over to be with Habiba Bal while she waits for her daughter to arrive. She called saying that her daughter isn't in Spain. She's been staying in Birmingham and she's on her way home to Cleevesford. I need one of you to interview Saira as soon as she arrives. Ask her everything she knows about Nell, and ask her about the letters she sent to Ross. It looks like they knew about each other, despite it being news to Habiba. I think Saira and Habiba might be in more danger than we first thought.'

FORTY-NINE

As Gina followed Jacob through the car park, the reporters all began shouting at once. A few specks of rain hit Gina's face.

'Is it Darrah Kelly? Did he kill Nell and Ross Craven?'

'Has he been charged?'

'What did forensics find?'

'What if you haven't got the right person and the killer is still out there?'

Gina stared at them and they paused, waiting for her to speak. 'You'll be updated in the next briefing.' She caught up with Jacob, not looking back and ignoring any further shouts. A few flashes went off, lighting up the night. Most of them would soon be gone until the next morning. Shirley Bretton had been left with an officer just in case Abigail did end up at the campsite, but Gina doubted that Abigail had any intention of turning up. The camper van had been nothing but a wild goose chase for them.

As she passed reception, she saw Darrah Kelly smirking. 'They're letting me go. See, I didn't do it.' He stared at Gina and laughed.

You fucking bitch, I'll kill you! The message that Darrah had sent to Nell still lingered at the forefront of Gina's mind. His solicitor had done her job and got him out, for now. He didn't kill Nell as his alibi had now confirmed. She'd caught up with the notes on the system while Jacob had driven them back. Gina passed Darrah swiftly so that he wouldn't be able to see how tightly clenched her fists were. Even if he didn't kill Nell, that message had probably scared the life out of her. She spared a thought for the terrified young mother who had turned all her cupboards out, thinking someone might be bugging her home or watching her. She was abusing caffeine so that she wouldn't fall asleep, just in case her stalker came into her home. All Nell wanted to do was protect her little boy and escape Abigail, instead she'd been murdered. It was also annoying Gina that she didn't have the name of Alfie's father.

She entered the incident room. 'What do we know?' she asked O'Connor.

'Wyre has headed over to Habiba Bal's place. Garth confirmed that the footage we have of Darrah Kelly is pukka, so we've had to let Kelly go, for now.'

'I just saw him leaving. He looked so smug but what can we do? Without evidence we can't keep him.' She pushed open the window slightly and watched Darrah leaving. A huddle of reporters gathered around him. He nudged through them and stood on the wall that surrounded the car park. They all shut up and held their cameras and boom mics out. 'Dammit. He's talking to the reporters.'

'I have been hauled into this station and questioned for something I had nothing to do with. I have an alibi so record that. My alibi has been verified so I am now free. Nell was my neighbour. Nell was my friend, and I would never hurt her. I looked after her dog and did a few jobs for her. That's what you get for being a nice person.'

'He forgot to tell them about the threatening message he sent to her. If only they knew.' Gina shut the window, not wanting to hear anymore. 'Right, we need to go back to the board.' She looked at Maeve and Saira's names. 'Nell had two half-sisters, one we know is Maeve and it looks like Nell had been communicating with Saira. We know at some point, Nell stopped using her smartphone and started using the burner phone. We haven't managed to locate her other phone and the thinking is she got rid of it when she left Abigail Bretton.'

'What do you think Ross's role is in this, guv?' O'Connor asked.

Gina bit her bottom lip and thought for a moment. 'Again, I only have theories right now. Why would Abigail kill Ross? I'm wondering if Ross knew that Abigail was being abusive towards Nell. Maybe he went over there to threaten Abigail. At first, we thought Ross was the threat but now I'm wondering if he was trying to protect Nell, which is why he could have been murdered. Ross was also seen hanging around Nell's flat if Darrah Kelly is to be believed, but then again I'd say Darrah is telling the truth. His description of Ross was accurate. Again, maybe Ross Craven was looking out for Nell. The big question we need to ask is, was Abigail the threat? Is she still a threat? Is she working with someone else? Is Darrah Alfie's father? Nell didn't believe he was. She was trying to contact someone at a hotel in Turkey who was, in Shirley Bretton's words, there to fix something. That brings us to the Turkish eye. Coincidence or clue? I don't believe in coincidences in this instance. The killer knew that Nell was trying to contact Alfie's father and they knew she met him in Turkey. She also thought he was now living in the UK. I think this rules Darrah out. Then we have Saira.' Everything whirled around her mind in a jumbled mess. 'We're missing something huge here and I can't put my finger on it. There are a lot of names on this board. O'Connor, Kapoor, can you go through each one and find out as much as you can. Search their social media too, every last bit of it.'

Kapoor nodded and began tapping away on her laptop.

The main phone rang. Briggs grabbed it. He listened and then turned to Gina. 'It's Wyre. Habiba Bal is in a right state. She can't get hold of her daughter at all.'

FIFTY

DIARY EXTRACT

A lot has happened but everything went to plan. When you give your all to a person and they treat you badly, you know you have to punish them. Ross Craven treated me so badly. When he threw that Turkish eye back at me, I knew then that all my love and help had been for nothing. He'd been to my house and I think he wanted to talk because when I confronted him in my garden, he went to say something but he stopped. I lost my mother, then he left me to fend for myself.

Murdering scum, Ross Craven was nothing. I thought he'd fill me with fear but there was nothing scary about him, nothing at all. I wonder how alike we are? I wonder if my angry side comes from him because I hate the world and most of the people in it. Most of all I hate Nell for the love he had for her. What was so bloody special about Nell?

I know he gave her diaries too and we both write our thoughts and feelings down like sad idiots. Maybe I should have seen her as a victim of his neglect too, but I didn't. All she was was a thorn in my side, something to come between me and my dad. The more I think about those stupid diaries, the angrier I get. To think both of us probably clung on to those cheap note-

books like they were precious. Ross was a cheapskate; I'll give him that. We were his children and that's all we got from him while growing up – cheap notebooks and promises that never came to fruition.

I was the one who was there for Nell, I listened as she went on and on about him and it irked me. For some reason, she said she'd be seeing Ross again. He killed her mother but she went on, saying that he's her father and that meant something. She claimed she was going to forgive him and that she wanted to listen to what he had to say. Why? Because he said he was sorry and that he hated himself for what he'd taken from her, that he'd acted in the spur of the moment when he accidentally killed her mother and that he will regret it forever. How could she have fallen for that? Well, I guess I did but I know better now. I tried to tell her how wrong she was but she turned on me. That's the thanks I got.

I called him Dad too, even though it felt alien to say that word after so long, but he didn't want my forgiveness. He didn't want anything from me. That's why I had to take the next step. I called him and asked him to meet me at Watcher's Way. I told him that Nell was in serious trouble and that I had her with me, and he had to come. I said if he didn't come, she'd get hurt. To make sure it would work, I actually went to Nell's flat, turned her phone on silent and hid it in a drawer. Then I upped my game and told him I'd hurt Nell if he didn't hurry. He knew I was serious because, as far as we were concerned, the apple really didn't fall far from the tree. We will both kill if we need to. When he arrived and found out I was alone, he started calling me all sorts. All hot and sweaty, he took his coat off and threw it to the ground. I'll confess, I cried as he insulted me but he didn't care. I was hoping that right then, he'd put his arms around me and tell me how much he loved me, but then he called me a psycho bitch and said my mum was as bad. Then he told me something else out of the blue that shocked me to the core.

That did it. For the first time in my life, I'd heard the truth straight out of his mouth. Right at that moment, at Watcher's Way, he knew that I now knew. He hadn't meant to say what he said but it was too late now. I also knew he still wanted to keep his secrets. No way did Ross want to go back to prison so he was never going to let me leave Watcher's Way alive. I still shake when I think about that moment. Blood pumped around my body, creating the deafening drumbeat in my ear with each rapid breath. Fight or flight. I remember glancing up at the crows in the trees above, their beady eyes on me, and thinking, I can do this. I have them on my side.

Ross then showed me that he was every inch the murderer when he lunged at me. He gripped my neck before pinning me against a tree. Little did he know that I'd been watching him. I knew everything about him.

I saw him but he never really saw the real me, which is why he didn't even consider what came next. Earlier, I'd placed a large smooth rock in one pocket and a knife in the other. However hard I tried, I couldn't move my trapped arm to get the knife. Rock it was. I pulled the huge smooth stone from my pocket. It's no use trying to prise the hands of the man trying to strangle you from your neck. It's a waste of energy. What I needed to do was to go straight on the attack. With every bit of strength, I hit him, then I hit him again and again and again, until I was spent.

The real me had awoken. It was then I knew that I was every bit as dangerous and volatile as Ross was. He had created the monster that I am, and I can't deny the monster living inside me any longer. Laughing as he took his last breath, I pulled out my knife. He failed to see himself in me and for that he was weak and I was strong. The crows squawked above, as if telling me to get the job done.

With perfect sight, he was blind to it all. There's only one thing for it and the birds are hungry. With every rough cut and *pull to get his eyeballs out, I did it. Then just to make sure they all got the bloody message; I carved an eye on a tree. I glance at my work. It was either me or him, and I chose me. I killed Ross Craven.*

No one will ignore me ever again.

It doesn't stop here. This is only the beginning because Ross's blood runs through mine but I am better than he ever was and I'm going to show Nell. Ross wanted her forgiveness and love so badly but he didn't want mine. I hate them. I am no longer content with messing with her fragile mind and making sure poor little Nell is losing it. It's taking too long and gives me no pleasure any more. A crow begins pecking at my offering and another joins it. Very soon, Ross's eyes are no longer looking at me.

Nell can't see what's right under her nose so I'm going to have to spell it out. Adios, Nell!

FIFTY-ONE

Habiba paced up and down her long living room carpet while Gina and Jacob sat on the settee. 'Ms Bal, can you tell us what you said to Saira when you spoke to her on the phone?'

'I was surprised when I couldn't hear the international dial tone. When she answered, I asked her what was going on. That's when she told me she was staying in Birmingham with a boy she'd met in Spain. Anyway, I decided not to have too much of a go at her because I had called to tell her about her father. A little later, she called me back and said she was coming home straight away. She should have been here ages ago and she's not. What if something's happened to her?'

Gina spotted Wyre standing outside talking to PC Smith. Normally she wouldn't be worried about someone being a little bit late, but Saira wasn't answering her phone and the circumstances were anything but normal. She turned back to Habiba. 'How is she getting here?'

'Train and then a bus. She said she'd be catching the train from Moor Street Station to New Street Station, then from New Street to Redditch Bus Station and lastly from the bus station to here. She said she'd be an hour and half but it's been three hours now. And her phone, she's not answering. That's what's worrying me the most. She's always glued to her phone. I've been calling non-stop and nothing. Her phone has gone dead.'

Gina did a quick check on Google Maps and Habiba was right about the journey and the time it should have taken. 'Can we check in with the various stations?' Gina asked Jacob.

'I'll ask Wyre to contact them to see if we can confirm that she got on the train. We'll be able to ask police and security there to check the CCTV.'

'Do you have a recent photo of her?'

Habiba grabbed a framed photo off her mantelpiece. 'This was taken at Christmas.'

Gina took a moment to take in the young woman wearing reindeer antlers and smiling for the camera, before Jacob took it and left to speak to Wyre.

'How did she seem when you spoke to her?'

Habiba tapped her nails on the windowsill as she watched Wyre, Jacob and Smith talking in the small front garden. 'I don't know. Weirdly, she didn't sound upset but I guess that's the way it is when you think your father abandoned you.'

Gina knew she needed to address Saira knowing Nell. 'Did you know that Saira was in touch with Nell?'

Habiba turned and furrowed her dark brows. 'She can't have been. She would have told me. Besides, I've only just found out about Nell.'

'I think they were going to meet which may have been partly why Saira came back early. Saira was also writing to Ross. It wouldn't have taken too much research to find out which prison Ross was detained in, that's if Nell didn't just tell her. I think Saira already knew about Ross's release.'

'That's how she found out. Nell told her everything.' The extent of Saira's secret slowly dawned on Habiba. Slamming her hand on the coffee table, Habiba kneeled in front of it. 'How could she have kept all this from me? Why?'

'How did Saira feel about Ross?'

She shrugged. 'We were both angry at him for just leaving us the way he did all those years ago, but I had no idea he was back in her life. He didn't say anything when we spoke and I don't know why he wouldn't. Something doesn't feel right about all this. Maybe she asked him not to say anything until she'd spoken to me. That's possible. Actually, he did quite often stare at me in the kitchen, like he wanted to say something, maybe he wanted to tell me. But none of that explains where she is now and why she's not answering her phone.'

Habiba picked up her phone and tried to call her daughter again and all she got was the dead tone again. Her jaw began to wobble. 'I just want her here with me.' She paused and scrunched her brow again. 'That's why Ross came here, wasn't it? He wanted to be there when Saira and Nell met up. Saira knew about Nell and she didn't want to hurt me by telling me. That's all. Who could have hurt her? Ross is dead and Nell is dead. Who wanted them dead? I just can't think of anyone.'

As Gina hunched over, she felt a twinge in her chest that reached deep within. She took a breath in the hope that it would go away but the pain just deepened. Jacob came back in. 'We've sent Saira's photo to Moor Street and they're reviewing the afternoon's CCTV. It could take a while.'

'Thanks. Have we tried to trace Saira's phone?'

'Wyre has been working on that too. It went completely offline around three hours ago.'

'That would be when she got to Moor Street Station. I know the signal is bad there but she would have regained it a short while into her journey.' Habiba glanced at her phone again.

Gina knew Habiba was right. Saira would have had an intermittent signal fairly soon after boarding the train.

Wyre ran in. 'Guv, Moor Street station have got back to us.

They have Saira on CCTV. She did get to Moor Street Station at the time she was expected and it shows her dropping her phone and it smashing.'

Gina turned to Wyre. 'See if you can track the rest of her route on CCTV. Contact the relevant stations and bus depots.'

Habiba stood. 'So where did she go? She should be here by now.'

'Does Saira know that Nell has been murdered? Did you tell her?' Gina asked.

Shaking her head, Habiba began to pick her nails. 'I only told her that her dad had been murdered. I was going to tell her more when she arrived.'

Gina stood and walked outside. 'I know there are officers on Nell Craven's road. Get them to look out for Saira Bal. She may have taken a diversion and headed to see Nell first, not knowing what has happened to her.'

Gina's stomach began to churn. Had the killer got to Saira first?

FIFTY-TWO

ELLYN

Ellyn sat on a stool at the island, working away on her iPad. She'd messaged DI Harte to update her, letting her know that all was okay at the vicarage and that Sally had headed to the church with a stand-in-vicar to set up for a wedding ceremony the following morning. Alfie had also fallen asleep in his cot a short while back. It was only her and Maeve. She finished by mentioning that she'd checked the area and no unexpected cars were in the car park and she'd seen no one suspicious hanging around.

'Can I get you a drink?' Maeve asked as she flicked the kettle switch.

'That would be lovely, thank you. Could I just have water?' Her throat was a bit on the dry side. She sneezed a couple of times and wiped her eyes. Her hay fever had started to play up earlier after her antihistamines had started to wear off.

Maeve placed a box of tissues in front of her. 'You might need these.'

'Thank you.' She hit send and blew her nose.

Maeve ran the tap and filled up a glass with water before

passing it to Ellyn. 'Do you mind if I pop upstairs and do a bit of work while Alfie is asleep?'

'Of course. I'll be fine here. In fact, I'll call Sally just to make sure she's okay. I know she said the other vicar would walk her back once they'd finished at the church, but I should double check. I'll call you if I need anything.'

'Great.' Maeve picked up her mug of coffee and left the room. 'I'll take the dogs with me.' She called them and they followed her up the stairs.

Ellyn heard a bedroom door slam closed and hoped it hadn't woken the toddler up. She didn't hear any cries from above. She glanced out of the kitchen window at the dark graveyard and shuddered. A slight rumble of thunder created an air of unease. She pulled the blind down and made sure the back door was locked. A gust picked up and she flinched as a bang in the living room filled downstairs. Running along the hall, she peered into the room and saw that the window that had been on the catch earlier was now flapping in the breeze. Alfie had been playing with it. Maybe he'd unclipped it. She leaned out and listened for any sounds. The bushes rustled and the lights were still on at the church. She could see Sally and a man of about seventy in one of the rooms, standing by the window gesturing pleasantly as they spoke. Pulling the window closed, she took a deep breath and phoned Sally. 'Hello, Sally, everything is fine here and Alfie is okay. I just wondered if you were coming back soon?'

'I shouldn't be too long now. I'm just going through tomorrow's schedule with Reverend Langham as he'll be conducting a wedding for me. I won't be more than half an hour, is that okay?'

'Yes, that's no problem. I know this is an inconvenience for you, but can you call me when you're ready to leave the church?'

'Not at all and of course I will. We're grateful to have you here,' Sally replied.

Ellyn ended the call with a couple of pleasantries. She wasn't happy about Sally leaving the house on her own while Abigail Bretton was still at large, but the church was close and she didn't want to leave Alfie and Maeve on their own either. Besides, she could watch Sally and the other vicar walking back once Sally called.

A bang came from the other end of the house. She walked towards the front door. The lounge was to her right but there was another door to the left of the stairs. Sally hadn't showed her that part of the house and Ellyn hadn't asked about it either. She turned her attention to the huge coat cupboard next to it. After opening it, she saw that there was nothing in there. It seemed ridiculous checking cupboards for noises but the banging window had spooked her. Then she checked the down-stairs toilet. Nothing looked tampered with and the tiny window was firmly closed. It had to have come from the other room. She pressed the handle. The door creaked and the room was in pitch darkness except for a tiny shaft of light from the hallway. All she could see was the top end of a twelve-seater long banquet table with hefty wooden carver chairs. Staring wide-eyed into the darkness, she heard another bang followed by a back-and-forth creaking sound. The hairs on her arms prickled and she shivered. She reached for the light switch but when she pressed, the light didn't come on. 'Hello.'

She snatched her phone and turned on her torch. The back window was wide open. She glanced to the left at the huge oversized mahogany Welsh dresser at the far end. The window creaked again.

Maybe Sally had opened it earlier. Ellyn took a few steps into the room, leading the way with her torch. She walked around the table, taking in the huge candelabra in the middle and the large silver serving bowls that adorned the table. On a normal day, she'd stop to admire such a decadent display, but right now her focus was on that banging window. A gust burst through, sending the window clanging against the wall and another rumble of thunder groaned.

Scurrying the rest of the way, she grabbed the window and closed it as best she could. That's when she noticed that the catch was broken. She stared out at the church. The lit-up room that Sally and the other reverend had been in was now turned off. Phone gripped ahead of her, she pointed the shaft of light and saw another door next to the dresser. Maybe it led to a cellar or maybe it was a cupboard. As she crept close to it, she placed her hand on the handle. Just as she went to press it down, she felt a knife in the back of her leg. She collapsed to the stone floor in agony, just in time to see the dark mass of a person climbing from under the table with a clenched fist. The figure smashed Ellyn's phone from her hand and it hurtled across the stone tiles, crashing into the fireplace. Within seconds, her attacker was straddling her and the knife came down again.

FIFTY-THREE

MAEVE

She could see that Matty had been intermittently typing a reply to her message for several minutes now. Considering the messages had been flying back and forth earlier, she wondered what was holding him up. She placed her phone down on her single bed in Sally's sparse guest room. At least the annex had a TV and Netflix. This room had nothing. She pulled her earphones out, sick of listening to the radio, and that's when she saw Jerry and Toffee loitering at the door with wagging tails. She wondered if Alfie had woken up. As she opened the door, the dogs scarpered down the stairs.

The door to the nursery was open. Maeve was sure it had been nearly closed when she came up the stairs. She heard rustling coming from downstairs. Sally must have come back. She crept towards the door and saw Alfie standing in his cot, giggling. 'Llolole mamman-man.'

She hurried over. He reached out, his little hands making a grabbing motion for her to pick him up. She lifted him and held him close to her chest. He yawned and used his balled-up fists to rub his eyes. 'Shall we sit in Aunty Maeve's room for a bit?'

'Lollo ollo.'

'What are you trying to say?' She used her index finger to pick a bit of sleep from his eyes and she smiled at him. He smiled back, not answering. She walked back to her room and placed him on her bed. Toffee ran back up the stairs and jumped up next to them, yapping, then he hurried over and licked Alfie's face. 'Toffee, stop it.' She lifted the little dog back onto the carpet but he continued to yap. After having enough, she ushered Toffee back out onto the landing and closed the door.

Alfie yawned again. She could tell he was still tired but not tired enough to be put back in his cot. Pulling him close, she lay on her bed and held him. His breathing deepened as his head sunk into her chest. She stroked his hair and unexpectedly tears began to prick and spill down her face. She knew then that she was ready to bring up Alfie. She was going to put her apartment on the market and do what Matty suggested. She'd look at houses close to the city and find the best nursery for her nephew to attend. They could do it together, both of them learning from each other. She didn't have the first clue about how to look after children but she knew she would do her best, like she'd always done in life. Guilt stabbed at her heart. Why hadn't she made time for Nell? Blaming her for their mother's murder had been silly and immature. It was now time to grow up. 'I'm going to do this, Nell, for you,' she whispered. She wasn't like Sally. She didn't believe Nell was in heaven or looking down on her, or even existing as a ghost with unfinished business. Her speaking aloud had been an affirmation, something she needed to say for herself.

Alfie placed his thumb in his mouth and began to suckle. Maeve hugged him closer and closed her eyes, knowing that if she had to be parted from this little boy, her world would collapse. Her phone beeped. She wiped the trailing tears away and sniffed before snatching her phone and reading the message from Matty.

Maeve, I really like you and I know we have something special, which is why I can't keep lying to you. I have to speak to you, in person, and it can't wait. Be in your annex in about fifteen minutes. Sneak out. I'll make sure no one sees me so you don't get into trouble. Xxx

Her muscles tensed. What had he lied about and what was so urgent it couldn't wait? She tried to call him but his phone was turned off. Something was seriously wrong.

FIFTY-FOUR

MAEVE

Alfie lay in her arms, gently blowing a spit bubble from the corner of his mouth. She lifted him and carried him downstairs, past the yapping dogs in the hallway. Toffee jumped at the front door and Jerry started snuffling at the bottom of the dining room door. She hurried into the kitchen to see if Ellyn would mind watching Alfie for a few minutes while she popped to get something from the annex. She hoped that Ellyn wouldn't try to follow her. That would scupper the plan to meet Matty and she really wanted to know what he had to say. Her stomach began to churn as she imagined all sorts. Was he married? She stopped dead. The kitchen was empty. 'Ellyn,' she called, but there was no reply. The FLO's glass of water and iPad had been left on the worktop. A message flashed up. Maeve had a quick glance before it vanished. It was from someone called O'Connor asking Ellyn how things were going at the vicarage. The screen went blank again. The back door was unlocked. Maybe Ellyn had popped to her car to get something or maybe she'd nipped to the church to walk Sally back.

With Alfie snuggled in her chest, Maeve hurried out into the dark to the annex, unlocking it and leaving the light off. The last thing she needed was to wake Alfie and tell Ellyn she had left the main house. She left the door on the catch, hoping that Matty would discreetly come in when he arrived. Placing Alfie down on the single bed, she watched as he snuggled up to the slight ruffle on the quilt and placed his thumb in his mouth.

Several minutes passed and it had been more like twenty-five minutes since Matty had messaged. She pulled out her phone and called him but it went straight to answerphone. Maybe he was still driving. She sighed and paced, knowing that she shouldn't really have left the house, but she had to know what Matty was going to tell her. Placing one of her neatly gelled nails into her mouth, she began to chew on the tip, a habit she'd broken many years ago that was now providing some comfort from the nervousness that seemed to be making her body tremble a little.

She opened the door a little and peered out across the dark graveyard, seeing things that weren't there; shapes in the darkness created by her own imagination. The bushes rustled, making her stiffen. 'Hurry up, Matty,' she whispered under her breath. A thin fork of lightning flashed across the sky, followed by a low rumble of thunder. She checked her phone again, and he hadn't called. Another ten minutes had passed and she heard the dogs barking in the vicarage again. It was no good, she had to get back. She sent him a quick message.

Sorry, Matty. I need to get back to the main house as the FLO is going to miss me. Maybe I can call you later or meet you in the morning?

She waited a few seconds but her message still hadn't been delivered. Something was wrong, she could tell. She bit off a huge strip of nail and flinched as it caught the skin on her finger at the same time. The dogs got louder and one of them began to howl.

She carefully lifted Alfie up again and left the annex while formulating an excuse in her head. That's it, she'd say she thought her earbuds were in the bedside drawer and just went to check. She closed the annex door then stopped dead as she heard a distinct rustling in the bushes that ran alongside the graveyard. Her heart began to bang and she quickened her pace as she held on to Alfie. Just on the verge of hyperventilating, she reached the back door of the vicarage, entered and pushed it closed before locking it. She'd left the light on but now it was off.

Ellyn's iPad lit up with another message from O'Connor. Holding Alfie with one arm, Maeve reached for the light switch and pressed, but the light didn't come on. The dogs barked like mad in the hallway. She needed to put Alfie down somewhere so she could use her phone. The settee, that's where she could pop him down. As she felt her way through to the lounge, she placed him down, carefully. He let out a slight murmur but carried on sleeping. The dogs whined and almost tripped her up in the dark.

She pulled her phone from her pocket and used the torch. That's when she saw Sally lying against the stairs, blood slipping down her face. Jerry was curled up next to her, licking her chin. Sally squinted at Maeve, looking confused but then her confused look turned into a wide stare full of fear. That's when she felt the hot breath of another person on the back of her neck. Without hesitating, she went to press DI Harte's number but the figure behind her hit her hand so hard the phone catapulted across the hallway floor, once again leaving her in darkness as it smashed.

Maeve froze, scared to turn, scared to move. Alfie began to cry from the living room and her heart sank. She had to fight, for him and for Sally. She swung around in the dark and went to punch the figure but she was instantly blocked and flung to the floor, her head crashing against the radiator's edge as she went down. Alfie cried even louder. The figure crouched down and a flash of lightning reached through the glass panel at the top of the door, lighting up her attacker for a second.

'Your bitch mum really deserved what she got. Nell and she took everything from me, and you did too. Now it's your turn to pay.'

The thwack to her head sent her world black to Alfie's scared cries. All she could think of was him and if he was safe, and if she'd ever see him again.

FIFTY-FIVE

Gina left Wyre sitting with an even more panicked Habiba. It had been hours and there had still been no sign of Saira. A few drops of rain began to fall as another rumble of thunder filled the sky. Jacob undid the two top buttons of his short-sleeved shirt. 'It's so stuffy.'

Jacob's phone beeped. He furrowed his brow as he read the message. Gina glanced through Habiba's window and watched as she stood in the lounge, gripping a balled-up tissue. She could see that Wyre was trying to reassure her, but it wasn't working. Jacob finished reading the message. 'What is it?' Gina asked.

'O'Connor can't get hold of Ellyn. Her phone has gone dead and she isn't answering his messages. He's going to try again now and call us back. It might be that she's just popped to the loo or something. Wait...' He looked at his phone. 'I have a message from Redditch Bus Station and there's CCTV attached.' He clicked on the link and stood next to Gina under a lamppost, then he pressed play on the footage.

They watched as it showed Saira entering the bus station an hour later than planned. 'She must have gone somewhere else first.'

They continued watching for a bit longer and then the footage flicked to another camera angle. 'Where's this?'

'I recognise it,' Jacob replied. 'It's the café in the bus station.' They watched as Saira sat with a drink and pulled a tablet from her bag before starting to tap away.

'Maybe she was trying to connect to the internet.' Saira continued to type in the video, then she stopped and bit her nails for a couple of minutes, like she was waiting for a reply. Then she typed again and scrunched her brows before leaving the café. Jacob clicked on the next video, showing Saira boarding the bus. 'Where did she get off?'

Jacob fast-forwarded until Saira stood, then he pressed play again. They watched her step off the bus at eight fifteen that evening.

'That was around the time that Habiba called us over. Where is she now?'

Jacob read the message that came with the footage. 'She got off the bus on Cleevesford High Street.'

Gina sighed. 'I can almost see the stop from here. Where the hell was she going?'

Gina's phone beeped. Her mystery messenger had made contact again. She opened the message and pressed play on the GIF. Happy anniversary filled the screen and that blended into a scene of a man proposing to a woman and what followed, chilled her to the core. Blood dripped over the image until the whole of her phone screen was red. She gasped and closed it. 'Is there more news?'

She shook her head. 'No, it's nothing.' It was far from nothing, she felt sick to the stomach. She now knew exactly what today meant. She nodded to Jacob to follow her back into Habiba's.

'Have you found her?' Habiba stopped dead in the middle of the lounge.

'We have CCTV of her getting off the bus at eight fifteen on Cleevesford High Street.'

'I don't get it!'

'Neither do we at the moment. Saira also stopped at Redditch Bus Station at a café and we think she may have needed to use the internet on her tablet as we know her phone was broken. Do you know if she has mobile broadband for her tablet?'

'No, she doesn't.'

Gina's heart started banging. Saira could have walked into some sort of trap. 'Did she mention anyone at all when you spoke?' The message whirled through her mind again. Blood down a screen.

Habiba shook her head and leaned on the fireplace. 'Where is she? Where is my daughter?'

'Do you have her boyfriend's name or contact details?'

'No,' she said with a quiver in her voice.

'What social media accounts does she have?'

'Err, Facebook and TikTok. She makes dance videos.'

Gina logged on to Facebook. 'What is her username?'

'StreetDanceGalSaira on TikTok and Saira Jane Kayleigh Bal on Facebook. Here she is on Facebook.' The phone shook in Habiba's hand.

Gina took Habiba's phone and scrolled through Saira's posts. 'You're not friends with her?'

Habiba shook her head. 'She said I'd ruin her street cred so I never friended her.'

'There's a young male who keeps liking her stuff.' She passed the phone to Wyre. 'Can you check out her TikTok too and try to contact Leroy Young. We need to ask him if Saira said anything about where she was going.' Gina sent Saira's profile link to Garth back at the station in the hope that he might be able to reach her or Leroy by message. She sent a quick message to O'Connor.

Just to update you, we haven't managed to locate Saira. She has been back in Cleevesford since eight fifteen. It's now eleven and no one has seen her since she got off the bus on Cleevesford High Street. Can you also get uniform to Sunshine Barn where Kira Fellows is staying? I can't take any chances.

O'Connor called as soon as she hit send. 'Excuse me, I have to take this.' Jacob followed her outside. 'O'Connor, have you spoken to Ellyn?'

'No, guv. I can't get hold of her and I've tried Sally too, and she's not answering either.'

'I'm heading to the vicarage right now. Send backup.'

FIFTY-SIX

As Jacob turned left at the next junction, Gina could see the church path glowing orange under its one and only outdoor streetlamp. The lit-up cross that once existed on the back wall had long gone so it was no longer a beacon in the night. She grabbed her phone and tried to call Sunshine Barn but the phone just rang and rang. Kira wasn't picking up either. Jacob pulled into the church drive and headed towards the car park.

PC Smith had already beaten them to it and another police car pulled in behind them. Gina spotted a Mercedes estate in the car park. She wondered if Abigail Bretton had hired one since they still hadn't found her. As soon as Jacob pulled the handbrake on, Gina got out of the car. 'Do we know who that vehicle belongs to?' She reached into the back seat of the car, pulled out a stab vest and began to put it on. Jacob came up beside her and grabbed a vest.

PC Smith glanced at her. 'Someone called Mathias Yilmaz.'

A sharp pain flashed through the core of her upper right chest and she gasped. The last message, she couldn't get it out of her mind. Did someone want her dead? Ignoring her own inner turmoil as best she could, she started to jog past the church towards the vicarage. Another rumble of thunder filled the air and she heard the dogs barking as they approached. She glanced back at the church and could see that the back door was closed and it was in darkness, just like the house.

Jacob walked over to the main window and peered in. 'No one in the lounge, guv.'

Gina hammered on the front door but no one answered. 'Smith, walk around, see if there is a way in. If not, we need to get this door open, asap.' PC Smith began to run around the back of the house. Gina banged again and peered through the letter box but she was faced with nothing but the bristles of the letter box hedgehog. She poked her finger through, hoping to get a glimpse of what waited in the darkness for them but all she managed to do was press the wet nose of a whimpering dog.

'Guv,' Jacob called, as he peered through a tiny window to the right of the house. He pressed the window and his hand reached through. 'The catch is either broken or someone has left it open. I'm going in.' He nudged the window again and just about managed to wedge himself through the small gap. 'The window catch is broken.' Then he was gone.

She waited a few seconds in the hope that he'd hurry and open the front door but all she heard was him calling from inside the room he'd just climbed into. She couldn't hear a word he was saying but she did sense the urgency in his voice from the way he was shouting. As Gina hopped over the mounds of uneven grass, she called out. 'What is it?'

'Get an ambulance here, now. I've found Ellyn. She's been stabbed in the torso and her ankle has been slashed. She's unconscious and she's lost a lot of blood.'

PC Smith hurried back towards Gina. 'It's locked round the back.'

'It's Ellyn,' Gina shouted. 'She's been stabbed. Can you get in there and help until the ambulance arrives?'

He nodded and began grunting and puffing as he struggled through the small gap.

Jacob opened the front door and the dogs barked around Gina's feet. 'I've left Smith with Ellyn. Any sign of the others?'

'I don't know. All the lights are out.' He grabbed his torch and held it in front of him. That's when they saw blood spray across the white radiator.

Gina ran in. 'Sally, Maeve...' No one called back and all Gina wanted to hear was Alfie's cries.

'Check all the downstairs rooms thoroughly and then check the annex. I'll head upstairs.'

Jacob ran into the kitchen as Gina ascended the stairs, taking two at a time. As she reached the top, she gasped for breath, each time she inhaled her chest twinged in protest of her heavy breathing. Something was very wrong and she really needed all this to be over so she could get checked out, but there was no way she'd let the team down, or Sally, Maeve and Alfie. They needed her. She went into every room and checked every cupboard. No one else was upstairs.

'There's no one down here or at the annex,' Jacob called up.

Gina hurried down using only the light of her torch.

Jacob continued. 'Ellyn's iPad is on the worktop and her phone is smashed to pieces in the dining room. There is also a smashed phone in the hallway. Oh, and I've shut the dogs in the kitchen for now.'

She peered into the dining room where she could see PC Smith comforting Ellyn, while pressing a towel into the wound on her bleeding torso. 'Is she okay?' Gina said in a hushed voice, trying not to alarm Ellyn even more.

Smith looked up at her from his knees as Gina pointed her torch at him; his eyes glassy, his forehead creasing as a worried expression spread through his whole face. 'We're going to make it, aren't we, Ellyn?' he whispered to the unresponsive woman, and he shook his head.

It felt like the floor had shifted beneath Gina's feet. They were losing Ellyn. Maeve, Sally and Alfie were nowhere to be seen. She flashed her torch around the highly decorated dining room and spotted the door next to the fireplace. A few smears of blood reached the wall next to the frame. She dashed towards it and opened it, revealing a set of steep stairs that she knew had to lead to a cellar. Jacob edged into the small space beside her. She pointed her torch downwards. That's when she saw someone lying in a heap at the bottom of the stairs, her arm bent in an unnatural position. 'Sally, Maeve...'

There was no answer. 'Smith, when help arrives, tell them that we have another patient, looks like a broken arm and a head injury.' The crumpled person remained still. She could see blood around the head of the victim. On close inspection, she could see it was Maeve. Their perpetrator was panicking now, Gina could tell. No longer did the killer take their time to position the body and remove their eyes. Or maybe there was no reason for it. Maybe Maeve was simply in the way of what the killer really wanted. Gina swallowed. Alfie. It had to be Alfie.

Carefully running down the stone steps, she reached the semi-conscious woman. Maeve murmured. 'Maeve, it's DI Harte and DS Driscoll. Help is coming. You're going to be okay.' Gina kneeled next to her and placed a gentle arm on Maeve's shoulder. Her stab vest crushed her chest as she settled onto her knees. She greedily gulped in some air before speaking. 'We can't find Alfie or Sally. Can you tell us anything?'

'Alfie...'

'Where is he?' Gina asked, desperate to know where the tiny dot of a boy was. 'Who did this? Who has him?' She caringly sat a little closer to Maeve.

'Mask... took Alfie. Sally...'

Maeve seemed to drift off into what could have been described as a peaceful sleep under normal circumstances. 'Maeve, wake up.' It was no good, Maeve was not going to be helping them at this moment. She looked up at Jacob. 'Someone has Alfie and from what I gathered; this person was wearing a mask of some sort.'

'Guv, the paramedics have arrived.'

'Help is here, Maeve. Hang on, okay? Alfie needs you.'

The knot in Gina's stomach grew. She only hoped that nothing had happened to him or Sally. They'd been too late to stop Ellyn and Maeve's attacks. She pictured a man called Mathias Yilmaz, unknown to them, or was Abigail Bretton behind everything, or were they both working together? She moved out of the way so that the paramedics could squeeze through. She went back up the stone stairs before following Smith and Jacob outside.

Gina's phone rang. 'O'Connor, what do you have?' She held a hand to her chest but kept going.

'Quick update, Saira Bal's boyfriend, Leroy Young, doesn't seem to know anything. He said he thought Saira was just popping home to see her mother, then coming back to his.'

Someone else was trying to call her, and she could see it was Wyre.

'Has tech had any luck with Saira's messages or her phone records?'

'Garth is still working on that. I should have answers soon. There is, however, more and it's regarding Kira Fellows. We sent uniform to check on her at Sunshine Barn. She hasn't turned up.'

After Wyre ended the call, Gina leaned on the wall and furrowed her brow as she quickly updated Jacob.

Then she saw the slightest flicker of light coming from Sally's office. 'The church. There's someone in there.'

FIFTY-SEVEN

Saturday, 6 July

Gina fought through the pain and ran to the church back door with Jacob hot on her heels. She heard Smith thudding behind them. 'Go around the front. I don't want anyone escaping.' Smith kept running. Gina heard sirens in the background. More help was on its way.

As she reached the back door, she nudged it and it creaked open. 'Hello,' Gina called as she entered. She poked a few fingers into the top of her stab vest to give her chest more room to expand as she gasped for air. 'Sally...' She listened out for Alfie's cries but she couldn't hear them. A clanging noise came from Sally's office. Gina went to jog in the direction of the sound but Jacob pulled her back.

'The killer could be in there and backup is close.' The sirens got louder. Smith was busy around the front and another officer had stayed at the house to assist just in case the perp showed up.

She stared at Jacob in the dark. 'You saw what happened to

Maeve and Ellyn. If Sally is in there with the killer...' She shook her head. 'It doesn't bear thinking about. We have to help her.' It would hurt like hell if she lost Sally. Gina trusted Sally and she loved their chats.

Jacob sighed. She could tell that he knew she was right. He nodded and followed her. 'We've got this.'

She took a deep breath and led him to the office door. Pressing her hand on the door handle, she felt her heart rate go through the roof. That's when she saw Sally holding a pencil torch behind her back while tied to the clothing rail where all her cassocks were hanging up. The whole room had been ransacked. There were textbooks, Bibles and notebooks all over the floor and all the bookshelves were empty. It was like there had been an explosion in a paper factory. Gina jumped over the mess and bent over to remove the gag from Sally's mouth, before untying the rope that bound her hands behind her back. Sally dropped the pencil torch into Gina's hand. 'Sally, who did this to you?'

Sally coughed and wheezed.

Gina turned to Jacob as she heard uniform shout that they were outside. 'Go see if there's anyone else in the church and get a paramedic here.'

'Did you see who it was, Sally?' Gina placed her arm around the vicar she considered to be a friend. She still had Alfie to find. She couldn't afford to crumble now.

After pulling bits of fibre from her mouth, Sally wiped her hand across her bloody head and grimaced. 'The person who attacked me had a mask on, like a balaclava but... actually, it was possibly tights with holes where the eyes were. Oversized hoodie, that's what she was wearing but the attempted disguise didn't matter. She couldn't hide who she was. I know who it was. Then the man came. I don't know the man.' Sally began to hyperventilate and cry. 'She took Alfie.'

Gina knew a panic attack when she saw one. 'You're going

to be okay, Sally. Just breathe and grip my hand. You're safe and we're going to find Alfie, I promise.' Gina held Sally's hand and hugged her while she sobbed.

As Sally's panic subsided, she reached around and passed Gina a notebook. 'It was all for this,' Sally managed to say in sporadic breaths. 'Alfie found a bracelet. It was back here. Nell must have hidden this on the day she was killed. I found it tucked against the wall behind all my clothes.' Sally gasped again. 'I thought she was going to kill me. I tried to protect Alfie but she tore him from my arms, threatening him with a knife as she frogmarched me to the church and tied me up. He was scared and crying and I couldn't help him. My head... I was so dizzy, I could barely stand and walk, let alone run or fight.' Tears flooded down Sally's face and into her lap.

'They left out the back just before you got here. I heard you all pulling up and I tried to make a noise but no one heard me. Then I managed to grab this torch she dropped when she was tying me up.'

'Who is she?' Gina had to work with what they had. The car in the car park belonged to Mathias Yilmaz and the masked attacker was a woman. Gina now had three missing women. Abigail, Kira and Saira. Abigail had been running from them. Kira hadn't arrived at Sunshine Barn and Saira had gone missing after stepping off a bus in Cleevesford. Which one of them had the man left with?

Sally blurted a name out just as a paramedic walked in, and Gina furrowed her brows. Sally blew out a breath and continued speaking. 'I know what Alfie meant when he babbled and I can't believe I didn't make the link. He kept saying ollolo, ollo. Things like that. It all makes sense, doesn't it?'

It made obvious sense to Gina now, but why had the woman killed Nell and Ross Craven?

She had no time at all to ponder that question. It could wait until they had her in an interview room. Alfie was her number one priority.

'Go, I'll be okay,' Sally said as a paramedic stepped over the scattered paper and books to help her with her bleeding head. 'Please don't let anything happen to Alfie. She had a knife. She will kill him; I know she will.'

FIFTY-EIGHT

'Guv,' PC Smith called. 'An officer has just found a teddy bear by the trees at the back of the graveyard.'

She closed the notebook, that she now knew was a diary, and ran with Jacob back towards the vicarage while telling him what she'd skim-read.

Smith lifted the small bear in a transparent evidence bag up towards her face.

'Where exactly did you find this?' Gina asked.

'I'll show you.' PC Smith led the way.

As they passed another PC, Gina slotted the diary into an evidence bag from her pocket and gave it to him. 'I need this booked in immediately.' She'd only flicked through the last couple of pages as she left the church but that told her all she needed to know. Ross Craven had lived so many different lives and told so many lies. His release from prison had obviously set off the chain of events before them. Right now, everything was coming to a head and her hands were shaking at the thought of Alfie being hurt. 'Take photos of the last few pages and send them straight to O'Connor, Wyre and Briggs. Also, we need a dog team.'

The PC nodded.

As they hurried around the back of the vicarage and skirted the graves, another two officers joined them. Gina could only hope that it hadn't been too long and that their perps hadn't escaped. That's when she heard a child's cry.

'Alfie,' she whispered to Jacob before she darted in the direction the sound had come from. As she nudged through a wall of nettles, scratching her hands to bits, she almost stepped into the dried-up brook. Stopping to get her breath back, she and Jacob listened for Alfie again but his cries had stopped. That's when she could hear nothing but her own heartbeat in her ears.

Thud, thud, thud.

She needed it to stop but it wouldn't. It got worse. She bent over in the hope that her heart would stop banging.

'Guv, I heard something coming from over there.' He pointed to her right and they both ran again.

Gina pushed with all she had, not even considering stopping again until she had Alfie safely in her arms. Branches whipped their heads, then a flash of lightning temporarily lit up the woods. That's when her eyes fixed on the man in the distance. 'Stop, police,' she yelled. The man continued to run, then Alfie cried again. It looked like the man was struggling with something or maybe he was hurting Alfie because all Gina could hear was shrill cries coming from the toddler.

'Mathias Yilmaz, stop. You are surrounded and you are under arrest for the child abduction of Alfie Craven. You do not need to say anything. But it may harm your defence if you do not mention when questioned something which you later rely on in court. Anything you do say may be given in evidence.' They needed him at the station for questioning. Gina had no idea who she could trust anymore but she wasn't taking any chances with the man in front of them.

With that command, he stood tall. His dark T-shirt hung

loose and he held his hands in the air. Gina heard rustling and Matthias glanced back. He spoke so fast she could barely take in what he was saying. 'I didn't do anything. I'm on your side,' he called. 'She's getting away. I came to see Maeve and I saw the woman leaving with Alfie, and he was crying like he didn't want to go with her. I knew Maeve was looking after Alfie with someone called Sally, and the woman who had him wasn't Sally. I called after her and she ran. That's when I knew something was wrong. I just managed to find her and you've let her go. Don't let her get away!'

Gina almost wanted to punch a tree. She turned to one of the PCs and stared back at Matthias, pointing her torch at him. 'Please take him in and get him interviewed immediately.' The PC cuffed him.

As he turned, he said, 'Be careful, she's dangerous and she has a knife.' He held his arm up and Gina saw the blood on his hand. 'She tried to stab me but I dodged the brunt of it. I am so scared for Alfie. Please save him, please.'

PC Smith reported back through the radio. 'Armed and dangerous... knife.' That's all Gina heard as they left.

Another cry came from ahead and rain began to fall. Thunder crashed. Gina flinched but headed towards the cry. Then the cries got louder, just as Hannah's had on that thundery night when Terry was threatening them. She swallowed and ploughed on. What was once her greatest fear was now being pushed aside and exchanged for strength. She saved Hannah that night by killing Terry and she was going to save Alfie. She wanted to roar as she burst through the stingers and shrubs, crashing through even more low-hanging branches with her arm up to block them. Jacob and the other officers were close behind. All those years ago, she'd been alone, but right now she had her team and she wasn't going to let Alfie come to any harm.

Pain stuck in her chest.

Her phone beeped again.

She was not stopping.

Alfie cried again, so she pushed harder.

Then she spotted the woman behind the diary entries, and all she wanted was to save Alfie.

The crying had stopped and Alfie was nowhere to be seen. 'Where is he?'

Kira didn't answer. The tights that had been pulled over her head when she had attacked Ellyn, Maeve and Sally were dangling behind her, still gripping onto her hair. Her oversized black hoodie was filled by her muscular, athletic frame. Gina knew exactly what Alfie had meant when Sally told her he'd been saying 'olllo lollo'. He was thinking about his little friend, Leo, every time he saw Kira. He had also said man. Gina understood that too. Kira could easily be mistaken for a man with the hoodie pulled up and her loose jeans on.

'Kira. Where's Alfie? I know you don't want him to get hurt and it's dangerous out here.'

Kira smirked and shrugged. Gina nodded to one of the PCs to skirt around them to look for Alfie, and to block Kira from escaping, but Kira was too fast. She darted like a greyhound in the opposite direction, jumping over a branch. Without considering whether she could catch Kira, Gina went after her. Kira yelled and it sounded like a tree branch had slapped her. That was Gina's opportunity to close the distance between them. She held her arms out again, blocking the branches from slapping her, and more rain began to fall.

'I'm right with you, guv,' Jacob called.

Another crash of thunder sounded and Gina smiled as she drew more strength from it. As she pushed through a tangle of gnarled wispy branches, her hand happened on the tights. She gripped them as she darted forward, not wanting to lose any evidence. Kira was almost in reach. Gina leaned out and grabbed Kira's ponytail, yanking her back onto the stinger carpet, but Kira jumped up and continued running. Gina dived forward, both feet momentarily off the ground before she landed on Kira, bringing her down and winding herself at the same time. Pain seared through her chest and she could hardly breathe.

'Get off me,' Kira shouted, as she went to poke her fingers into Gina's eyes. Suddenly the tables were turned as Gina tried to take some air in. The woman wrestling her was pure muscle. Kira was now on top of Gina. She then pressed her thumbs into Gina's eyes and Gina tried to kick and punch.

Gina couldn't get Kira off her, however hard she tried. 'Jacob, get her off me.' She hoped he was nearby. Exhaling, she turned over gasping for air, just as Kira was pulled off her by Jacob and PC Smith. It took both of them to drag her off Gina and Smith's nose was bleeding. Kira was wriggling and snarling like a rabid animal as she shouted obscenities at them all.

Gina coughed and lay there as her blurry vision cleared. She screamed out as the sharpest pain yet tore right through her chest. She could hear bits of Jacob reading Kira her rights for the murders of Nell and Ross, then the unlawful wounding of Sally, Maeve and Ellyn. And, then the kidnapping of Alfie. Tears slipped from Gina's eyes as she struggled to breathe. Poor Ellyn, their lovely FLO might be dead. And Alfie, he was somewhere in the woods alone.

To her left, she heard rustling. Grabbing a tree stump, she roared as she fought the pain. Her eyes were sore and scratched. Every bit of her body hurt and her hands were shredded by all the stingers and branches, but she wasn't going to stop until she found Alfie. She staggered forward holding her torch out and parted two bushes. That's when she saw the toddler sitting on a tuft of grass, playing with a bloodied knife. Next to him was a baseball bat. Gina calmly walked towards him, gently taking the knife before dropping it next to the bat. Just further back, she could see the bonnet of a car, and she knew it was Kira's.

Little droplets of rain gripped Alfie's long eyelashes. His little button nose was red and he held his hands up to Gina, wanting her to take him away from all the chaos. She reached down and cried slightly as she lifted him and hugged him close. 'It's okay, Alfie. You're safe now. You're safe.' She bobbed him up and down, not wanting to let him go. He might be safe but he'd now lost his mum and she had no idea how Maeve was doing. Maybe he'd lose her too and be all alone in the world, all because one little girl never received any love from her father.

FIFTY-NINE

Gina leaned against the back door of the vicarage, watching as Alfie was placed into Sally's arms. The dogs yapped around her feet. PC Smith came out.

'I've just spoken to a paramedic,' he said. 'Sally is being collected in a short while. She wouldn't go to hospital until she knew Alfie was okay. She's called a reverend named Ernie and he is going to go with them to the hospital.'

'And Maeve?'

'She definitely has a broken arm and concussion. She's already gone to Cleevesford General. A police car has followed and officers will be staying with them to gather evidence and report back. Wyre is on her way to Cleevesford General, so she can interview Maeve and Sally. As for Ellyn...' PC Smith's Adam's apple bobbed as he swallowed hard. He closed his eyes for a second and took a deep breath. 'She's lost a lot of blood. We don't know.' He shook his sadness away and the last thing Gina needed was to start tearing up. 'Anyway, I best get back in there, see what's happening.'

O'Connor was phoning her. 'What do you know? Any news

on Saira or Abigail?' Gina genuinely feared for their safety, especially as Saira would have been one of Kira's targets.

'Uniform have only gone and picked Saira up at Sunshine Barn. She got out of an Uber and they saw her knocking at the door from their car. She said Nell told her to come there but she doesn't have the Snapchat messages any longer. She'd been messaging back and forth with someone who called themselves Nell. Earlier, the person sending the messages gave her Kira's address but then changed their mind later in the day, telling her to go to the barn. Basically, it's Kira pretending to be Nell.'

'She was going to kill Ross's other daughter. Saira has been lucky,' Gina replied.

'It looks that way. Saira had no idea Nell was dead. She's being brought into the station with her mother to give a statement. I'll happily interview her as soon as she comes in. That's where we are with Saira.'

Jacob walked towards Gina and passed her a bottle of water. She nodded in thanks. 'What about Abigail Bretton? Any sign of her?'

'No, guv.'

'Now we know everything Kira said was to throw us off track...' Something struck Gina. 'It's obvious now. Leo never had a stomach bug on the morning of Nell's murder. Kira had opportunity and now I've read some of her diary, I know she had motive. She was just so believable. How did we let her slip our radar?' Gina frowned as she took in a gulp of water. 'She never lied about seeing Abigail talking to Darrah Kelly. She used the photos of Abigail loitering around to misdirect us. What if she didn't lie about Abigail turning up at hers a few hours ago? What if Abigail knocked on her door, went in, and...' She looked up at Jacob. 'Are uniform still on Kira's road?'

'No, they left a while ago,' O'Connor replied.

'Get an ambulance and uniform over to Kira Fellows's flat

immediately.' She ended the call and after reading between the lines, Jacob knew exactly what was coming next.

Gina quickly updated PC Smith. All she could think about was Shirley Bretton and how horrible it would feel to tell her that Abigail had been murdered. Abigail was clearly no angel, in fact, she seemed downright abusive, but Shirley loved her daughter. She feared what they were about to find at Kira's flat, but was Abigail dead or alive?

SIXTY

Jacob whizzed round the streets, following the blue lights of the police car in front of them. Finally, he pulled up with a jerk of the car outside Kira's flat. Gina felt another searing pain rip through her as she went to follow PC Ahmed holding a battering ram, but this time she couldn't hide it. She doubled over and pulled a pained face. Jacob came beside her. 'Do you think you need to wait this one out, guv?'

She literally wanted to cry and scream in pain. 'No, I want to get in there and find Abigail. It's just indigestion.'

Jacob frowned as PC Ahmed hit the door with the battering ram. Once again, neighbours began to amble onto the street in track bottoms and pyjamas. Elaine and Reg hurried over, him rubbing his eyes and her talking to someone on her phone about what was going on.

'It looks like more than indigestion, guv. I'm no doctor, but you're getting worse.'

She forced her hunched-over body to straighten up. 'I'm okay, see.' He went to speak but she interrupted. 'I will see a doctor tomorrow, I promise. It's nothing, really, but I'll go if it makes you happy.'

He leaned in. 'It's not about me being happy. We're a team, a family. We look out for each other and I wouldn't be doing my job if I didn't point out that you absolutely look like shit and need a doctor.'

She felt touched by his concern. 'Let's get this over with and I meant what I said. I promise, I'll get an emergency appointment tomorrow.' With her last word, PC Ahmed had managed to take the door down and the air filled with gasps and phone camera flashes. Another police car pulled up and two officers ran out and ushered the crowd back. Gina let Jacob lead this time. She doubted that anyone would want to fight or wrestle her now but if they did, she knew Jacob could handle them.

'Abigail,' Jacob called. 'Police.'

PC Ahmed led the way. He turned on the light and waited for them to pass. She stepped in and looked to her left, at the kitchen they'd sat in to talk with Kira only a few days ago. As they walked along the hall, she saw a poster stuck to the cupboard door. They hadn't ventured this far into Kira's flat. It contained information like the Wi-Fi code for the flat and who to contact in an emergency. She recognised the logo on the poster. Stay With Us Holiday Lets. It had a smiling sun in the corner of the page.

'This isn't even Kira's flat.' Gina shook her head. Where the hell had Kira come from? Another thought struck her. How could she have done all that and risked losing everything, including her own son. 'Abigail,' Gina called.

'There's no one in the living room,' Jacob said.

Gina stared at the settee. The bowl that Kira had left next to Leo was still there. She thought of Alfie, saying ollol all the time. Kira had taken Leo with her while she sneaked around looking for her diary. She'd probably been entering through the window with the broken catch or just brazenly walking in through the back door. She'd broken into the church to look for the diary that Nell had left there and, in the process, took one of the candlesticks and assaulted Sally so that it would look like a burglary. If that was the case, what did she do with the candlesticks?

Jacob passed her and nudged the bedroom door open. 'Abigail,' he called. 'Clear.' Gina peered over his shoulder and thought it odd that Kira had a really old, battered doll on her bed, wearing a pinafore dress with the name Suki sewn on the front.

Gina pushed the bathroom door open and flicked the light switch. That's when she saw Abigail trussed up in the bath. Eyes closed; she seemed still. Gina ran over to her. 'Abigail, it's the police.' There was no movement but Gina could see that Abigail was breathing. Then she saw the sleeping tablets on a shelf above the sink. She reached for her pulse. It was slow but steady. 'She needs medical help.'

Jacob left to get a paramedic and PC Ahmed waited with her.

'Abigail, can you hear me.' Gina began to untie all the rope. As it unravelled, Gina waited with her until the paramedic came in. She leaned back and a cupboard door handle stabbed her. She turned and opened it. That's when she saw the silver candlestick neatly placed on top of a small pile of towels. She slipped on a pair of latex gloves and rummaged amongst the towels. She lifted one up and underneath was a black cord necklace, like the one Ross had been wearing minus the Turkish eye. Next to it was a roll of washing-line cord, just like what was used to strangle Ross. She tiptoed to look on the higher shelf. There was a permanent marker, possibly used to draw the eyes, and a bottle of rat poison. Then she saw a really battered old notebook with a horse on the front. She took the book and opened it before reading the child's handwriting.

My name is Kira and my daddy just gave me this book. He said it's for writing the things I do in and it is called a diary. I was scared because he upset Freeloader the dog and came to the back door, but then he hugged me. Nanny was at work and told me not to answer the door but it's okay because it's Daddy. I only remember Daddy a bit. When I was littler, we went on holiday and we walked and looked at the sea with Mummy. I am sad now because my mummy is dead. She died when we were on that holiday and then Daddy left us. My sister didn't care because she didn't like Daddy but I did care because I wanted Daddy to stay with us and look after us. Nanny said it wasn't our fault that Daddy left and she said she didn't know where he had gone and Nanny doesn't like him. She doesn't talk to me and my half-sister, Vonnie, about it. He said he would come back again. He said he would hide until I was on my own and I can't tell Vonnie or Nanny as it's our secret. I feel special that we have this secret and he called me my special name. He called me Bright Eyes because my eyes are special and they are like his. Me and Suki are going to play with Freeloader now because Vonnie will be home soon. And I am going to hide my special secret horse diary under my bed where Nanny will not look. He didn't leave me. I am so happy. Bye, bye, Diary. I will write in you again soon. I will do it for Daddy, like he said, because one day we can read it together.

Gina exhaled and closed the diary. The paramedics carried Abigail out on a stretcher. Jacob came over. 'They think she's just sedated from the tablets and there are two missing from the pack. They're taking her to Cleevesford General to be kept under observation. Some of the cord and rope used to tie her up has cut into her skin so they'll clean her up too.'

Gina gripped the diary. Along with the other diary that Sally had found, they suggested that Kira was Ross's daughter too. Kira was the one who'd struggled most with his abandonment; the little girl whose mother had died, whose father had left them. Bright Eyes – that name sent a shiver through her.

Kira must have been his first child. She was definitely older than Nell. Ross must have left Kira after her mother had died and moved on to Nell and Maeve's mother. Then he killed her and moved on to Habiba when he was on the run, then Habiba gave birth to his third daughter, Saira. Why did he abandon Kira? That was another story and maybe the answer had been written in the other diary that had been hidden in the church.

SIXTY-ONE

Gina inhaled and a sharp pain struck, along with twitching muscles. Her phone lit up. Several emails pinged through on her personal account, all from odd-looking email addresses. She silenced her phone and turned it over. Interviewing Kira was her priority and she needed it to be over fast so she could rest before calling the doctor.

Kira slouched back in the standard issue track bottoms and grey T-shirt that she'd changed into after being booked in. A young, male duty solicitor sat next to her, yawning, his tie crooked. The tape was running and Jacob and Gina sat there, hoping Kira would talk soon. So far, she'd remained silent, not even saying no comment.

'Miss Fellows, you have been arrested for the murders of Ross and Nell Craven, amongst other things of which DS Driscoll has just read out to you. We'll start with the murders.' Gina swallowed back her anger, knowing that they'd received no news on Ellyn. It was getting harder to ignore the tugging pain in her chest, the light-headedness that was playing with her sense of balance, but she was nearly done with Kira and she wanted the whole story. Her victims deserved that much.

Besides, she was sure Kira was about to crack. She couldn't remain silent forever.

Kira shrugged and began to pick dirt from her fingernails.

Gina's heart began to bang as she imagined dragging Kira by the neck and demanding that she tell all. But instead, she was going to present Kira with some evidence. 'We found several items in your flat.' Gina placed the photos down on the desk showing the candlesticks, the necklace cord, the washing line and the rat poison, and she described each one for the tape. She held the photo of the horse diary back. 'Tell us about these items?'

Rolling her eyes, Kira sat up straight and placed her hands gently in her lap. 'You already know everything.'

The solicitor looked like he had nothing to add and Gina could tell that he mostly wanted to go back home to bed. The evidence they had against Kira was watertight and the statements that Wyre had taken from Sally and Maeve had confirmed everything. Kira just couldn't help herself when it came to muttering away as she hurt them.

'Why?' Gina knew why but she wanted Kira to talk.

The stony look on Kira's face began to break as her lower jaw trembled. 'I just wanted him to choose me. He was meant to choose me...'

'Ross Craven?'

She nodded.

'For the tape, Kira Fellows has just nodded,' Jacob said.

'I was the only one who bothered with him while he was in prison. When he got out, we were meant to spend time together and get to know each other again but...' She began to sob. 'He let me down, just like when I was growing up. It was hard back then and I begged him for help with things that Nan couldn't afford but he never helped. He should have helped me; he was my dad and all he gave me was notebooks. Then that was it, I felt so alone, like I was missing inside. Then he stopped visiting me when I was little. I now know that was when Nell came along. When he wrote back to me from prison, I no longer felt missing. I felt as though I belonged.' She paused. 'I don't know what I did wrong. It wasn't me, it was him. Was he sorry? No.'

'What do you mean by it wasn't you, it was him?'

Kira closed her eyes and shook her head. 'I can't talk about it. I promised that I'd never tell. It's a secret.'

Gina exhaled. It was being made easier now that Kira had confessed to Ross's murder but she knew Kira had so much more to say. 'What is the secret, Kira?'

'Not allowed to say. Not allowed to say. Not allowed to say,' she kept repeating as she pulled her knees onto the chair and hugged them as she rocked slightly.

'Kira?'

'Huh?' She stopped rocking.

'What is the secret? Is it something you were arguing with Ross Craven about on Cleevesford High Street around midnight on Sunday the twenty-third of June?'

She shrugged. 'Yes, but I can't say.' She burst into tears. 'He said he'd kill Nanny, Freeloader and Vonnie and I didn't want Leo to get hurt. Nanny is dead now. He can't hurt her but I wanted to protect Vonnie and Leo.'

Gina made a note to speak to Leo's father after the interview. 'Ross Craven is dead, Kira. He can't hurt your family.'

'He's always here. I feel his presence all around me. I can still hear his voice. I can smell him. He is the shadow in the corner of every room. He will never leave. Do you believe in ghosts?' After rubbing her damp eyes on her knees, she looked up with a smirk. 'He called Nell Bright Eyes, too. I was never special to him. We were all a secret from each other and I hated her, then I found out about Saira and it blew my mind.' She paused.

'Tell me about Saira.'

'We've been in touch.'

'Saira thought she was communicating with Nell yesterday, but it was you pretending to be Nell, wasn't it?'

'So, Nell was dead. I know Nell had been in touch with her. My dad couldn't help but mention her either. He told me he was staying with Saira's mother. I got her number from Nell's phone and I wanted to see her for myself. I wasn't going to hurt her.'

Just like all the others Kira wasn't going to hurt, Gina thought. 'You knew where Ross Craven was staying.'

'You know, I was so intrigued by Saira that I followed Ross back to Saira's mother's house and I sat watching them from the garden.'

'How did Ross's coat get in their garden?'

'Would you believe me if I said Saira's mum put it there?'

Gina wiped her clammy forehead and raised her brows.

'I put it there because I didn't know what to do with it.'

Gina swallowed. 'You hoped Ross Craven would get the blame for Nell's murder, that's why you left the knife in the pocket. We know that Ross was killed before Nell.'

'I'm no scientist. I was scared and lost, okay?' Kira snapped. 'I was upset because of Nell and him. She had started to receive calls from our dad while he was still in prison. I don't know how she first connected with him. Maybe she wrote, I don't know. I so wanted him to love me as much as he loved Nell because I kept his secret. You know what? He went to her. I gave him that Turkish eye.' She shrugged. 'Nell gave it to me. She got it from her travels. That really pissed me off. I gave her hints as to who I was but she wouldn't see or maybe she didn't want to see. I promised Ross that I wouldn't reveal that we were sisters until he'd had a chance to tell her himself. But I felt he was never going to tell her. There was never a right time. I hoped she'd see. It was like I was invisible to Dad and Nell. I mean, we had the same eyes, the eyes I've now come to hate. I can't even look at myself in the mirror now.'

Gina listened while Kira rambled on. 'Why did you kill Nell?'

'I didn't want to. She found my diary when she used my loo that morning, and she knew everything. She knew I'd killed our dad and it dawned on her that she was my half-sister. I told her that he deserved it and that I'd done us both a favour, but she wasn't having any of it. I didn't mean to do what I did after that.'

'What did you do?'

'I just wanted her to stop. Her shouting was scaring Leo and Alfie. I dragged her into the kitchen and begged her not to report me. I mean, I helped her. I found her a flat away from that abusive bitch she was living with. I took my time in getting to know Nell. First online and then in real life. We became friends and I hoped we'd get closer but, in that moment, I saw her in me and both of us in Ross, and I realised she was just like him. She was about to ditch me too so I grabbed a knife and held it to her throat. I didn't mean to. It was an impulse thing. I just wanted her to listen but she wouldn't. She fought me, grabbed Alfie and left with my stupid diary. I was so sure she was going to call the police. I shouted after her, saying we're sisters and that I was sorry.

'For the next hour or two, I paced, thinking you lot were going to come, but you didn't. I saw Nell return from the church so I barged into her flat, left Alfie in the hall and dragged her into the garden. Then I asked her where my diary was and I saw red when she said she'd hidden it somewhere I'd never find it. Somehow, she must have thought I wouldn't hurt her if she had that hidden as insurance, but Bright Eyes kept running through my mind and the rest is a blur. I had the knife I'd used to remove Ross's eyes with in my pocket.' She looked down again. 'I had to stop her from talking. She pleaded for her life and told me that the diary was somewhere in the church grounds.'

'So, you hit her, then you strangled her to death and removed her eyes?'

Kira nodded. 'I got carried away. She made me do it. She should have just given me my diary back and understood why I killed our dad, but no. You know, in the run-up to all this, she was all up for learning to forgive him. I know this because I set up a couple of hidden cameras in Nell's flat and I'd hear her talking on that bloody basic phone. I had to know how she and Ross were getting on. It was killing me, not knowing. I'd see him hanging around by hers, not quite able to knock and I didn't want him to. Then he'd loiter and watch me, and I even found him in my garden, but he'd never come in. It was as if he was being disloyal to bloody Nell. I wanted him to spend time with me and hurry up and tell her that we were sisters. I thought things would somehow fall into place and he would love me because I'd been speaking to him longer than she had.' She frowned and paused. 'I didn't mean to hurt the vicar. She's been so kind to me but I had to find my diary and while I was rummaging in the night, she came into the church so I tried to make it look like a burglary.'

Gina felt her knuckles clenching. 'And you went back last night and attacked her again. Why did you do that?'

'I told you. I wanted the diary. When I went back to take another look, Maeve and another woman were there. They just got in my way so I did what I had to do. I wanted the diary, then I was going home.'

'You're not registered as living anywhere. Where is home?' Gina's chest spasmed again. She took a deep breath and Jacob gave her a look from the corner of his eye.

'Home is where Alfie and I were going to live.' Kira let her legs slip off the chair and she sat hunched over. 'That's never going to happen now.' She sniffed and looked up.

'Where is your son, Leo?'

She bit her bottom lip and scrunched her brows. 'He's not my son. Leo is my nephew. My sister picked him up and took him home. She had to work away recently so I've been looking after him. Vonnie has him back now. I told Vonnie I had a flat and that Leo could stay with me, to help her out.'

'But it's not your flat? It's more of a temporary holiday let. You rented it, knowing it was close to another flat that was free. You also recommended the other flat to Nell because the person who owns the one you were renting owns both.'

Kira pressed her lips together. 'Let's just get this over with. I'm tired of running, tired of lying and tired of life. I did it. I did all you said I did. I killed Ross. I took his coat after and I put it in Habiba's garden, and I killed Nell. I hurt Maeve because, well... her mum took my dad. I posted a horrible note through her letter box. I followed her a little because I just wanted to know if I'd got to her. I even sat next to her at a canal café.' Kira let out a laugh. 'I even dressed Leo up in little girl's clothes to try and hide who I was, who we were, and I spoke to her. That just made me hate her more.' She began to cry. 'I poisoned the crows and used the dead ones to scare Maeve. Happy now?'

Gina wanted to frown but refrained from showing Kira how she felt. She hadn't heard anything from Maeve about the crows. Instead, she let Kira fill the silence. Her story was coming out in jumbled pieces but it was coming out, and Gina was glad about that.

'I climbed in through Sally's broken window and the other woman was there. I hurt her and I'm sorry. Is she okay?'

Gina felt sticky and undid her top buttons.

Jacob interjected. 'She is actually a family liaison officer called Ellyn, and no, she's not okay.' He shook his head and Gina knew he was finding it harder to conceal his anger than she was. One of their team was on death's door and it was all down to the woman in front of them.

'Well, I didn't set out to hurt her. I don't even know her. Please tell her I'm sorry.' She paused. 'I attacked Maeve and left her in the cellar. I made Sally come with me. I didn't want to hurt her with the knife, I just wanted the diary. That's why I tied her up at the church. I knew she'd be okay; I just needed enough time to get to my car with Alfie. Tell them I did not intend to hurt anyone, isn't that what you all look for when charging people, the guilty mind? It was an accident.' She nudged her solicitor. He whispered, then sighed. 'I only wanted to kill Ross and then I wanted my diary. It's Nell's fault she's dead, not mine. If she hadn't hidden my diary, none of this would have happened.'

'Tell me about Abigail Bretton?' Gina shifted the underside of her bra in an attempt to relieve the pressure on her chest, then she exhaled slowly to try and get rid of the deep sickening pain, but nothing was working. It was hot, so hot.

Kira grimaced and folded her arms. 'She just came by demanding to know what had been going on between me and Nell before she was murdered, and the crazy bitch lunged at me in my own home, so I pushed her away. Take note that I was trying to defend myself at this point. I even helped the woman. Nell was torn on the day she moved out of Abigail's house and she felt bad for completely cutting Abigail off. She really regretted getting rid of her phone and Alfie was missing Abigail, so I dropped an anonymous note through Abigail's door with Nell's new phone number on it. I now realise that was a stupid thing to do.' Kira smacked her lips. 'You know, Abigail lied to Nell, telling Nell to meet her for a day out and Abigail didn't go. She was trying to get into Nell's flat, probably to wait for her until she got back, to scare her or drag her back home, but Darrah saw her so that ruined whatever plan she had. Anyway, when I pushed Abigail, she hit her head. She seemed disorientated and I didn't know what to do with her. I thought people might have seen her coming to mine and there she was, in a heap on my floor, so I called you and said I'd seen her. I was just going to leave her in the bath until I'd left the area with Alfie. She would have woken up and escaped.' She paused. 'Where's Alfie's dad?'

'What do you know about him?'

'The man who was chasing me said he was Alfie's dad but a dad isn't someone who abandons their child. I was going to make sure Alfie never got abandoned like I was. I was going to love him forever and he was going to be all mine.' Kira stood.

'Miss Fellows, please sit,' Jacob said as Gina tried as hard as she could to fight the intense pain. Every time she breathed in, it felt like a lightning strike in her chest.

'No.' She began to pound on the door. 'I told you everything. Ross made me do it. He didn't pay for his biggest crime so I made him pay.' She screamed and pounded.

'What do you mean, Kira?'

Jacob stood and went closer towards her, and the solicitor moved to the other corner of the room. 'I think my client has had enough. Stop the interview.'

A wide-eyed Kira balled-up her fist, then she slammed it into the wall with a sickening crunch and let out a primal cry. 'You want to know his secret?'

Gina's pain intensified to the point she couldn't catch her breath. She had to leave the room. Hot beads of sweat formed at her brow. She was having a heart attack; she went to get up but her vision prickled. Her legs went tingly and she collapsed onto the floor.

SIXTY-TWO

DIARY EXTRACT

I can't stop thinking about what my dad said when he confessed. He was so heartless. That's how I know I've done the right thing. I mean, he attacked me too. I had no choice.

I am going to write his secret down because I need to let it go, then I am going to destroy this page. I might tell, I might not, but the power to choose is now mine.

I was only five when I heard Mum and Dad arguing. Vonnie was older and she'd stayed behind to play with a friend she'd met back at the caravan park. Mum had made a picnic to take to the top of the cliff. Mum also had this aversion to sand, almost a phobia, so whenever we went to the beach, we'd enjoy the sea a bit further back from everyone else. I was so young; I remember trying to feed Suki the doll a bit of chocolate eclair while sitting on the rug. It wasn't a very nice day and the beach below wasn't even a proper beach. It was more just sea crashing against rocks. I'd heard snippets of their argument and one name I remember was Lynette.

When Mum came back over, all teary and red-faced from where my father had slapped her, I asked her who Lynette was and she ignored me and cried. I looked down at my doll, not knowing what to do. I remember Freeloader whining next to her and trying to nudge his head under her arms, but she told him to go and lie down. I put Suki down and crawled on my knees until I reached Mum. I placed my arms around her and she hugged me tighter than she'd ever hugged me before.

I now know who Lynette was. Lynette was Nell's mum. Dad was having an affair with her. He wanted to leave us for Lynette. Of course, I didn't know about Nell until recently because Dad never told me when he made those secret visits.

Mum went back over to him and began shouting again. Just as I looked up from Suki, I saw my mum tumbling over the edge of the cliff and Dad still had his arm out. Did he push her? Back then, I hadn't been sure. I remember wishing Vonnie had been with me as I cried for Mum.

Soon after the funeral, after the 'accident', my dad sold the house and before I knew it, he had ditched me and Vonnie with Nan. Nan had said she never wanted him to darken her door again, that he'd ran off with some woman and ditched us. I never did get any more details. All I know is that Nan struggled until she died. It was hard for her bringing us up on a shoestring and that was all down to Dad and his other family. I know now that Dad chose Nell and Maeve over me and Vonnie.

He'd turn up now and again when Nan was out. He'd give me those stupid diaries and ask me about that day on the cliff. It was the same conversation we'd had at the cliff, then at home before the police came, then before speaking to everyone else. Each time, I'd slip in that I saw him arguing with Mummy but I didn't tell anyone, like he asked. He said I was being good because if anyone found out, the people I loved would get hurt and he didn't want that. I was scared all the time, so damn scared of saying something I shouldn't, just in case Vonnie went over the cliff, or Freeloader. After all, I'd seen Dad kill Mum.

The other night, I had to tell him that I did see him pushing Mum off the cliff. He killed her. I told him everything I saw that day and it made me sick to my stomach to openly speak the truth. Why did I do it? Because he put me second again.

He killed my Mum for Lynette, Maeve and Nell.

I should tear this page out now and burn it. Damn it. Why does he still have this power over me? He's dead. I killed him but he's still in my head, talking to me and I can't ever get him out. He's telling me, 'Tear it out. Do it, Bright Eyes. Do it?'

Perhaps, I will.

Maybe one day I will tell his secret. He murdered my mother!

EPILOGUE

Gina stood next to the hospital bed as the doctor gave her the all clear for discharge. She began reading all the emails once again and it made her blood boil. Someone had leaked her private email address to some dubious site. She read the subject lines again and fought the sickness that had climbed up her throat. It was as if Terry was alive again.

Murder role play, sex game. Yes please.

Slag, I'm hard for you.

Tie me up and punish me.

Address, please????

I'm going to debase you, whore! Address?

Where live?

Jacob entered just as she yelped while pulling her T-shirt on. She ditched the hospital gown on the end of the bed. Her phone kept beeping with more emails. She turned it to silent and with trembling fingers, she placed it in her pocket.

'Knock, knock,' Jacob said from behind the curtain.

Gina took a deep breath and pasted on a false smile before swiping it open. 'I've got the all clear.'

'Really. I didn't expect to be able to see you. I tried calling but they said they'd only speak to family. Why are you dressed? Is this usual protocol a few hours after a heart attack?' He frowned.

'It wasn't a heart attack. I had an X-ray. Apparently, I have a really bad intercostal muscle strain, whatever that is. Diving at suspects over the past few days has likely caused it.' She didn't mention her heightened anxiety from the messages. 'And when I ended up on the floor with Kira, that was it, the injury took an even worse turn. I am in pain but at the same time, I am so relieved.' She felt a lump in her throat. During the interview, she really thought she was going to die.

'So, what happens next, guv?'

'I shouldn't do anything for a couple of weeks. I'll need physio, but I'm going to be okay. I'm made of tough stuff, you know that. I'll probably avoid any wrestling and diving in future though, and I'm going to eat better food. My cholesterol is a little high. I'm turning over a new leaf.'

'Good for you.'

'How are things with the case? I've logged on to the system and I see that Sally has been discharged, Maeve is still in hospital and I couldn't see how Ellyn or Abigail were.'

'Abigail was fine after the tablets wore off and I know she's now under arrest for everything she did to Nell. I don't know how Ellyn is,' Jacob replied. 'I was heading to critical care next.'

Gina winced and started walking towards the ward door. 'No point wasting time. My discharge papers are going to be a good hour yet. Nothing fast happens in hospitals. Let's go and see our patients.'

'Guv, shouldn't you be resting. I can do that.'

She turned to look at him. 'I'm bored, Jacob. I can't sit in a waiting room for an hour looking at four walls. The Wi-Fi is non-existent and it's full of ill people.' She also needed a distraction from the messages, while she worked out what to do.

'Okay, but I'm not responsible if you have a relapse.'

Gina had a quick word with a nurse at the nurses' station and they left the secure ward. 'Where are they keeping Maeve?'

'Ward four. She's due to have surgery on her arm later today.'

Gina checked her watch. It was almost one. 'We best hurry then.'

As they approached ward four, Gina showed the nurse at the desk her identification and they were led to a side room. Gina knocked.

Maeve smiled and beckoned them in. 'One of your DCs filled me in on everything. It's a lot to take in. Please tell me you're keeping that woman banged up.'

Gina nodded and almost wanted to say ouch at the pain that caused, but held back. 'She's in a cell and she's been charged. How are you doing?'

'Surprisingly, I feel relieved it's over and I just want to get back to my life, and I want to take my nephew home as soon as I'm allowed. I've decided I can't rehome Toffee with strangers. Nell loved that dog so much. I owe it to her to take care of him, and Alfie loves him too.'

Gina wondered if Maeve knew that the man they'd caught in the woods last night, Mathias Yilmaz, was claiming to be Alfie's father. He was soon discounted as a suspect and had been released at around five in the morning after being interviewed. He told them that he'd moved back to Birmingham after completing the upgrade on the computer system at the hotel chain in Turkey, where he'd met Nell. He said that a previous colleague had called from there to say that Nell had been trying to find him and that she had given them her sister's details as she didn't have a permanent address. A bit more research had led him to Maeve. Then he saw that Maeve's company was looking for the very expertise he had to offer. As soon as he'd found out that Nell had been murdered, he'd been shocked but couldn't bring himself to say anything to anyone as he feared he'd become a suspect. He said he had been trying to find the right moment to tell Maeve, which was why he was there that night. Gina was about to discuss Mathias with Maeve when he appeared at the door, knocking.

'Matty,' she shrieked. 'I'm so happy to see you.'

'Can you give us a few minutes, please?' Matty asked.

Jacob left the room and Gina followed. They stood outside while Mathias started to speak.

'Maeve, I came over last night because I had something really important to tell you. It's about Alfie…'

Gina pulled the door closed.

'Guv, I wanted to hear the next bit.'

'Their business, Jacob.'

'Killjoy.'

'Let's go and see if we can get news on Ellyn.'

As they headed out of ward four and back onto the main corridor, Gina saw Sally and Alfie. She walked up to them. 'Hello, Alfie,' Gina said as she smiled at the toddler. 'How are you, Sally? I was going to pop by later.'

'My door's always open for you, Gina, you know that. It would be lovely to unpack all that has happened this week. Even vicars need to talk sometimes.'

'Great, but I might have to insist we snack on carrot sticks and not cake.' Gina yelped as she dropped her arm too fast.

'Are you okay?' Sally asked.

'Yes, just a badly torn muscle and high cholesterol but we

can save these conversations for when we have our carrot sticks. Are you both going to see Maeve?'

Sally nodded. 'I thought this little one should see how his aunt is doing.'

'She has a visitor.' Gina thought it best to warn Sally.

'Oh, maybe I should come back.'

Mathias came around the corner and frowned, giving nothing away. He nodded and passed them. 'Looks like she's free now and I think she'd probably like to have a friend to talk to,' Gina said.

'We best be on our way then. See you soon, Gina.'

Jacob led the way to critical care. Once buzzed in, all they could hear was the beeping of machines. Gina flagged down a passing nurse and asked for Ellyn.

'Are you a relative?' she asked.

'No, she was injured in the line of duty. Cleevesford Police.'

'She's just come out of surgery. It went well, that's all I can say. I suggest you come back later when she's awake, then you'll be able to speak to her. She's going to be okay.' The nurse smiled.

As they left the ward, Gina turned to Jacob. 'I haven't been able to stop thinking about what Kira wrote about Ross Craven pushing her mother off the cliff.' She took a couple of breaths. 'That's where it all started. I do feel a bit sorry for the little girl who witnessed that. He played with her mind and her emotions for years.'

'Nothing is ever black and white, is it?' Jacob sighed.

'It certainly isn't.' Gina checked her watch again. 'I best get back to the waiting room, ready for my discharge papers.'

'And I best get back to the station. There's a shedload of paperwork to do.'

'Call me later with updates.'

'You really aren't able to have any downtime, are you?' He smiled. 'I will do.'

Gina quickly sent Hannah a message, telling her what had happened and not to panic because she was okay. Then she ambled back to the waiting room. Half an hour passed and she'd been told her discharge papers would be yet another hour. She tried to use her phone but the signal was at zero. She leaned her head back against the wall, enjoying the coolness of the rotating fan that had been positioned in the corner of the room. People came, people went. She felt her phone vibrate in her pocket. She knew the emails wouldn't stop. She swallowed and felt her head beginning to ache with it all.

'Gina.' She knew that voice.

Without opening her eyes, she stayed in the same position. 'If you've come to tell me off for doing my job, I suggest you walk straight back out of that door,' she said to Briggs.

'I come bearing gifts.'

He sat beside her. She opened her eyes and saw all the sweets and chocolates he was holding. 'I can't have any of that, but it was a kind thought.'

He frowned. 'It wasn't a heart attack.'

'I didn't say anything before but my cholesterol is a bit high and I automatically assumed I was having a heart attack. Well, it felt like a heart attack.' She paused and looked away. 'I thought I was going to die. I've never felt pain like it. Right in my chest.' Tears began to slip down her cheeks.

'Come here.' Briggs drew her close, and she leaned into his chest.

'Can you wait with me and drive me home in a bit.' She knew she'd have to tell him about the emails and messages later but right now, she couldn't do it.

He stroked her hair. 'I'll do more than that. If it's okay, I'd like to take you home, then I'll go shopping and buy some ingredients for a lovely salad and I'll make it.'

A nurse entered. 'Ms Harte, your discharge papers are ready.'

'Let's go,' she said as she took the papers and followed him out of the hospital. It was time to go home. For just a second, she allowed herself to enjoy being cared for and she tried to imagine how at peace she'd feel, if she hadn't received those messages. She already knew that their evening was ruined. She sighed. Maybe she should tell him now, that would be the right thing to do. 'Chris.'

'Yes.' He held out a hand to help her up even though she didn't need help.

She pulled her phone from her pocket, ready to show him the messages, then she changed her mind and popped it back in. 'Thank you, for being here.' She couldn't tell him. Not yet. She forced away the impending panic by breathing in and out. As they left the hospital, Gina forced her tears back. Time healed everything, that's what people said. They were wrong. Time just made it worse. The baggage she was carrying was breaking her back and there was no cure. She couldn't report it as she would end up losing everything. Briggs could lose everything, too. She quickly glanced at the latest email as Briggs put her bag in the car.

From: VenMan

To: GinaH

Subject: Bitch needs to pay. Likes it rough. (Dark web dox: call to action). Check out Men-R-Takin-It-Back.

Stephen was back and the game he was playing made Gina wonder how she could even begin to fight him. She knew this was just the start and she was petrified of where it would end.

'Gina, do you need a hand?' Briggs called from across the bonnet of the car.

She wanted to scream yes, but instead she got into the car,

she put her seat belt on, stared out of the windscreen and swallowed down her tears. It was the beginning of a new chapter, one she wished she could close the book on, but right now she was at the mercy of someone whose hatred of her ran so deep he'd stop at nothing to see her suffer to the end.

A LETTER FROM CARLA

Dear Reader,

I'm really happy and grateful that you decided to read *One Last Prayer*.

If you enjoyed *One Last Prayer* and would like to keep up-to-date with all my latest releases, just sign up at the following link where you can also get a free copy of my short story, *Their Broken Hearts*. Your email address will never be shared and you can unsubscribe at any time.

www.bookouture.com/carla-kovach

I enjoyed exploring a lovely new set of characters alongside my trusty police team. Sally, the vicar, has been screaming at me for ages (in my head), pleading for a bigger role, so I had to oblige. I know I put Gina through the wringer with her health and that came from a personal place. I had chest pains in my late thirties and I managed to get the full works at the doctor's surgery. I received an emergency appointment and an ECG. It turned out to be a pulled muscle but it really felt like a heart attack was coming on. I remember having pains when inhaling and then those pains reached right through my chest. Then weirdly, anxiety came into play which made things even worse. Gina's injury was a lot worse than mine because she does way more than me. She runs after suspects and hauls herself over fences. It's not surprising that she suffered such a bad injury in this book.

Whether you are a reader, tweeter, blogger, Facebooker, TikTok user or reviewer, I really am grateful of all that you do and as a writer, this is where I hope you'll leave me a review or say a few words about my book.

Thank you,

Carla Kovach

 facebook.com/CarlaKovachAuthor

 x.com/CKovachAuthor

 instagram.com/carla_kovach

ACKNOWLEDGEMENTS

I'd like to say a mahoosive thank you to everyone who has helped to bring *One Last Prayer* to life. Editors, cover designers, and all the people working in every aspect of publishing from admin to management. They are all a part of this big team and I'm so proud to be a part of team Bookouture.

My editor, Helen Jenner, is brilliant and I couldn't have written this book and all my others without her valuable insight. Thank you.

I'm grateful to Lisa Brewster for the cover design. I absolutely love it.

The Bookouture publicity team are the best. Publication day is always super special because of them.

Many thanks to the blogger and reviewer community. I know there are millions of books out there so it means a lot that they chose mine.

Much gratitude to the Fiction Café Book Club. It's such a haven and so supportive of authors.

I also adore being a member of the Bookouture author family. The fellow author support is incredible. My other author friends are lovely too. Authors are amazing.

My beta readers, Derek Coleman, Su Biela, Abigail Osborne, Jamie-Lee Brooke and Vanessa Morgan, are all brilliant and I'm thankful that they read my work at different stages before publication. Super thanks to Anna Wallace for the proofreading.

I'd love to give special thanks also to Jamie-Lee Brooke,

Abigail Osborne – again. And also, thanks to Julia Sutton. I love our 'Hot Dog Cringey Crew' support group where the four of us chat about our work and check in bi-weekly. Sorry, the name of our group is an in-joke. Also thank you, Abbie, for lending me your name for this book. I hope you like Abigail.

I'd like to give special thanks to expert, Stuart Gibbon, of Gib Consultancy. Without his policing expertise I'd definitely be making a mess of the police procedures and charges. Any inaccuracies are definitely my own.

Lastly, humongous thanks to my husband, Nigel Buckley, for the coffee, the admin, handling my website and a whole host of other jobs I'm terrible at, and mostly for being there for me throughout the whole process.

PUBLISHING TEAM

Turning a manuscript into a book requires the efforts of many people. The publishing team at Bookouture would like to acknowledge everyone who contributed to this publication.

Audio
Alba Proko
Melissa Tran
Sinead O'Connor

Commercial
Lauren Morrissette
Hannah Richmond
Imogen Allport

Cover design
The Brewster Project

Data and analysis
Mark Alder
Mohamed Bussuri

Editorial
Helen Jenner
Ria Clare

Made in United States
Orlando, FL
16 October 2024

52748627R00200